William Cleaver Wilkinson

The epic of Paul

William Cleaver Wilkinson

The epic of Paul

ISBN/EAN: 9783743368439

Manufactured in Europe, USA, Canada, Australia, Japa

Cover: Foto ©Andreas Hilbeck / pixelio.de

Manufactured and distributed by brebook publishing software (www.brebook.com)

William Cleaver Wilkinson

The epic of Paul

THE EPIC OF SAUL.

BY

WILLIAM CLEAVER WILKINSON.

FUNK & WAGNALLS.

NEW YORK:
18 & 20 ASTOR PLACE.
1891
LONDON:
44 FLEET STREET.

PRINTED IN THE UNITED STATES.

CONTENTS.

THE EPIC OF SAUL.

SAUL of Tarsus, brought up at Jerusalem a pupil of Gamaliel, the most celebrated Rabbi of his time, from setting out as eager but pacific controversialist in public dispute against the preachers of the Gospel, changes into a virulent, bloody persecutor of Christians, and ends by abruptly becoming himself a Christian and a teacher of Christianity. THE EPIC OF SAUL tells the story of this.

PROEM.

SAUL in the council Stephen's face saw shine
As it had been an angel's, but his heart
To the august theophany was blind —
Blinded by hatred of the fervent saint,
And hatred of the Lord who in him shone.
What blindfold hatred such could work of ill
In nature meant for utter nobleness,
Then, how the hatred could to love be turned,
The proud wrong will to lowly right be brought,
And Paul the "servant" spring from rebel Saul —
This, ye who love in man the good and fair,
And joy to hail retrieved the good and fair
From the unfair and evil, hearken all
And speed me with your wishes, while I sing.

BOOK I.
SAUL AND GAMALIEL.

SAUL visits Gamaliel to submit a forming purpose conceived
by him of entering into public dispute with the Christian
preachers. Gamaliel disapproves; informing Saul that the
Jewish rulers are about to apply against those preachers the
penalties of .the law. These men accordingly arrested and
arraigned, the Sanhedrim hold a council on their case, at
which Caiaphas advises accusing them to the Romans as seditious ; Mattathias urges stoning them out of hand ; Shimei
recommends pursuing against them a policy of guile.

THE EPIC OF SAUL.

SAUL AND GAMALIEL.

GAMALIEL sat at evening on his roof
And deeply mused the meaning of the law.
The holy city round about him lay
Magnificent, encircled with her hills.
Beyond the torrent Kedron, sunken deep
Within his winding valley, Olivet
Leaned long his shaded ridge against the east,
Distinct in every olive to the sun.
Nearer, amid the city, chief to see,
The glory of the temple of the Lord!
The seat was noble for a noble pile:
The summit of Moriah, levelled large,
Spread larger yet, outbuilt on masonry
Cyclopean, or more huge, pillar and arch
Fast-founded like the basis of a world.
A world of architecture rested there —

Temple, and court, and long-drawn colonnade
On terrace above terrace ranged around,
Cloister, and porch, and pendent gallery,
Height, depth, length, space, and splendor, without end,
Glittering its stones of lustre purest white,
And stately portals rich with gems and gold :
The setting sun now smote it that it blazed.
The sight was torment to Gamaliel's pride,
Torment with pleasure mixed, but torment more,
As there he sat upon his roof alone.

Tall, and erect in port, unbent his form
With all that weight of venerable years,
His head with almond-blossom glory-crowned,
And bosom overstreamed with silver beard,
Gamaliel stood before his countrymen
Their stay, their solace, and their ornament,
One upright pillar in a fallen state.
Fallen, for Rome had pushed her foaming wave
Of conquest far into the East, and laid
Judæa under deluge, quiet now,
But deep, of domination absolute —
A weight as of the sea upon her breast.
Jerusalem was glorious to behold,

Girdled with guardian mountains round about,
And sunlit with her temple in the midst.
Alas, but more her glory, more her shame!
For all her glory was the Roman's now,
The queen a vassal at a tyrant's feet,
She Cæsar serving who should serve but God.
And, worse disgrace than heathen servitude,
There recreant Jews were found, and more and more,
Who their hearts sold to their captivity,
And abjectly gave up the ancient hope
And promise, dawning-star of prophecy,
That yet to captive Israel should arise
Messiah, King of kings and Lord of lords,
To break the yoke from off His people's neck
And gift them with the empire of the earth —
This crown of Israel's hope gave up, to choose,
Instead, for captain and deliverer, one
Base-born, from Galilee, consorting friend
With publicans and sinners, hung at last
Convicted malefactor on the cross!

   Such thoughts and tortures exercised the mind
Of grave Gamaliel on his roof that eve.
He felt the burden of his name and fame

Weigh heavy, his renown of sanctity,
With wisdom, rife so wide, and holy zeal.
His head declined upon his bosom, there
Amid the evening cool unheeded, he,
Gray reverend teacher of the law, sat mute,
Rapt over the writ parchment on his knees,
And read, or thought, or thought and read, and
    prayed.
The veil was on the old man's heart; he saw
Unseeing, for the sense from him was sealed.

In words like these his prayer and plaint he poured:
" Hath God forgotten to be gracious?   Will
Jehovah cast us off forevermore?
We groan, O Lord, Thy people groan, beneath
The yoke of the oppressor.   It is time,
Lo, bow Thy heavens and come avenging down !
Appear Thou for Thy people !   Visit us !
Not only the uncircumcised are come,
And heathen, into Thine inheritance,
But of Thy chosen seed are risen up
False children unto Abraham, to vex
Our nation's peace and shame us to our foes.
The son of Joseph suffered his desert,

Accurséd, on the tree, pretender vile,
Who out of Nazareth came forth to claim
Messiahship, the gift of David's line,
And trailed a glorious banner in the dust,
The banner of the hope of Israel.
That day, too long expected, yet shall dawn
And true Messiah, girded on His thigh
His sword athirst for alien blood, shall ride
Conquering and to conquer over all
The necks of these His enemies and ours.
How long, Lord God of Sabaoth, how long?
For now that hated false Messiah's name
Is preached, the dead for re-arisen to life,
The crucified for glorified, to men,
And ICHABOD is written everywhere
On all that was the boast of Israel.
O Thou that overthrewest the harrying horde
Of Pharaoh whelmed beneath the entombing sea,
Rise, overwhelm Thine enemies, restore
The glory and the kingdom to Thine own !"

Gamaliel prayed, and knew not that his prayer
Found voice and smote at least an earthly ear.
"Amen !"   Gamaliel started as he heard

The voice of Saul responding fervently.
Saul had been pupil to Gamaliel,
Loyal and loving, and he now was friend
Familiar, whom, as guest, unbidden oft
And unannounced, that famous Pharisee
Welcomed to share his most seclusive hours.
" My son!" " Rabboni!" mutually they said.

The younger to the elder now had come,
A thought to purpose quickening in his breast.
He too was Hebrew patriot, and he yearned
With anguish like his master's, yet at once
Sharper than his, and more accessible
To hope, as well his livelier youth became
And native blood more nimble in his veins —
Saul also, with Gamaliel, yearned and burned,
Beholding prone his country in the dust,
Under the grinding heel of Roman power —
And Messianic glory turned to shame !
Saul's first wish was to bring his brethren back
Stung to their pristine, proud, prophetic hope
Of a Messiah born to regal robes,
Swaying a sceptre, seated on a throne,
Crowned with a crown of myriad diadems,

Symbol of lordship that should myriad tribes
Mass in one mighty empire of mankind.
He felt the soul of eloquence astir
Within him, and he longed to be at war,
In words that flamed like lightning and that smote
Like thunder-stones, against those grovelling men
Who Israel taught to grovel at the feet
Of Galilæan Jesus crucified,
Accepted for the Christ, forsooth, of God !
Such wish, becoming purpose, Saul has brought
This evening to Gamaliel, with high hope,
Hope high, but vain, to disappointment doomed,
Of grateful gratulant words to hearten him,
Approving and applauding his desire,
Won from the wisest in Jerusalem.

   Thus minded, Saul, blithe, eager, sanguine, bold,
With yet a grace of filial in his mien,
As toward a master had in love and fear,
Said :
        " Teacher, what I came to learn from thee,
Already, having marked thy prayer, I know.
God hear thee out of Zion in thy prayer !
God bring to naught the counsels of His foes !

Now know I, and rejoice to know, that thou,
My teacher in the blessed law, wilt say,
'God speed thee, son,' in what I seek to do.
For, lo, I seek to serve the suffering cause
Of truth wounded and bleeding in the street.
Love of my country burns me as with flame
Imprisoned and living in my very bones —
My country, and my countrymen.   This land
To me is lovely like a bride beloved —
Beloved the more, unutterably wronged !
Her trodden dust is dear to me.   Not I,
As do my brethren on her bosom born,
Equably love her with composed and calm
Affection sweet.   That homesick longing bred
With boyhood in Cilicia haunts me yet,
To heighten love with anguish, and more dear
Make the dear soil of this my fatherland.
A passion, not a fondness, is my love ;
And for my countrymen to die, were sweet —
Such blind abandonment of love usurps
My being for my kinsmen in the flesh.
Would God I might in very deed pour out
This blood, no vain oblation, to redeem
My bondmen brethren and to purge this land !"

In speech no farther — though in passionate tears
The strong man vented still his else choked heart.
Gamaliel, with wise senior sympathy,
Sat silent, waiting till that burst were past.
Then gravely :
              " Yea, my son, I know thy zeal,
And praise it.   Such as thou, in number more,
Might somewhat ; such as thou, alas, are few."

His master's praise Saul took as check and chill,
Uttered with that insinuated sense
Of sage discountenance to his youthful zeal.
He shrank, but braced himself, and gently said :
" But, father, not by many or by few
Is our God bound to working.   Many or few
To Him is one.   Nay, were there none save me,
Were I alone among my brethren, I,
Alone among my brethren, yet would dare."

Against the vernal aspiration warm
Of Saul's young blood and tropic temperament
Gamaliel's aged, wise, sententious phlegm,
And magisterial manner though benign,
Abode unmoved, inert, insensible ;
Like an ice-Alp that freezes on its cheek

A breath of spring soft blowing from the south.
With viscid slow demur the old man spoke,
And downcast heavily shook his hoary head:
  "To dare is cheap and common with our race,
We are few dastards; did not Judas dare?
And Theudas? But their daring came to naught.
Wisdom with daring, fortitude to wait,
We need, son Saul; the daring that must do,
And cannot wait, has wrought us sumless ill."

  Damped, but remonstrant, Saul still plied his plea:
"And yet but now, 'How long,' I heard thee cry,
'How long, Lord God of Sabaoth, how long?'"

  "Yea," said Gamaliel, "that I daily cry."

  "Thy counsel and thy praying how agree?"

  "Men I bid wait; wait not, I pray my God."

  "Were this not well, O master calmly wise,
In trust that God will rouse him at my cry,
To rouse myself and strongly side with God?
I cannot rest in peace; I hear the woe
Denounced for such as safely sit at ease
In Zion.   Let me do as well as pray."

  Saul's rising zeal once more the master checked:

" Praying is doing, likewise waiting works ;
But what, son Saul, is in thine heart to do?
I cherished better dreams, my son, for thee,
Than to behold thee leading to their doom
One helpless, hopeless, hapless company more,
Insurgent out of season against Rome,
Confederate sons of folly and of crime ! "

    Rebuke like this Saul brooked it ill to hear ;
With filial sweet resentment he replied :
" And cherish other dreams, I pray thee, father !
No man-at-arms am I to challenge Rome ;
Though not even Rome should daunt me, called of God
To front her with but pebble from the brook,
Like David, in her plenitude of power.
Rome rules us, and I grieve, but I rejoice :
I grieve that we are such as must be ruled,
And cannot rule ourselves ; but I rejoice,
Since such we are, that we are ruled by Rome.
The strongest and the wisest is the best
To serve, if one must serve.   Alas, my country !
Her face is in the dust because her heart
Grovels, and therefore on her neck the heel.
So, not to rid us of the Roman. I

Labor with this desire, but to erect
The dustward spirit of my countrymen.
This people knowing not the law are cursed ! "

    By instinct wise of policy unmeant,
Saul, in his last half-maledictory words
Of vehement passion edged with bitterness,
Had struck a chord that answered in the breast
Of the habitual teacher of the law.
" Yea," said Gamaliel, " now art thou true son
And utterest wisdom.   Make them know the law.
With both my hands I bless thee speaking thus.
The law shall save them, if they know the law. "

    Saul knew it was Gamaliel's wont that spoke,
His life-long wont of reverence for the law
And trust in its omnipotence to serve
Whatever need befell his nation — this,
Rather than any fresh, fair-springing sense
Of hope in him auxiliar to his own.
Yet, in despair of better heartening now,
And self-impelled to ease his laboring mind,
He, fixed and faltering both, with courteous phrase
Premised of teachable assent sincere
To smooth somewhat thereto his doubtful way,

Frankly a hearing for his counsel sought :
" I ever heard thee, father, teaching that,
And I believe it wholly, mind and heart ;
But something now I did not learn from thee,
Hearken, I pray, and weigh if it be wise. "

But less like one who hearkened as to weigh
A counsel shown, Gamaliel now to Saul
Seemed, than like one who sat behind a shield
In opposition, a broad shield of brow
Immobile, placid, large circumference,
And orb of diamond proof, between them hung
There on the housetop still in dim twilight,
Ready to quench in darkness any ray
Of word or sign from him that should aspire
To reach an understanding guarded so —
Such to Saul seemed Gamaliel now, while yet,
Despite, repressed but irrepressible,
That strenuous strong spirit thus went on :
" Deeply I have desired to know my time
And not to waste my strength beating the air.
Are not men's needs other with other times ?
No more perhaps in peaceful shelters now
Sacred to sacred studies, synagogue

Retirements, where our doctors of the law
Propose in turn their sage conclusions, heard
By questioning disciples — here perhaps
No more is truth most truly taught to men.
Some, it may be, might well go forth to stand
Even at the corners of the streets and cry.
Folly amain preaches to gaping crowds,
And shall not wisdom cry?   My heart is hot,
Amid the multitude they make their prey,
To meet these false proclaimers to their face,
And stop their mouths, with Moses and with all
The prophets and the Psalms, from uttering lies. "

Gamaliel heard, and like a lion stood,
That shakes his dewy mane from slumber roused ;
The old man loomed in action nobly tall,
As thus, with weighty gesture, in a voice
Solid with will, he gently, sternly spoke :
" Nay, Saul, my son,. thy zeal misguides thee now --
Thy zeal, and peradventure some conceit
Of wisdom wiser than thine elders.   Thou,
Consenting thus to parley with the fool
According to his folly, like becomest.
This is a time to answer otherwise

Than with the wind of words against their words
Of wind, as equal against equal matched.
Those wresters of the law must feel the law
Smiting their mouths shut with the heavy hand.
With blows, not words, vain fools like these are taught.
Go thou thy way, to-morrow shalt thou see
Hap other far than that thou hast devised
Befall those evil men of Galilee.
Our chiefly prudent, watchful for our weal,
Will stop their mouths profane and make an end."

Saul chode his tongue to silence, but his heart
Set stern in resolution touched with pride,
As, after decent pause, he took farewell.

The master and the pupil parted thus,
And both were blind to that which was to be ;
For both would change, but change in converse ways,
Gamaliel gentle grow, and Saul grow hard.

That morrow, Peter with his brethren all,
Apostle preachers of the Gospel, felt
The heavy hand Gamaliel shadowed fall
Indeed upon them into dungeon thrown.
But thence by night the angel of the Lord,
Opening the doors, delivered them, and bade

Boldly into the temple take their way
And there preach Christ to all the worshippers.
With the first flush of morning, their swift feet
Shod with the sandals of obedience,
They hasten to fulfil the angelic word.
Meanwhile the Sanhedrim for counsel met
Concerning those their prisoners, and the state,
The vexed state, of the Hebrew commonwealth,
Sent pursuivants to fetch them from their cells
And station them in presence to be judged.
But those despatched to bring them came and said,
" We found, indeed, the prison safely shut
And all the keepers keeping watch and ward
Without before the doors; but entering in
To find our prisoners, prisoner found we none. "

The captain of the temple, the high-priest,
And all that council mused in maze and doubt —
Gamaliel most, guessing the finger of God.

But now comes one who brings a fresh report ;
" Behold," said he, " the men ye put in bond
Are standing in the temple teaching there. "
Forthwith the captain of the temple goes,
His band attending, and, no violence shown —

For fear was on them of the people, lest
They stone them — leads the Galilæans in.

   Robed venerably each in rich array
Of purple, and fine linen, glistering white
And broidered fair, their flowing garments fringed
With large expanse of border and with cords
Of blue adorned, broad their phylacteries,
The council of the seventy sat severe
Within their council-hall in solemn state.
A semi-orb they sat, or crescent-wise,
And in the midst, between the horns, were placed,
Under their beetling frown, the prisoners.
Awful these felt the presence of the place,
And, while the high-priest of their nation, throned
Middle and chief among the councillors,
Denouncing asked : " Did we not straitly bid
Forbear to teach in this accursèd name ?
And, lo, ye fill Jerusalem with bruit,
And seek to bring on us this person's blood ! " —
While thus, sternly, he spoke, those simple men
Felt the heart fail within them and the tongue
Cleave to the mouth's dry roof.   He ceasing, back
Their spirit came, and Spirit not their own,

The Holy Ghost of God, flooded their souls,
As when into a bay the ocean pours.
Then Peter and his brethren boldly spoke :
" Fathers and brethren, hearken to our words :
God needs must we, rather than men, obey.
That Jesus whom ye crucified and slew,
Him did the Lord God of our sires raise up,
And at His own right hand exalt to be
Both prince and saviour, to bestow on us
Repentance and forgiveness of our sins.
Of these things all we stand here witnesses ;
Nor we alone, for with us witnesseth
God's Spirit bestowed on whoso Him obeys. "

Something not earthly in those prisoners' mien
A tone of more than human in their words,
A majesty, as of omnipotence
Patient within them, ready to break forth,
But patient still, to brook how much was need —
So much, no more ! — this awed one watchful heart
Prepared amid that council now to heed ;
Gamaliel inly pondered, ' Is it God ? '
The clear simplicity, the perfect faith,
The steady, prompt obedience, the serene

Courage that dared, without defying, all
The terrors brandished by the Sanhedrim —
This spirit, strange in those despiséd men,
As with a soft and subtle atmosphere
Enfolding and suffusing him, subdued
The solid temper of his mind, the strong
Set of his resolution grim relaxed,
Undid the hard contortions of his nerves,
And supple made the will so firm before.
His steadfast poise of confidence perturbed,
Gamaliel trembled with uncertainty.

Otherwise Saul; he, merged in different thought,
Eluded quite that penetrative spell.
Unconscious of the Holy Ghost, he strove
Blindly against Him, like the rest, though not
Yet, like the rest, with zeal of violence
To do the prisoners harm or shed their blood ;
With such zeal not, but with ambitious pride
Of wisdom unawares puffed up to show
His prowess in the Scriptures, and to earn
A high degree surpassing all his peers.
His fellow-councillors concerting how
To quench this propagandist fire in blood,

Saul said within his heart :

       ' Nay, nay, instead,
Might I but once these bold presumers face
Amid the idling crowds they feed with lies,
How, from the law itself, whereof, untaught
Therein, they prate, would I, in open test
Of argument, confute them to their teeth !
Their own ill-wielded weapons from their hands
Seen wrenched and turned against them, surely then
Not only would these brawlers cease, but all
Would laud and magnify the glorious Word
Of God, thus shown, well wielded, capable
Of wreaking its own vengeance on its foes.'

  These twain such counsel in their secret breast
Held diverse, while that strife of words went on.

  Not what, in present need, behooved to do —
A full and fell accord conjoined them there ! —
Was doubt or question to the Sanhedrim ;
But in what chosen way their chosen goal,
The doom of death for those accursèd men,
With safe sure speed, most prudently, to reach —
This doubt embroiled a vehement debate.

One argued thus his sentence and advice —
Caiaphas he, high-priest that lately was,
Reputed statesman politic and wise:
" We are a subject nation ; government
Is for this present slipped from out our hands.
Chafe how we may, how will it otherwise,
Ours is a state of vassalage to Rome.
Death in our hearts and death upon our tongues,
Denounced amain against our enemies,
Is futile — thunder bare of thunderbolt.
We make ourselves a laughter — unless we
Warp toward our end with wisdom ; who is weak
Well needs be wise, to win — wisdom is power.
To kill and keep alive, by process due
Of law, no longer appertains to us,
That right being forfeit to our conqueror ; this
Must we not let our honorable pride,
Justly indignant, and our holy zeal
Incensed for God, bribe us to blink.   But slave,
If wise, may make a foolish master serve.
Break we proud Rome to do our task for us.
True triumph, when we wield the tyrant power
Itself of domination over us
A weapon in our hands to work our will !

" I counsel that we seek and find firm ground
Of mortal accusation, before those
Who rule us, against these audacious men,
As teachers of seditious doctrine meant
To undermine allegiance, and at length
Prompt insurrection and a state of war.
Rome then will stamp our troublers out of life,
And we, well rid of them without annoy,
Besides shall safely reap from her the praise,
Ill-merited, of fealty to her right —
Praise that sometime hereafter may be gain
Of vantage, if sometime hereafter come
Fit season to fling off her hated yoke."

Such words of weight spoke Caiaphas, and ceased
Those words, not idle, fell as falls the steel
Smiting the flint; a sparkle keen of fire
Flew forth, found tinder ready, and flashed up
In instant flame.   A patriot malcontent,
Fiercely, irreconcilably, a Jew,
Was Mattathias; Mattathias said:
" Yoke by whom hated?   Surely not by him
Who tamely brooks to talk of earning praise
For loyalty from Rome!   Nor more by those

Who patient sit to hear such counsel broached!
Nay, men my brethren, that I did not hear!
Sure, son of Abraham never have I heard
Own himself slave, and meekly speak of Rome,
As of a master!   This I will not hear!
I could not hear it!   Speech of such a strain
Were like a river of molten metal poured
Red-hot into my ear to quench the sense!
Stone-deaf am I to craven treachery
From one of my own fellow-councillors here!
I only heard my brother say, ' Let us
Arise and stand for God!'   Lo, I arise
And stand, with him, with all!   There is a law,
Ancient and unrepealed, wholesome and good,
To stone for blasphemy.   Blasphemers these,
What wait we? We have hands, and there are stones,
Let us this instant forth and stone them, stone
Unto the death!"

                    The clenched hands, and the fierce
Menace of husky tones, half-choked, and teeth
Gnashing, and brow braided with swollen knots,
Were more than words to speak the murderous will.

The prisoners listened with suspended breath :

They deemed a dreadful doom indeed was nigh.
Instinctive instant fear, forestalling faith,
With sudden loud alarum startled them,
And for one moment violently shook,
In them, all save the basis of the soul —
One moment — then they sped themselves with prayer,
Ran to the shelter of the promises,
And were at peace !   In that secure retreat
Withdrawn, the secret place of the Most High,
The angel of the Lord encamping round,
Composédly at leisure they looked out
And saw the wicked plot against the just,
Vainly, and gnash upon him with his teeth !
Within their hearts they knew his day would come.

The speaker still stood leaning imminent,
His posture instigation, while a hiss
Of hot adhesion ran increasing round —
But skipped Gamaliel, skipped the musing Saul
With one beside, scarce daring to be dumb —
When, in his place, slowly, by soft degrees,
With furtive look and gesture, to his feet
Stealing, half stood, half crouched, a speaker new.
This was one Shimei, an abject man,

Abject in spirit, though in wit not dull,
And capable of long malevolence
Fed on resentments such as abjects feel.
Saul listened, but Gamaliel bowed in prayer,
As Shimei thus, obliquely, sneering, spoke :
" Stoning is pleasant, doubtless, when, as now,
One's sense of righteousness is much engaged.
The reflex satisfaction to be had
From accurately casting a choice stone
To break the teeth of the ungodly, is
Superlative, perhaps the very highest
Relish attainable to mortals here.
The consciousness of sympathy with God
Always exhilarates delightfully ;
But in particular if the sympathy
Be exercised in such a case as this,
Where the most glorious of God's attributes,
His justice, is involved.   Borne far above
Pity, or any weakness of the sense,
You only feel a rapture of divine
Approval of the law you execute.
So subtly strong and sweet possesses you
The instinct to indulge your appetite
For righteousness, you might almost mistake

Your pleasure for the pleasure of revenge.

 " But let revenge be for the heathen, who
Know not Jehovah and His law contemn.
Jehovah's chosen we, our sentiment
Purged of all personal bias of mere hate,
We simply wash our feet in wicked blood
With pleasure — pleasure naturally enhanced,
If we have spilled said wicked blood ourselves.

 " Yea, stoning gratifies the pious mind
Profoundly — grant the stoning be by you ;
By you, not to you ; being stoned, I judge,
Is less satisfactory.   On this point who doubt
Or differ, have their opportunity
To clear their minds by prompt experiment —
They need but act upon the last advice ;
For — grant our gracious masters smiled and pleased
To let us play a prank of self-misrule,
This once, wilful, but harmless, in their view,
Which might even turn out comedy for them —
Yet, stoning these, we should ourselves get stoned,
With expedition — past all chance of doubt.
Our friend, the vehement adviser here,
Might peradventure go himself as blithe

To be stoned by the people, as to stone
These pestilent fellows — for the glory of God.
But, then, more clearly how the glory of God
Would be subserved thereby, the rest of us,
Colder in heart perhaps, but certainly
Cooler in head, would wish to be advised,
Before we take our lives into our hands
To wreak the righteous judgment of the law
On favorites of a fierce and fickle mob
Whose palms, unless I much misread the signs,
Already itch for stones to throw at us,
While we sit here and talk of throwing stones
At whom they love and honor.

        " Give them line
This wild Jerusalem mob, and they will change
Their mood.   Remember how it chanced but late
With Jesus Nazarene.   Hailed yesterday
Messiah, King of kings and Lord of lords,
Ovation of hosannas greeting him
From thousand times a thousand throats — to-day,
A malefactor hooted through the streets,
With ' Crucify him ! Crucify him !' cried
In multitudinous chorus like one voice —
The mouths to-day and yesterday the same.

Their second tune indeed we set for them
And sang precentors — but how well they joined!
In due time pitch them the like tune again,
And doubt not they will sing it with full breath.

 " Not that I hence advise to wait remiss;
My counsel is no less from sloth removed
Than hostile to crude, hasty violence.
Only, shun public note ; with proper quest,
Ways may be found, ways pregnant too, that make
No noise.   The nail that went so shrewdly through
Siscra's temples made no noise.   It sped
Softly, but sped surely, and found the quick
Secret of life.   Are there not Jaels yet?
You have guessed what I advise.   The end you seek
Is holy; holy hold whatever means
Shall lead thereto.   Let us commit this thing
To those the wisest found among us, few
Better than many, charging them to choose
Some suitable silent means of silencing
These praters, without stir or scandal made,
Likest the ways of nature, hint, perhaps,
Conveyed of overruling providence
At work through nature for revenging crime.

" For me, I seek no honor at your hands :
I do not court responsibility ;
I am least wise among you ; yet a trust
Imposed were duty sacred in mine eyes."

As, should along a living bosom warm
With youthful life-blood coursing joyously,
A deadly serpent, with protracted, cold
Belly incumbent, glide, beneath that touch
And creep the conscious flesh would creeping shrink,
And all the genial current in the veins
Curdle ; so now, at Shimei's words, much more
At signs in him that spoke beyond his words,
The accent of the voice, the look, the port
Of figure, sinister suggestion couched
In action or grimace, there came a chill,
A shudder, of reaction and collapse
Over the council late with zeal aglow.
Even Mattathias, who, in attitude
Of menace, after Shimei arose,
Some space still stood — he, too, while Shimei
Was speaking, felt the evil spell and sank
Into his seat.   With one accord they all,
When Shimei ceased, a gloomy silence kept.

Gamaliel did not lift his head, but groaned
Audibly now, though gently, in his prayer.

From such a source such sound made seem yet more
Ominous the spell which hushed that council-hall.

BOOK II.
SAUL AND THE SANHEDRIM.

THE Sanhedrim still in session on the apostles' case, Saul speaks ; first scornfully repudiating for himself Shimei's proposal of guile, and then impressively announcing his own purpose, now fully mature, to controvert the Christian preachers in open argument before the people. After a pause following Saul's speech, Gamaliel speaks in favor of letting the prisoners go free. Other councillors express their sentiments. A scourging of the utmost severity being proposed, Nicodemus, with bated breath, deprecates first a cruel infliction, and then any infliction at all. Release after scourging is finally resolved upon.

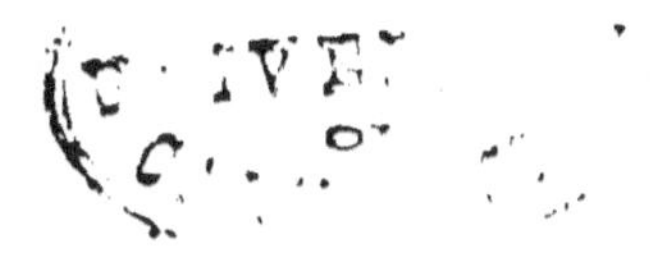

SAUL AND THE SANHEDRIM.

Dumb-struck and stirless long the Sanhedrim —
Instinctively abhorrent from the part
Of that base councillor — at last there rose
A new assessor in the midst to speak.

A young man he, who, in the general thought,
Wherever moving, round about him wore
A golden halo of uncertain hope
And prophecy of bright futures.   Aspect clear
And pure; straight stature; foothold firm and free;
The bloom of youth just ripening to the hue
Of perfect manhood upon cheek and brow;
Lip mobile, but not lax — capacity
Expressed of exquisite emotion, will
Elastic and resilient, tempered true
To bend, not break, and ultimately strong;
Glances of lightning latent in the eye,
But lightning liable to be quenched in tears;
The pride of every Hebrew, such was Saul.

A stir of expectation broke the hush
Of that strange silence, ere his opening words:
" That I, the youngest of this order, thus
Should rise for speech — and that beloved gray head
Before me bowed, unready yet — might seem
Unseemly.   But to speak after he speaks,
My own reveréd guide, the guide of all,
Would be, should I then speak to differ, more
Unseemly still.   And what I have to say,
Being my thought, burns in me to be said,
Approve, condemn, who will ; God bids me speak."

Gamaliel raised his head and looked at Saul.
Saul felt the look, and hardened his will, but not
His heart, to meet it.   Turning so, he saw,
Not what he inly braced himself to bear,
Warning, rebuke, anger to overawe,
Reproach, appeal, dissuasion, pain confessed
At filial separation, grasp of will
At old authority elapsed — of these,
Naught ; only a pathos of perplexity,
A broken, anguished, groping childlikeness,
Desire of any help, and hope of none —
Saul will hereafter understand it all ;

He simply marks it now compassionately
In wonder, pausing not, and thus, with loth
Allusion to the last advice, proceeds:
" But other speech my lips refuse, until
I purge my conscience by protesting here,
For me, I spurn, scorn, hate, loathe utterly
The devil and devilish lies.   I have no qualms
At blood, but I love truth, and qualms I own
At falsehood, practised in whatever name ;
Damnable ever, then thrice damnable,
Damning a holy cause it feigns to serve !"

A flush of warm revival in the breasts
Of some that listened answered to such words.
But one there was, that vile adviser, felt
A gripe of mortal hatred at his heart.
He, by Gamaliel's eye not unobserved,
Behind a black malignant scowl which, like
That murk emission of the cuttle-fish,
Flushed from his heart his face to overspread
And hide his thought, sat fostering the wound
Of Saul's disdainful noble words—a wound
To rankle long in the obscene recess
Of that bad bosom, and therein to breed

At last an issue foul of fell revenge ;
In purpose fell, though in fulfilment foiled.

But Saul, magnanimously heedless, deigned
Nor glance at him nor thought of consequence.
Elate with the elixir of his youth,
And buoyed with confidence exultant now
By the rebound of his beginning, buoyed
Besides with sympathy, he passed along,
Yet, master he, not mastered, of his mood,
Curbed strongly his strong passion and delight
Of power, and, calm with self-possessing will,
Force in him to have sped a thunderbolt
Stayed back from sudden waste, to be sent on
In fine diffusive throb — as farther thus :
" Enough of that ; I did but purify
My soul with words.   I feared some inward stain
From only listening, if I listened only,
And did not speak, when base was proffered me.

" Hear now what I propose.   What I propose
Is not advice ; advice I neither give
Nor ask.   I do not ask it, for my heart
Is fixed ; duress of conscience presses me,
With flesh and blood forbidding to confer.

I must do what I shall, in man's or devil's
Despite.   I trust I speak not thus in pride.
Not therefore that the census of your yeas
Or nays may guide me, but that ye may weigh
What force my purpose now unfolded owns
To sway your present counsels, hear and judge.

" Ye know, and all Jerusalem, that Saul
Has counted nothing worthy to be prized
Beside the learning of the law of God.
For this, a boy, from yon Cilician lands
I came ; for this, I have consumed my youth.
What envied gains of knowledge I have made,
Sitting a student at Gamaliel's feet,
Befits me not to vaunt ; these, small or large,
Belong to God and to my nation, being mine
Only to use for Him and them.   I see
Plainly how I must use my trust from God.
Wherefore are we assembled ?   Wherefore, save
Because these sciolists pervert the law,
Deceived perhaps, deceiving certainly ? "

Scarce waved a careless hand in sign at them —
Toward the apostles, still in presence there,
Saul deigned not to divert his scornful eyes :

"Shame is it if I, knowing the law indeed,
Am less than match for these untutored minds,
Amid the flocking fools they lead astray,
To controvert their hateful heresies.
Herewith then I proclaim my ripe resolve
To undertake, against the preaching liars,
On their own terms, a warfare for the truth.
Let it be seen which cause, in open list,
Is stronger, truth from heaven or lie from hell!

" Brethren and fathers, as ye will, consult ;
The youngest has his purpose thus divulged."

As when a palm diversely blown upon
In a strong tempest of opponent winds,
Now this way, and now that, obedient
To each prevailing present urgency,
Leans to all quarters of the firmament
By turns, but quickly, let a lull succeed,
Upright again, shows every leaf composed ;
So now the council, long enough between
Opinion and opinion buffeted,
While Saul was speaking took a little ease,
No new advice proposed, to breathe again,
Steady itself, and come to equipoise.

Some thought that Saul had spoken proudly; some,
That pride became his worth; some held that he
Would make his vaunting good; some feared his plan
Savored of youth and rashness; others deemed
Public dispute mistaken precedent
Teeming with various mischief — sure to breed
Insufferable pretensions in the crowd,
So taught to count themselves fit arbiters
On Scriptural or traditional points of moot,
And, by close consequence, a serious breach
Endanger in their own authority;
Yet others felt, whatever fruit beside
Was borne of Saul's proposed experiment,
Two things at least were safe to reckon on —
In its own dignity, the Sanhedrim
Must needs incur immedicable hurt, ·
So plainly scandalous a spectacle
Exhibiting, a councillor enrolled
Of their own number stooping to debate
On equal terms with ignorant fishermen;
Then, on their side, those flattered fishermen,
Far from indulging proper gratitude
For being publicly confounded quite
At such illustrious hands, would be instead

Inflated out of measure, nigh to burst,
With added pride at complaisance so new
From their superiors, while the common herd
Would give them greater heed accordingly.

Such things diverse they thought, and silence kept,
Saul's colleagues in the Sanhedrim; they all
Together felt that Saul in any wise
Would go Saul's way; they therefore silence kept.

One man alone, by age and gravity,
And reverence his in ample revenue,
Was easy master of the Sanhedrim:
On him the council rested and revolved,
As on a fixéd centre and support.
And now, 'Gamaliel! let us hear at last
Gamaliel's word,' was suddenly the sole,
The simultaneous, silent thought to all.
The eyes of all concentred instantly
Upon Gamaliel found that saint esteemed
And sage already stirring as to rise.
Their readiness to hear, with his to speak,
Timed so in perfect reciprocity
And exquisite accord responsive, marked
That fleet meet moment for the orator,

Which, conscious half, but half unconscious, he,
Gamaliel, wielded by the Holy Ghost,
Was now to seize and use for God so well.

The hoary head, the mien of majesty,
The associative power of ancient fame,
His habit and tradition of command,
Their instinct, grown inveterate, to obey,
Always, wherever he arose to speak
Among his brethren, won Gamaliel heed.
But now, a certain gentle winsomeness,
Born of a certain wavering wistfulness,
Qualified so a new solemnity
Of manner, like a prophet's, felt in him,
That awe came on his hearers as from God.
Gamaliel first bade put the prisoners forth,
In keeping, out of audience, and then said :
" My brethren : Saul my brother — son no more
I name him, since he parts himself from me
In counsel — yet I love him not the less — "

A tremor of sensation fluttered through
The council, with these words, and at Saul's heart
Pausing, infixed, then healed, a subtle pang
Of sweet remorse and gracious tenderness —

" Yea, not the less for this love I my son,
My brother, while I honor him the more.
Yea, and not wholly does he part himself
From me ; in deepest counsel we are one.
Saul seeks to honor God obeying Him,
The same seek I ; are we not deeply one?
And ever I have taught obedience
To God as the prime thing and paramount ;
Disciple therefore still to me, and son,
Is Saul, even in this act and article
Of his secession from his master's part ;
Saul and Gamaliel both, and all of us,
I pray my God to save from self-deceit !
I shudder while I pray, ' Deliver me,
O Lord, deliver, from the secret sin
Of false supposed obedience masking pride !'

" Late, I was sure, as Saul is sure to-day.
I thought, and doubted not, we ought to do
Even what ye now are bent to bring to pass.
My way was not Saul's way, but rather yours ;
To me it seemed plainly, as seems to you,
Wiser to save the body by some loss,
If loss were need, of limb.   Unfalteringly,

The knife would I myself with mine own hand
Have wielded to cut off these members, judged
Unsound and harmful to the general health,
Forever from the congregation.   Now,
I feel less sure, Gamaliel feels less sure.
I wish — brethren, I think I wish — to be
Obedient; though deceitful is the heart
Above all things and wicked desperately —
What man can know it ? — yet I think I will
Obedience.   That was a pure word — the mouth
However far from pure that uttered it —
' To God rather than men must we obey.'
Saul was true son of mine to turn from me
To God — if haply he to God indeed
Have turned from me, and not from me to Saul,
Not knowing !   Might I also turn, even I,
Gamaliel from Gamaliel, unto God !
I dread to trust myself, lest I, myself
Obeying, misdeem myself obeying God.

   " Hearken, my children.   These accuséd men
Unlikely, most unlikely, choice of Heaven
To be His prophets, seemed, and seem, to me.
I look at them and find no prophet mien ;

I listen and their Galilæan speech
Offends me ; and far more the scandal is
To think what message they propound to us.
Their person and their message I reject —
Reject, or if reject not, not receive.
And yet, my brethren, yet, I counsel you,
Beware !   What ye intend, accomplished once,
Were once for all accomplished, not to be
Undone forever.   Ye consult to slay,
And find your purpose hard to come by.   How,
If, having slain, to your repentance, ye
Consulted to bring back to life again ?
Were that not harder yet ?   Wherefore, I say, take heed,
Ye men of Israel.   Remember how,
A generation gone, Theudas arose,
Proud boaster and asserter of himself,
Who drew his hundreds to his standard ; he
Was slain, and all his followers came to naught.
Some space thereafter, out of Galilee
Judas arose and mustered to his side
Many adherents ; but he perished too,
And all that clave to him were far dispersed.

"This therefore as to these is my advice :

Refrain your hands from them ; let them alone.
Know, if their deed and counsel be of men,
Its doom is certain, it will come to naught ;
But if it be of God, strive how ye may,
Ye cannot overthrow it.   Well take heed,
Lest haply ye be found to fight against
God.   For myself, when close upon the heels
Of what was wrought mysterious in the escape
Of these our prisoners from that warded keep
Fast-barred, I heard their answer to our sharp
Inquest and blame, I felt as felt of old
That prophet chanting his majestic strain,
' The Lord is in His holy temple, let
The earth, let the whole earth, before Him keep
Silence.'   My soul kept silence and still keeps.
And silence keep, all ye, before the Lord !
For the Lord cometh, lo, He cometh swift
To judge the earth !   And who of us shall bide
The day of His approach ?   Not surely he
Then found in arms against God and His Christ !"

    Gamaliel spoke and ceased ; but, while he spoke,
His speaking was like silence audible,
Rather than sound of voice ; and when he ceased,

His silence was as eloquence prolonged.

Awhile the council sat as in a trance,
Unable or unwilling to bestir
Themselves for speech or motion.   But not all
Are capable of awe.   Some present there,
Either through sad defect of nature proof,
Or through long worldly habit seared and sealed,
Against the access of heavenly influence,
Bode unaware of anything divine
Descended near them — carnal minds, immersed
In sense, from shocks of spirit insulate,
Calm, discomposure none from things unseen,
The faculty for such experience lost,
Pitiably self-possessed ! and God Himself
So nigh to have possessed them !

These a space
Waited to let the power a little pass,
Wrought by Gamaliel on the council ; then
With tentative preamble, one of them
Said that Gamaliel's words were words of weight,
Weight well derived from character like his —
Whereat the speaker paused, with crafty eye
Cast round from countenance to countenance,

To read how much he safely might detract,
By open difference or by sly demur,
From the just value and authority
Of mild Gamaliel's sentence.   But small sign
Saw he to hearten him in hope of ebb
To the strong tide still standing at full flood
That set in favor of the prisoners.
He feebly closed with wish expressed — and wish
It was, not hope — of hope no grounds he saw —
That some means might be found to save the shocked
And staggering dignity — a dignity
Ancient and sacred — of the Sanhedrim
From sheer shipwreck.

                Some slight responsive stir
Under such spur to pride emboldened one
To trust they should at least sharply rebuke
The prisoners, and take bond of word from them
Not further to disturb the city's peace.
Another following said, that had been tried
Already once, with what result accrued
Was plain to see.   And now the Sanhedrim,
Through various such suggestion commonplace,
Relaxed somewhat from their late mood so tense,
Grew readier to approve his voice who said :

"The first offence we deemed condignly met
With reprimand from us, and interdict.
Those gentle means the prisoners once have scorned,
And to our face assure us they will scorn.
Now let such contumacious insolence
Toward just authority too meek, be met,
If not with death deserved, at least with stripes
So heavy they shall wish it had been death."

Such truculence renewed provoked a new
Reaction. This, that councillor less stern
Noted — who, with Gamaliel and with Saul,
Refrained, when all the others hissed applause
To Mattathias — noted, and with thrift
Converted into opportunity.

A wary spirit Nicodemus was,
With impulses toward good, but weak in will,
And selfish as the timid are. His heart
Was a divided empire in his breast,
Half firm for God, but half to self seduced.
His fellows trusted him accordingly;
Hate him they could not, but they did not love.
Some guessed him guilty of discipleship
To Jesus, secretly indulged through fear.

This their suspicion the suspect in turn
Suspected, and the uneasy consciousness
Made him more curious than his wont to move
By indirection toward his present aim.
What he wished was, to serve the prisoners
And not disserve himself — a double end,
Rendering his counsels double ; but as such
Could speak, now Nicodemus rising spoke.
With sinuous slow approach winning his way
Devious whither he wished to go, like those
Creatures that backward facing forward creep
And seem retiring still while they advance,
So Nicodemus wound him toward his goal,
Well-chosen, as he said :

      " Let us be wise ;
Beyond our purpose were not well to go,
Were foolish. Cruelty is not, I trust,
Our spirit ; God is just, but cruel not.
Let us, God's sons, be just indeed, like God,
But then, like God, also not cruel. Stripes
Are heavy, howsoever lightly laid
On freeborn men. The shame is punishment ;
A wounded spirit who can bear? Through flesh
You smite the smarting spirit, every blow.

Remember too that lacerated flesh
Has lips to plead with, makes its mute appeal
To pity — eloquence incapable
Of being answered, charging cruelty ;
Whereas the bleeding spirit, bleeding hid,
No cruelty imputes, reports no pain,
But, pith of self-respect clean gone from one,
Glazes the eye, dejects the countenance,
Changes the voice to hollow, takes the spring
Out of the step, and leaves the man a wretch
To suffer on an object of contempt
More than compassion — hopelessly bereft
Of power to captivate the public ear,
Which ever itches to be caught the prey
Of orator full-blooded, iron lungs,
Brass front, a lusty human animal.
Such make of men, through shame of public stripes,
Transformed to eunuchs — this, sure, were enough ;
Nay, for our purpose, more than more would be.
And even so much as this, yea, lightest stripe,
Drawing a sequel such as I have said —
Brethren, for me, my soul revolts from it ;
I feel it cruel, fear it impious.
Behooves we ponder well Gamaliel's word ;

And, if to slay were haply against God
To be found fighting, why not, then, to scourge?"

"Such fine-spun sentiment," another now,
Concurring, though sarcastically, said,
" In pity of the victim of the scourge
For suffering inwardly endured through shame,
Supposes that your victim is endowed
With some small faculty for feeling shame,
Which in the present case asks evidence.

" Still, I too take the clement part, and say,
If only for Saul's sake, let these go free
Of any but the lightest punishment.
Saul will desire for foemen hearts as strong
As may be, to call out that strength in him
Which we well know, for their discomfiture.
Even thus, he may prefer some other foe
Than men disparaged by the brand of blows
Upon their backs, some fairer, fresher fame,
His gage of battle to take up, and be
By him immortalized through overthrow
Experienced, such as never yet was worse."

Divergent so in view or motive, they
Agreed at last to let the prisoners go

With stripes inflicted, and a charge severe
Imposed to speak in Jesus' name no more.
These so released departed thence with joy,
Rejoicing to have been accounted meet
For Jesus' sake to suffer shame.　Nor ceased
Those faithful men to preach and teach as erst,
Both in the temple and from house to house,
Daily still sounding forth Jesus as Christ.

But Saul withdrew deep pondering in his mind
How he might best his plan divulged fulfill.

BOOK III.

SAUL AGAINST STEPHEN.

STEPHEN, as a Christian preacher of brilliant genius and of growing fame, is selected by Saul to be his antagonist in the controversy resolved upon by him. To a vast concourse of people assembled in expectation of hearing Stephen preach, Saul takes the opportunity to address an impassioned and elaborate appeal, with argument, against Stephen's doctrine. His hearers are powerfully affected ; among them, he not knowing it, Saul's own beloved sister Rachel.

SAUL AGAINST STEPHEN.

LIKE a wise soldier on some task intent
Of moment and of hazard, who, at heart
Secure of prospering, yet no caution counts,
No pains, unworthy, but with wary feet
Explores his ground about him every rood,
.All elements of chance forecalculates,
Draws to his part each doubtful circumstance;
Never too much provided, point by point
Equips himself superfluously strong,
That he prevailing may with might prevail,
And overcome with bounteous victory;
So Saul, firm in resolve and confident,
And inly stung with conscience and with zeal
Not to postpone his weighty work proposed,
Would not be hasty found, nor rash, to fail
Of any circumspection that his sure
Triumph might make more sure, or wider stretch
Its margin, certain to be wide.

Some days

After the council, he, with forecast sage
And prudence to prepare, refrained himself
From word or deed in public ; while, at home,
Not moody, but not genial as his use,
His gracious use, was, self-absorbed, retired
In deep and absent muse, he nigh might seem
A stranger to his sister well-beloved,
Wont to be sharer of his inmost mind.

Inmost, save one reserve.   He never yet
Had shown to any, scarce himself had seen,
The true deep master motive of his soul,
That fountain darkling in the depths of self
Whence into light all streams of being flowed.
Saul daily, nightly, waking, sleeping, dreamed
Of a new nation, his belovéd own,
Resurgent from the dust consummate fair,
And, for chief corner-stone, with shoutings reared
To station in the stately edifice —
Whom but himself?   Who worthier than Saul?

This beckoning image bright of things to be —
Audacious-lovelier far than might be shown
To any, yea, than he himself dared look,

With his own eyes, steadfast and frank upon—
Was interblent so closely in his mind
With what should be the fortune and effect
Of his intended controversy nigh,
That, though his settled purpose to dispute
He had for public reasons publicly
Declared, he yet in private, of that strife,
Still future, everywhere to speak abstained,
Abiding even unto his sister dumb.

Rachel from Tarsus to Jerusalem
Had borne her brother company, her heart
One heart with his to cheer him toward the goal
Of his high purpose, which she knew, to be
Beyond his equals master in the law.
Alone they dwelt together, their abode
Between Gamaliel's and the synagogue
Of the Cilicians.   Beautiful and bright
His home she made to him, with housewife ways
Neat-handed, and with fair companionship.

The sister, with that quick intelligence
The woman's, first divined, for secret cause
Of this her brother's travailing silentness,
That he some pregnant enterprise revolved;

Then, having, with the woman's wit, found means
To advise herself what enterprise it was,
She, with the woman's tact of sympathy,
In watchful quiet reverent of his mood,
Strove with him and strove for him, in her thought,
Her wish, her hope, her prayer; nor failed sometimes
A word to drop, unconsciously as seemed,
By lucky chance, that might perhaps convey
A timely help of apt suggestion wise
To Saul her brother for his purpose, he
All undisturbed to guess that aught was meant.

At home, abroad, reserved, Saul not the less
All places of men's frequence and resort
Still visited, and mixed with crowds to catch
The whisper of the people; active not,
But not supine, observing unobserved
As if alone amid the multitude.
The brave apostles of the Nazarene
He heard proclaim their master Lord and Christ,
And marked their method in the Scriptures; not
With open mind obedient toward the truth,
But ever only with shut heart and hard,
Intent on knowing how to contradict.

Meanwhile the novel doctrines spread, and found
New converts day by day, and day by day
Proclaimers new.   Of these more eminent
Was none than Stephen, flaming prophet he,
Quenchless in spirit, full of faith and power.
Him oft Saul heard, to listening throngs that hung
Upon the herald's lips with eager ear,
The claim of Jesus to Messiahship
Assert, and from the psalms and prophets prove.

In guise a seraph rapt, with love aflame
And all aflame with knowledge, like the bush
That burned with God in Horeb unconsumed,
The fervent pure apostle Stephen stood,
In ardors from celestial altars caught
Kindling to incandescence—stood and forged,
With ringing blow on blow, his argument,
A vivid weapon edged and tempered so,
And in those hands so wielded, that its stroke
No mortal might abide and bide upright.
Stephen is such as Saul erelong will be
Risen from the baptism of the Holy Ghost !

Saul felt the breath of human power that blew
Round Stephen like a morning wind, he felt

The light that lifted and transfigured him
And glorified, that bright auroral ray
Of genius which forever makes the brow
It strikes on from its fountain far in God
Shine like the sunrise-smitten mounta'n peak —
Saul felt these things in Stephen by his tie
With Stephen in the fellowship of power;
Kindred to kindred answered and rejoiced.
But that in Stephen which was more and higher
Than Stephen at his native most and highest,
The inhabitation of the Holy Ghost —
This, Saul had yet no se ..se to apprehend.
The Spirit of God, only the Spirit of God
Can know; the natural man to Him is deaf
And blind.   Saul, therefore, seeing did not see,
And hearing heard not.   But no less his heart,
In seeing and in hearing Stephen speak,
Leapt up with recognition of a peer
In power to be his meet antagonist
And task him to his uttermost to foil.
Beyond Saul's uttermost it was to be,
That task! though this of Stephen not, but God.

Still goaded day by day with such desire

As nobler spirits know, to feel the strain
And wrestle of antagonistic thews
Tempting his might and stirring up his mind,
Saul felt, besides, the motion and ferment
And great dilation of a patriot-soul,
Magnanimous, laboring for his country's cause.
He thought the doctrines of the Nazarene
Pernicious to the Jewish commonwealth,
Not less than was his person base, his life
Unseemly, and opprobrious his death.
He saw, or deemed he saw, in what was taught
From Jesus, only deep disparagement
Disloyally implied of everything
Nearest and dearest to the Hebrew heart.
The gospel was high treason in Saul's eyes;
Suppose it but established in success,
The temple then would be no more what erst
It was, the daily sacrifice would cease,
The holy places would with heathen feet
Be trodden and profaned, the middle wall
Of old partition between Jew and Greek
Would topple undermined, the ritual law
Of Moses would be obsolete and void,
Common would be the oracles of God.

To all divulged, peculiar once to Jews—
Of Jewish name and nation what were left?
Such thoughts, that seemed of liberal scope, were
  Saul's,
Commingled, he not knowing, with some thoughts,
Less noble, of his own aggrandizement.

It came at length to pass that on a day
The spacious temple-court is thronged with those
Come from all quarters to Jerusalem,
Or dwellers of the city, fain to hear
Once more the preacher suddenly so famed.
Present is Saul, but not as heretofore
To hearken only and observe; the hour
Has struck when his own voice he must uplift,
To make it heard abroad.
       He dreamed it not,
But Rachel too was there, his sister.   She
Had, from sure signs observed, aright surmised
That the ripe time to speak was come to Saul.
In her glad loyalty, she doubted not
That he, that day, would, out of a full mind,
Pressed overfull with affluence from the heart,
Pour forth a stream of generous eloquence —

Stream, nay, slope torrent, steep sheer cataract,
Of reason and of passion intermixed —
For such she proudly felt her brother's power —
Which down should rush upon his adversaries
And carry them away as with a flood,
Astonished, overwhelmed, and whirled afar;
Rescued at least the ruins of the state!
So glorying in her high vicarious hope
For Saul her brother, Rachel came that morn
Betimes and chose her out a safe recess
For easy audience, nigh, and yet retired,
Between the pillars of a stately porch,
Where she might see and not by him be seen.

   Thence Rachel watched all eagerly; when now
The multitude, expecting Stephen, saw
A different man stand forth with beckoning hand
As if to speak.   The act and attitude
Commanded audience, for a king of men
Stood there, and a great silence fell on all.
Some knew the face of the young Pharisee,
These whispered round his name; Saul's name and
      fame
To all were known, and, ere the speaker spoke,

Won him a deepening heed.

　　　　　　　　　Rachel the hush
Felt with a secret sympathetic awe,
And for one breath her beating heart stood still;
It leapt again to hear her brother's voice
Pealing out bold in joyous sense of power.
That noble voice, redounding like a surge
Pushed by the tide, on swept before the wind,
And all the ocean shouldering at its back,
Which seeks out every inlet of the shore
To brim it flush and level from the brine —
Such Saul's voice swelled, as from a plenteous sea,
And, wave on wave of pure elastic tone,
Rejoicing ran through every gallery,
And every echoing endless colonnade,
And every far-retreating least recess
Of building round about that temple-court,
And filled the temple-court with silver sound —
As thus, with haughty summons, he began :
" Ye men of Israel, sojourners from far
Or dwellers in Jerusalem, give heed.
The lines are fallen to us in evil times:
Opinions run abroad perverse and strange,
Divergent from the faith our fathers held.

A day is come, brethren, and fallen on us—
On us, this living generation, big
With promise, or with threat, of mighty doom.
Which will ye have it?   Threat, or promise, which?
Yours is the choosing—choose ye may, ye must.

" Abolish Moses, if ye will; destroy
The great traditions of your fathers; say
Abraham was naught, naught Isaac, Jacob, all
The patriarchs, heroes, martyrs, prophets, kings;
That Seed of Abraham naught, our nation's Hope,
Foretold to be an universal King;
Make one wide blank and void, an emptied page,
Of all the awful glories of our past—
Deliverance out of Egypt, miracle
On miracle wrought dreadfully for us
Against our foes, path cloven through the sea,
Jehovah in the pillar of cloud and fire,
And host of Pharaoh mightily overthrown ;
The law proclaimed on Sinai amid sound
And light insufferable and angels nigh
Attending; manna in the wilderness;
The rock that lived and moved and followed them,
Our fathers, flowing water in the waste—

Obliterate at a stroke whatever sets
The seal of God upon you as His own,
And marks you different from the heathen round —
Shekinah fixed between the cherubim,
The vacant Holy of Holies filled with God,
The morning and the evening sacrifice,
Priest, altar, incense, choral hymn and psalm,
Confused melodious noise of instruments
Together sounding the high praise of God ;
All this, with more I will not stay to tell,
This temple itself with its magnificence,
The hope of Him foreshown, the Messenger
Of that eternal covenant wherein
Your souls delight themselves, Who suddenly
One day shall come unto His temple — blot,
Expunge, erase, efface, consent to be
No more a people, mix and merge yourselves
With aliens, blood that in your veins flows pure
All the long way one stream continuous down
From Abraham called the friend of God — such blood
Adulterate in the idolatrous, corrupt
Pool of the Gentiles — men of Israel !
Or are ye men ? and are ye Israel ?
I stand in doubt of you — I stand in doubt

Of kinsmen mine supposed that bide to hear
Such things as seems that ye with pleasure hear!

  " Say, know ye not they mean to take away
Your place and name ?   Are ye so blind ?   Or are
Ye only base poor creatures caring not
Though knowing well ?   Oft have ye seen the fat
Of lambs upon the flaming altar fume
One instant and in fume consume away ;
So swiftly and so utterly shall pass,
In vapor of smoke, the glorious excellency,
The pomp, the pride, nay, but the being itself,
Of this our nation from beneath the sun,
Let once the hideous doctrine of a Christ
Condemned and crucified usurp the place
In Hebrew hearts of that undying hope
We cherish of Messiah yet to reign
In power and glory more than Solomon's,
From sunrise round to sunrise without end,
And tread the Gentiles underneath our feet. "

  Indignant patriot spirit in the breast
Of Rachel mixed itself with kindred pride
And gladness for her brother gleaming so
Before her in a kind of fulgurous scorn

Which made his hearers quail while they admired;
She could not stay a sudden gush of tears.

But Saul's voice now took on a winning change,
As, deprecating gently, thus he spoke:
" Forgive, my brethren, I have used hot words
Freely and frankly, as great love may speak.
But that I love you, trust you, hope of you
The best, the noblest, when once more you are
Yourselves, and feel the spirit of your past
Come back, I had not cared to speak at all.
I simply should have hung my head in shame,
Worn sackcloth, gone with ashes on my brow,
And sealed my hand upon my lips for you
Forever.   Love does not despair, but hopes
Forever.   And I love you far too well
To dream despair of you.   Bethink yourselves,
My brethren !   Me, as if I were the voice
Of your own ancient aspiration, hear.
Bear with me, let me chide, say not that love
Lured me to over-confidence of you.

" Be patient now, my brethren, while I go,
So briefly as I may, through argument
That well might ask the leisure of long hours,

To show from Scripture, from authority,
From reason and from nature too not less,
Why we should hold to our ancestral faith,
And not the low fanatic creed admit
Of such as preach for Christ one crucified.
Be patient—I myself must patient be,
Tutoring down my heart to let my tongue
Speak calmly, as in doubtful argument,
Where I am fixed and confident to scorn."

As when Gennesaret, in his circling hills,
By wing of wind down swooping suddenly
Is into tempest wrought that, to his depths
Astir, he rouses, and on high his waves
Uplifts like mountains snowy-capped with foam ;
So, smitten with the vehement impact
And passion of Saul's rash, abrupt
Beginning, that mercurial multitude
Had answered with commotion such as seemed
Menace of instant act of violence:
But, as when haply there succeeds a lull
To tempest, then the waves of Galilee
Sink from their swelling and smooth down to plane,
Yet deep will roll awhile from shore to shore

That long slow undulation following storm ;
So, when, with wise self-recollection, Saul,
In mid-career of passionate appeal,
Stayed, and those gusts of stormy eloquence
Impetuous poured no longer on the sea
Of audience underneath him, but, instead,
Proposed a sober task of argument,
The surging throng surceased its turbulence,
And settled from commotion into calm ;
Yet so as still to feel the rock and sway
Of central agitation at its heart,
While thus that master of its moods went on :
"What said Jehovah to the serpent vile
Which tempted Eve ?   Did he not speak of One,
Offspring to her seduced, Who should arise
To crush the offending head ?   No hint, I trow,
Of meekness and obedience unto death
Found there at least, death on the shameful tree,
Forsooth, to be the character and doom
Of that foretokened Champion of his kind,
That haughty Trampler upon Satan's head !

"To Abraham our father was of God
Foretold, ' In thee shall all the families

Of the earth be blessed.'   What blessing, pray, could come
Abroad upon mankind through Abraham's seed,
Messiah, should Messiah, Abraham's seed,
Prove to be such as now is preached to you,
A shame, a jest, a byword, a reproach,
A hissing and a wagging of the head,
A gazing-stock and mark for tongues shot out—
Burlesque and travesty of our brave hopes
And of our vaunts, shown vain, rife everywhere
Among the nations, that erelong a prince
Should from the stem of Jesse spring, to sway
An universal sceptre through the world?

"Did God mock Abraham?   Did He mean, perchance,
That all the families of the earth should find
Peculiar blessedness in triumphing
Over that puissant nation promised him,
His progeny, to match the stars of heaven
For multitude, and be as on the shore
The sands, innumerable?   Was such the sense
Of promise and of prophecy?   Behooves,
Then, we be glad and thankful, we, on whom

The fullness of the time now falls, to be
This blessing to the Gentiles.   But ye halt,
Beloved.   Slack and slow seem ye to greet
The honor fixed on you.   Why, hearken !   Ye,
Ye, out of all the generations, ye
Fallen on the times of Jesus crucified,
May count yourselves elect and called of God
To bless the Gentiles, in affording them
Unquenchable amusement to behold
Your wretched plight and broken pride !   Now clap
Your hands, ye chosen !   Let your mouth be filled
With laughter, and your tongue with singing filled !

     " Nay, sons of Abraham, nay.   No mocking words
Spake He who cannot lie, Lord God of truth
And grace.   He meant that Abraham's race should
     reign
From sea to sea while sun and moon endure.
And ever a blessing true it is to men
To bend the neck beneath an equal yoke
Of ruler strong and wise and just to rule.
Then will at last the Gentiles blesséd be
In Abraham, when, from Abraham's loins derived
Through David, God's Anointed shall begin,

In David's city, His long government
Of the wide world, and every heathen name
Shall kiss the rod and own Messiah king.

" Our father Jacob, touched with prophecy,
Spake of a sceptre that should not depart
From Judah until Shiloh came, to Whom
The obedience of the peoples was to be ;
A sceptre, symbol of authority
And rule, law-giving attribute, resort
Of subject nations speeding to a yoke —
Such ever everywhere in Holy Writ
The image and the character impressed
On God's Messiah, hope of Israel.

"What need I more ? Wherefore to ears like yours,
Well used to hear them in the temple chants
Resounded with responsive voice to voice,
Rehearse those triumphs and antiphonies
Wherein Jehovah Father to His Son
Messiah speaks : ' Ask Thou of Me, and I
To Thee the heathen for inheritance
Will give, and for possession the extreme
Parts of the earth.   Thou shalt with rod of iron

Break them, yea, shatter them shalt Thou in shards,
Like a clay vessel from the potter's hand.
Be wise now, therefore, O ye kings, be ye
Instructed, judges of the earth.   Kiss ye
The Son, lest He be angry, and His wrath,
Full soon to be enkindled, you devour.'
Tell me, which mood of prophecy is that,
The meek or the heroic ?   Craven he,
Or king, to whom Jehovah deigns such speech,
Concerning whom such counsel recommends?

"'Gird Thou upon Thy thigh Thy sword, O Thou
Most Mighty,'— so once more the psalmist, rapt
Prophetical as to a martial rage,
Breaks forth, Jehovah to Messiah speaking —
'Gird on Thy glory and Thy majesty ;
And in Thy majesty ride prosperously,
And Thy right hand shall teach Thee terrible things.
Sharp in the heart of the king's enemies
Thine arrows are, whereby the peoples fall
Beneath Thee.'   Such Messiah is, a man
Of war and captain of the host of God.
Nay, now it mounts to a deific strain,
The prophet exultation of the psalm :

' Thy throne, O God,' it sings — advancing Him,
Messiah, to the unequalled dignity
And lonely glory of the ONE I AM,
Audacious figure — close on blasphemy,
Were it not God who speaks — to represent
The dazzling splendors of Messiahship.

" Let us erect our spirits from the dust,
My brethren, and, as sons of God, nay, gods
Pronounced — unless we grovel and below
Our birthright due, unfilial and unfit,
Sink self-depressed — let us, I pray you, rise,
Buoyed upward from within by sense of worth
Incapable to be extinguished, rise,
Found equal to the will of God for us,
And know the true Messiah when He comes.
Be sure that when He comes, His high degree
Will shine illustrious, like the sun in heaven,
Not feebly flicker for your fishermen
From Galilee to point it out to you
With their illiterate ' Lo, here !' " Lo, there !' "

At this increasing burst of scorn from Saul,
'Exultant like the pæan and the cry

That rises through the palpitating air
When storming warriors take the citadel,
Once more from Rachel's fixéd eyes the tears
Of sympathetic exultation flowed —
The sister with the brother, as in strife
Before the battle striving equally,
Now equally in triumph triumphing.

But Saul, his triumph, felt to be secure,
Securer still will make with new appeal:
" If so, as we have seen, the Scriptures trend,
Not less the current of tradition too —
No counter-current, eddy none — one stress,
Steady and full, from Adam down to you,
Runs strong the self-same way.   Out of the past
What voice is heard in contradiction ?   None.

" Turn round and ask the present ; you shall hear
One answer still the same from every mouth
Of scribe or master versed in Holy Writ.
Tradition and authority in this
Agree with Scripture, teaching to await
For our deliverer an anointed king.
What ruler of our people has believed
In Jesus, him of Nazareth, Joseph's son,

As Christ of God?   If any, then some soul
Self-judged unworthy of his rulership,
Secret disciple, shunning to avow
His faith, and justly therefore counted naught —
Ruler in name, in nature rather slave.

  "And now I bid you look within your breast
And answer, Does not your own heart rebel
Against the gospel of the Nazarene?
'Gospel,' forsooth !   Has God, who made your heart,
Provided you for gospel what your heart
Rejects with loathing ?   Likely seems it, pray,
Becoming, fit, that He Who, on the mount
Of Sinai once the law promulging, there
Displayed His glory more than mortal eye
Could bear to look upon or ear to hear —
Who in the temple hid behind the veil
Shekinah blazed between the cherubim —
Nay, tell me, seems it tolerable even
To you, that your Jehovah God should choose,
Lover of splendor as He is, and power,
To represent Himself among mankind
Not merely naked of magnificence,
But outright squalid in the mean estate

And person of a carpenter, to die
At last apparent felon crucified?
Reason and nature outraged cry aloud,
'For shame!   For shame!' at blasphemy like this.'

    A strange ungentle impulse moved the heart
Of Rachel to a mood like mutiny,
And almost she "For shame!" herself cried out
In echo to her brother's vehemence;
While murmur as of wind rousing to storm
Ran through the assembly at such words from Saul,
The passion of the speaker so prevailed
To stir responsive passion in their breasts.
This Saul perceiving said, in scornful pride,
Fallaciously foretasting triumph won :
" Ye men of Israel, gladly I perceive
Some embers of the ancient fire remain,
If smouldering, not extinguished, in your breasts.
I will not further chafe your noble rage.
You are, if I mistake not, now prepared
To hear more safely, if less patiently,
The eloquence I keep you from too long.
Let me bespeak for Stephen your best heed."

    And Saul, as if in gesture of surcease,

A pace retiring, waved around his hand
Toward Stephen, opposite not far, the while
His nostril he dispread, and mobile lip
Curled, in the height of contumelious scorn ;
And Rachel, where she stood, unconsciously,
The transport of her sympathy was such,
Repeated with her features what she saw.

BOOK IV.

STEPHEN AGAINST SAUL.

Stephen, following Saul, turns the tide of feeling overwhelmingly in the opposite direction. Saul, however, but he almost alone — for even his sister Rachel has been converted — stands out defiant against the manifest power of God. Shimei appears as an auditor watching with sinister motive the course of the controversy.

STEPHEN AGAINST SAUL.

THE tumult grew a tempest when Saul ceased:
No single voice of mortal man might hope,
Though clear like clarion and like trumpet loud,
To live in that possessed demoniac sea
Of vast vociferation whelming all,
Or ride the surges of the wild uproar.
What ailed thee, O thou sea, that thy mad mind
So suddenly was soothed?   Did ' Peace, be still!'
Dropping, an unction from the Holy One,
Softly as erst on stormy Galilee,
Wide overspread the summits of the waves
And sway their swelling down to glassy calm?
Stephen stood forth to speak, and all was still.

Before he spoke, already Rachel felt
A different power of silence there, and sense,
Within, other than sympathetic awe;
This felt she, though she knew it not, nor dreamed
It was the Holy Ghost sent down from heaven!

" Brethren"—so Stephen, not in confidence
Of power his own, but in full faith of power
Bestowed, began—" God's thoughts are not our
        thoughts,
Neither our ways His ways; for as the heavens
Are than the earth more high, so than our ways
More high are His, and His thoughts than our thoughts.
Our valued wisdom folly is to God
Full oft; then most, when folly seems to us
God's wisdom.   Have ye yet to learn that God
Rejoices to confound the vain conceit
Of man ?   The Scriptures, then, search ye with eyes
Blinded so thick ?   It is Isaiah's word :
' Jehovah, yea, hath poured upon you all
The spirit of deep sleep, and hath your eyes,
Those prophets of the soul that might be, closed,
Also your heads, meant to be seers, hath veiled ;
And vision all is now to you become
Even as the words of a shut book and sealed.
Therefore Jehovah saith, For that this people
Draw nigh to Me in worship with their mouth,
But have their heart removed from Me afar,
While all their fear of Me is empty form
Enjoined of men, and idly learned by rote—

Behold, a thing of wonder will I do
Among this people, wonder passing thought,
And perish shall the wisdom of their wise
And prudence of their prudent come to nought!'

" Brethren, that was man's wisdom which just now
Ye heard, and were well pleased to hear, from Saul.
Hearken again, and hear what God will speak."

At the first word that fell from Stephen's lips,
An overshadowing of the Holy Ghost
Hung like a heaven above the multitude;
With every word that followed, slow and full,
That awful cope seemed ever hovering down
Impendent nearer, as when, fold to fold,
Droops lower and lower a dark and thunderous sky.
The speaker used no arts of oratory;
Only a still small voice, not wholly his,
Nor wholly human, issuing from his lips,
Only a voice, but eloquence was shamed.
And Stephen thus his theme premised pursues:
" Rightly and wrongly, both at once, have ye
This day been taught of God's Messiah; King
He is, as Saul has said, but in a sense,
And with a highth and depth and length and breadth

And reach immense of meaning, that nor Saul,
Nor ye, nor any by the Holy Ghost
Untaught, have yet conceived.   Not of this world
His kingdom is.   The pageant and the pomp,
State visible, and splendor to the eye,
Are of this world that vanishes away,
And of the princes of this world that come
To naught.   His glory whose the kingdom is
Whereof I speak, no eye hath seen, no eye
Can see.   That vision is for naked soul.

 " The lordship and authority which craves
Obeisance of the knee, the lip, the hand,
And the neck breaks to an unwelcome yoke,
But traitor leaves the hidden heart within,
Rebel the will insurgent, infidel
The mind, the critic reason dissident,
And violated conscience enemy —
Such rule is but the hollow show of rule,
A husk of vain pretence, the kernel gone.

 " No earthly kingdom such, Messiah's is,
Of nations hating and yet serving Him —
Trampled into the dust beneath His feet,
And either cringing or else gnashing rage.

A kingdom here on earth of heaven to found,
From heaven to earth God's true Messiah comes;
A kingdom built of meek and lowly hearts
By Monarch meek and lowly to be ruled;
A world-wide kingdom and a time-long reign.
This kingdom new of heaven on earth commenced
Will gather Jew and Gentile both in one,
Whereso, of high or low, of rich or poor,
Heart ready to receive it shall be found,
In time or clime however hence afar.
For hear Him speak, the High and Lofty One
Who maketh His abode eternity :
' Lo, in the high and holy place dwell I,
Likewise with him of meek and contrite mind.'

" In those words were foreshown the things which
    are,
Brethren, and kingdom which we preach to you,
Messiah here indeed, His reign begun,
Invisible but glorious, on the earth.
He that hath ears to hear, lo, let him hear,
And hail the one right Ruler come at last ;
Who rules not nations, masses of mankind
Only, with indiscriminate wide sway

Imperfect though to view magnificent,
By many an individual will unfelt;
But seeks His subjects singly, soul by soul,
And over each, through all within him, reigns.
Jew must with Gentile, heart by heart, submit
To own Messiah thus his Lord and King,
Throning Him sovereign in the realm of self,
The empire of a humble, contrite mind.

   " No other rule is real than rule like this,
The true Messiah's rule, which well within
The flying scouts and outposts of the man,
Wins to the midmost seat and citadel
Of being, where the soul itself resides,
And tames the master captive to its thrall.
Then sings the soul unto herself and says,
' Bless thou, Jehovah, O my soul, and all
That is within me, bless His holy name!'
Filled is the hidden part with melody.
For joyfully the reason then consents,
The mind is full of light to see, and says
'Amen!' the will resolves the opposite
Of its old self, won by the heart, which, more
Than mere obedience, loves; conscience the while

Delightedly infusing all delight,
And Holy Spirit breathing benison.

"Such subjugation is a state of peace;
But peace, stagnation not, nor death. You live
And move and have your being evermore
Fresher and deeper, purer and more full,
Drawn in an ether and an element
Instinct and vivid with God. The appetites
Are subject servitors to will, the will
Hearkens to reason and regards its voice—
Reason which is the will of Him who reigns,
Your reason and His will insensibly
Blending to grow incorporate in one.
Such is the kingdom of the Christ of God.
You easily miss it—for it cometh not
With observation; you must look within
To find it—pray that you may find it so."

A mien of something more than majesty
In Stephen as he spoke, transfiguring him;
Conscious authority loftier than pride;
Deep calm which made intensity seem weak;
Slow weight more insupportable than speed;
Passion so pure that its effect was peace,

Beatifying his face; betokened power
Beneath him that supported him, behind
Him that impelled, above him and within
That steadied him immovable, supplied
As from a fountain of omnipotence;
An air breathed round him of prophetic rapt
Solemnity oppressive beyond words
And dread communication from the throne,
Moved near, of the Most High, which only not
Thundered and lightened, as from the touched top
Of Sinai once in witness of the law —
Such might, not Stephen's, wrought with Stephen
     there
And laid his hearers subject at his feet.

Saul saw the grasp secure that he had laid
Upon his brethren's minds and hearts — to hold,
He proudly, confidently deemed, against
Whatever counter force of eloquence —
This tenure his he saw relaxed, dissolved,
Evanishéd, as it had never been.
Perplexed, astonished, but impenetrable,
Though dashed and damped in spirit and in hope,
Angry he stood, recoiled upon himself.

But Rachel had a different history.
She felt her inmost conscience searched and known ;
Sharper than any sword of double edge,
The Word of God through Stephen pierced her heart,
And there asunder clove her self and self.
She heeded Stephen's warning words ; she looked
Within, she pressed her hand upon her heart
And prayed, " O God, my God, my fathers' God,
Thy kingdom — grant that *I* may find it *here !* "
So praying she listened while farther Stephen spoke :
" That such a Ruler should be such as He
Whom we proclaim, the Man of Nazareth,
The Carpenter, the Man of Calvary,
Affronts your reason, tempts to disbelief —
Doubtless ; but all the more shown absolute
His sovereignty, transcendent, passing quite
Limit of precedent or parallel,
As nothing in Him outwardly appears
To soothe your pride in yielding to His claim.
Always the more offended pride rebels,
Is proved his triumph greater who subdues.
Deep is our human heart, and versatile
Exceedingly, ingenious past our ken,
Inventive of contrivances to save

Fond pride from hurt.   But here is no escape ;
Pride must be hurt and bleed, unsalved her wounds,
She may not conquer crouching, she must crouch
Conquered ; nor only so, she must be glad
To be the conquered, not the conqueror ;
Thus deeply must the heart abjure itself,
Thus deeply own the mastership of Christ.
Christ will not practise on your self-conceit
And lure you to obey illusively.
Obedience is not obedience
Save as, obeying, you love, loving, obey —
The chief of all obediences, love."

  Such serene counter to his own superb
Disdain of Jesus wrought on Saul effect
Diverse from that meanwhile in Rachel wrought.
She yielded to exchange her standing-ground,
And ceased to hold her centre in herself.
Centred in God, she all things new beheld
Translated by the mighty parallax.
Open she threw the portals of her soul
And gave the keys up to her new-found King.

  But Saul more stubbornly than ever clamped
His feet to keep them standing where they stood.

Haughty, erect, rebuffing — he alone —
He still stared on at Stephen, who Saul's scorn
Felt subtly like a fierce oppugnant force
Resistlessly attractive to his aim,
As, suddenly soon borne into a swift
Involuntary swerving of his speech —
Himself, with Saul, surprising — he went on :
" Such lord, requiring such obedience,
In Him of Nazareth, a man approved
Of God by many mighty works through Him
Among you done, this day I preach to you,
My brethren all — my brother Saul, to thee ! "

Therewith full round on Saul the speaker turned
That self-same instant, the seraphic sheen
Brightened to dazzling upon Stephen's face ;
Saul standing there, transfixed to listen, blenched,
As if a lightning-flash had blinded him.
Then, prophet-wise, like Nathan come before
King David sinner, Stephen, his right hand
And fixed forefinger flickering forth at Saul,
An intense moment centred upon him,
Sole, the converging ardors of his speech —
As who, with lens of cunning convex, draws

Into one focus all the solar rays
Collected to engender burning heat.

Rachel, who saw Saul blench, and full well knew
What pangs on pangs his pride could force him bear —
He smiling blithely while he inly bled —
Watched, with a heart divided in sore pain
Between the sister's pity of his case
And sympathy against him for his sake,
As Stephen thus his speech to Saul addressed :
" Yea, to thee, Saul my brother, in thy flush
And prime of youth and youthful hope, thy joy,
Thy pride, of all-accomplished intellect,
And sense of self-sufficing righteousness —
To thee, thou pupil of Gamaliel, thee,
Thou Hebrew of the Hebrews, Pharisee,
Against the gust and fury of thy zeal,
And in the teeth of thy repellent scorn,
Jesus the crucified I preach *thy* lord.
Blindly with bitter hate thou ragest now
Against Him ; but hereafter, and not long
Hereafter, thou, despite, shalt lie prostrate
Before Him and beneath Him in the dust,
Astonished with His glory sudden shown

Beyond thy power with open eye to see.
Lo, by the Holy Spirit bidden, I
This day plant pricks for thee to kick against.
Cruel shall be the torture in thy breast,
And unto cruel deeds thou didst not dream
The torture in thy breast will madden thee —
The anguish of a mind at strife with good,
A will self-blinded not to cease from sin.
Nevertheless at length I see thee mild —
Broken thy pride, thy wisdom brought to naught,
To thyself hateful thy self righteousness,
Worshipping at His feet whom late thou didst
Persecute in His members, persecute
In me. Lo, with an everlasting love
I long for thee, O Saul, and draw thee, love
Born of that love wherewith the Lord loved me
And gave Himself for me to bitter death."

Rachel her prayer and love and longing joins,
With tears, to Stephen's, for her brother, who,
Conscious of many eyes upon him fixed,
Far other thought, the while, and feeling, broods.

As captain, on the foremost imminent edge
Of battle, leading there a storming van

Of soldiers in some perilous attack,
Pregnant with fate to empire, if he feel
Pierce to a vital part within his frame
Wound of invisible missile from the foe,
Will hide his deadly hurt with mask of smile,
That he damp not his followers' gallant cheer;
Thus, though with motive other, chiefly pride,
Saul, rallying sharply from that first surprise,
Sternly shut up within his secret breast
A poignant pang conceived from Stephen's words,
Resentment fated to bear bitter fruit,
But melt at last in gracious shame and tears.

With fixéd look impassible, he gazed
At Stephen, while, in altered phase, that pure
Effulgence of apostleship burned on:
" Nor, brethren, let this word of mine become
Scandal before your feet to stumble you
Headlong to ruin —' gave Himself for me
To bitter death '—implying it the Christ's
To suffer death in sacrifice for sin.
This is that thing of wonder prophesied,
Confounding to the wisdom of the wise;
A suffering Saviour, a Messiah shamed.

Monarch arrayed in purple robes of scorn,
With diadem of thorns pressed on His brow,
And in His hand for sceptre thrust a reed —
The Lord of life and glory crucified !

" Dim saw perhaps our father Abraham this,
Through symbol and through prophecy contained
In smoking furnace and in blazing torch
Beheld, that evening, when the sun went down
And it was dark.   The smoking furnace meant
The mystery of the Messiah's shame
To go before His glory typified
In the clear shining of the torch ablaze.

" Of the same mystery of agony
In sorrow, shame, and death, forerunning dark
The bright and brightening sequel without end
Of the Messiah's work, Isaiah spake,
When he foresaw His coming day from far.
The eagle vision of that seer was dimmed
With tears, like Jeremiah's, to behold
What he beheld — Messiah's visage so
Marred more than any man's, and so His form
More than befell the sons of men.   He read,
Within the mirror of his prophecy,

Astonishment depicted in the eyes
Of many—in the eyes of which of you,
My brethren?—at a spectacle so strange.
The melancholy prophet saw a gloom
Of unbelief darken the world. 'What soul,'
Wails he, ' is found to credit our report?
To whom has been revealed Jehovah's arm
In such a wise outstretched to save?'   Heart-sick
At what, too clearly for his peace, he sees,
Isaiah, turning from his vision, cries
In pain—consider, brethren, whether ye
Unwittingly fulfil what he portrays!—
' He was despised, rejected was of men,
A man of sorrows and acquainted well
With grief; as one from whom men hide their face,
Despised was He, and we esteemed Him not. '

    "Now our own gospel hear Isaiah preach,
The good news that such sufferings borne by Him,
Messiah, were for you, for us, for all :
' Surely our griefs they were Messiah bore,
He carried sorrows that were due to us.
Yet we, alas, of Him as stricken thought,
Smitten of God, and for affliction marked!'

"Would God, my brethren, ye who hear these
		things,
This day, were minded as the prophet was
Who thus from God reported them to you !
He but foresaw them, and he saw them ; ye
Saw them, and did not see !   And yet, even yet,
Look back, as forward he ; lo; touch your eyes
With eyesalve that ye be not blind, but see !
See, with Isaiah, how Messiah was
' Wounded for your transgressions, bruised so sore
For your iniquities, how chastisement
On Him was laid that peace should bring to you,
How stripes whereby He bled to you were health.'

" Meekly and thankfully Isaiah sinks
Himself, one drop, into the human sea,
And says 'we,' 'our,' and 'us'—do ye the same.
O brethren, if this day ye hear His voice,
A whisper only in your ear from heaven,
I pray you, harden not your heart.   Confess
Your fault, and say with your own prophet, ' We,
All we, like sheep, have gone astray, astray,
And God on Him hath laid the sin of all.'"

At such expostulation and appeal

Ineffable, found hidden in the words
Of prophecy, Rachel her heart felt fail
Into a pathos of repentance sweet
With love and soft sense of forgiveness, bought
For her at cost so dear!—and she dissolved
In sobs and tears of sorrow exquisite,
Better than joy, and uncontrollable.
The mastership of Jesus now to her
Merged in the sweetness of His saviorship;
The duty of obedience to a Lord
All taken up, transfigured, glorified,
In the transcendent privilege of love.
Never such grief in joy, such joy in grief,
Was hers before—for self was wholly slain
And her whole life grew love unutterable.

Yet longed she, with a hope that half was pain,
For Saul, while Stephen brokenly went on:
"O ye to whom for the last time I speak,
My heart is large for you, it breaks for you,
And melts to tears within me while I plead.
I pray you, I beseech you, in Christ's stead,
Be reconciled to God.   Hearken this once
And answer, Were it set your task, in choice

Few words to frame the image and the lot
Of Jesus whom ye slew, how otherwise
More fitly could ye do it than was done
Aforetime by Isaiah when he wrote
Prophetically thus of Christ to be:
' Oppressed He was, yet He abased Himself
And opened not His mouth ; even as a lamb
Led to the slaughter, as a sheep before
Her shearers speechless, so He opened not
His mouth.   His grave they with the wicked made,
And with the rich they laid Him in His death. '
Say, brethren, was not Jesus very Christ ?

  " But, that ye err not, Messianic woe
Is not the end ; a-glorious change succeeds.
Isaiah chanted it in sequel glad
And contrast of the sorrow-laden strain
That mourned Messiah's sufferings ; hear the song :
' When thou, Jehovah, shalt His soul have made
An offering for sin, Messiah then
The endless issue of His pain shall see ;
Still on and on He shall His days prolong,
And in His hand the pleasure of the Lord
Shall prosper ; of the travail of His soul

He shall see fruit and shall be satisfied.'
So, with rejoicing too serenely full
For exultation, sang Isaiah then
Of Messianic glory following shame.

"And now, concerning Jesus whom ye slew,
Know, brethren, that He burst the bands of death,
Which could not hold the Lord of life in thrall.
Know that He, having risen, rose again,
Ascending far above all height, and led
Captive captivity; attended so
With retinue of deliverance numberless,
He entered heaven a Conqueror and a King;
Before Him lifted up their heads the gates,
The everlasting doors admitted Him.
There sits He now associate by the side
Of His Almighty Father, Lord of all.
For to Him every knee shall bow, in heaven,
On earth, and every tongue confess that He,
Jesus, is Lord; Jehovah wills it so.

"Fall, brethren, I adjure you, haste to fall
Betimes upon this stone and bruise your pride;
Wait but too long, this stone will fall on you:
Not then your pride, but you, not bruised will be,

But ground to undistinguishable dust."

So Stephen spoke ; and ceased, as loth to cease.

The moments of his speaking had been like
A slow and dreadful imminence of storm.
With those august and awful opening words
Of his, which were not his, but God's, it was
As when an altered elemental mood
Usurps the atmosphere; the winds are laid,
Clouds gather, mass to mass, anon perchance
Roll back, disclosing spaces of clear sky,
But close again, deeper and darker, full
Of thunder, silent yet, of lightning, leashed
From leaping forth, but watchful for its prey.
Such had been Stephen's speaking, boded storm ;
His ceasing was the tempest burst at last—
A silent tempest, silent and unseen,
Rending the elements of the world of soul !

Meanwhile the angels in attendance there,
Watching with eyes that see the invisible
Things of the spirit of man within his breast,
The posture and behavior of the mind,
Had seen exhibited amidst that late

Motionless multitude of souls suspense
With supernatural awe, a spectacle
Of consternation and precipitate flight
To covert, such as sometimes is beheld
In nature, when a mighty tempest lowers,
And man, beast, bird, each conscious living thing,
Shuddering, hies to hiding from the wrack.
With wild inaudible outcry heard in heaven,
That shattered congregation, soul by soul,
Each soul its several way, fled, to find shroud
From spiritual tempest hurtling on the head,
Intolerably, hailstones and coals of fire.

But one excepted spirit stood aloof,
Scorning to join the fellowship of flight.
Like a tall pine by whirlwind lonely left
Upon his mountain, forest abject round,
This man dared lift, though sole, a helmless brow
Of stubborn hardihood to take the storm.
Others, dismayed, might flee to refuge ; Saul,
Not undismayed, fronted the wrath of God.

Shimei alone there neither stood nor fell ;
By habit grovelling, on his belly prone,
Already prostrate he had thither come.

Incapable of awe from good inspired,
He, abject, but without humility,
Ever, by force of reptile nature, crawled;
And now had crawled, as, dusty demon's-heart
And vitreous eye of basilisk, he still —
With equal, though with different, enmity,
Devising death for Stephen in his mind,
And studying slow prolonged revenge for Saul —
Watched all, whatever chanced to either there;
But most, malignantly delighted, watched
Deepen the settled shadow on Saul's face
Cast from the darkness of his inner mood.

BOOK V.

SAUL AND SHIMEI.

SAUL, sullen, gloomy, and chagrined, over his discomfiture recently experienced, is visited, in his self-imposed seclusion at home, by Shimei, who, always by nature antipathetic to Saul, hates him virulently now for the affront from him received publicly in the late council. Shimei exasperates Saul with sneering, pretended sympathy for him over his defeat at Stephen's hands ; at the same time disclosing the plot he has himself concocted, involving subornation of perjury, with alleged connivance on the part of the Sanhedrim in general, for the stoning of Stephen. Shimei gone, Saul, in the open court of his dwelling, sits solitary, brooding in the depths of dejection over the fallen state of his fortunes.

SAUL AND SHIMEI.

As if one, from some poise of prospect high,
Should overlook below a plain outspread
And see a bright embattled host, in close
Array of antique chivalry, supposed
Invincible, advancing, panoplied,
Horseman and horse, in steel, and with delight
Of battle pricked to speed, he — while that host,
Swift, like one man, across the field of war,
With pennons gay astream upon the wind,
And arms and armor flashing in the sun,
Moved to the sound of martial music brave —
Might ask, " What strength set counter could with-
      stand
The multiplied momentum of such blow ? "
And yet, as, let a rock-built citadel
Upspring before them in their conquering way,
And, through embrasures in the frowning wall,
Let enginery of carnage new and strange,

Vomiting smoke and flame from hellish mouths —
Let cannon, with their noise like thunder, belch,
Volleying, their bolts like thunderbolts amain
Among those gallant columns, then would be
Amazement seen, and ruinous overthrow ;
So, late, to Saul's superbly confident
Assay of onset all seemed nigh to yield,
Till that the wisdom of the Holy Ghost,
Through Stephen speaking, made the utmost might
Of eloquence ridiculous and vain,
So was the duel all unequal, joined
By Saul with Stephen on that fateful day.
Though not ill matched the champions' native force
And spirit, and not far from even their skill,
Equipment disparate of weaponry —
Human against Divine, infinite odds ! —
Made the conclusion of the strife foregone.
Had mortal prowess against prowess been
Between those twain the naked issue tried,
Saul, with his sanguine dash of onset, might
Perchance have won the day — through sheer surprise
Of sudden and impetuous movement swift
Beyond the other's readiness to oppose
An instantaneous rally of quick thought

And lightning-like alertness of stanch will
Mustering and mastering his collected might.
But the event and fortune of that hour
Resolved no doubt which combatant excelled
In wit or will or strength or exercise.
Stephen was fortressed round impregnably,
Saul stood in open field obvious to wound ;
Saul wielded weapons of the present world,
Celestial weapons furnished Stephen — nay,
Weapon himself, the Almighty wielded him.

Saul knew himself defeated, overwhelmed.
By how much he had purposed in his heart,
And buoyantly expected, beyond doubt
Or possible peradventure, to prevail,
More than prevail, triumph, abound, redound,
And overflow, with ample surplusage
Of prosperous fortune far transcending all
Public conjecture of his hoped success ;
By so much now he found himself instead
Buried beneath discomfiture immense
And boundless inundation of defeat.
For multitudes of new believers won
To Stephen's side from Saul's thronged to the Way,

Storming the kingdom of heaven with violence.
It was a nation hastening to be born,
Like Israel out of Egypt, in a day.   .
As Israel out of Egypt were baptized
To Moses in the cloud and in the sea,
So Israel out of Israel Saul now saw
Baptized obedient into Jesus' name.
Dissolving round about him seemed to Saul
The earth itself with its inhabitants,
And, to bear up the pillars of it, he
A broken reed that could not stand alone !

But, while thus worsted Saul forlornly felt
Himself, he by whom worsted missed to know.
His challenge was to Stephen ; how should he
Guess that in Stephen God would answer him ?
Unconsciously with God at enmity,
But with God's servant Stephen consciously,
Saul chafed and raged in proud and blindfold hate ;
Half yet, the while, despising too himself,
Detected hating thus, by his own heart
Detected hating, his antagonist,
For the sole blame of visiting on him
The fortune he had purposed to inflict.

Saul in such mood of rancor and remorse
Commingled — both unhappy sentiments
Still mutually exasperating each
The other — Shimei came to him.
                                    Now Saul
And Shimei were two opposites intense
In nature, never toward each other drawn,
But violently ever sent asunder;
Yet chiefly by repulsion lodged in Saul,
Spurning off Shimei, as the good the evil;
For Saul instinctively was noble, frank,
And true, as Shimei instinctively
Was false, profound in guile, to base inclined.
But strangely, since that council wherein Saul
Fulmined his shame on Shimei's proffer vile,
Shimei had felt the other's scorn of him
A force importunate to tempt him nigh —
Perverse attraction in repulsion found! —
As evil ever struggles toward the good,
Not to be leavened with virtue issuing thence,
But leaven instead to likeness with itself.
So Shimei came to Saul, as knowing Saul
Spurned him avaunt with loathing; in degree
Attracted as he was intensely spurned.

He fain would feast his malice on the pride,
Seen writhing, fain would make it writhe the more,
Of Saul in his discomfiture.

                      With mien
Demure of hypocritic sympathy,
The nauseating vehicle of sneer,
Malignly studied to exacerbate
The galled and angry feeling in Saul's mind,
He thus addressed that haughty Pharisee:
" The outcome of your effort, brother Saul,
To vindicate the cause of truth and God —
And therewithal justly advance somewhat
Your individual profit and esteem
As rising bulwark of the Jewish state,
Whereby so much the better you might hope
Hereafter to promote the general weal —
This spirited attempt, I say, of yours
Has in its issue disappointed you,
You, and your friends no less, who, all of us,
Together with yourself, refused to dream
Aught but the most felicitous event
To enterprise with so much stateliness
Of dignity impressively announced
By you, and show of lofty confidence.

By the way, Saul, the grand air suits your style
Astonishingly well ; I should advise
Your cultivation of it.   Why, at times,
When you display that absolutely frank
And unaffected lack of modesty
Which marks you, really, now, the effect on me,
Even me, is almost irresistible ;
I find myself well-nigh imposed upon
To call it an effect of majesty.

   " But, to sustain the impression, Saul, it needs,
Quite needs, that you somehow contrive to shun
These awkward misadventures ; the grand air
Is less impressive in a man well known
To have made a bad miscarriage, such as yours.
For in fact you — with sincere pain I say it —
But served to Stephen as a sort of foil
To set his talent off and heighten it.
You must yourself feel this to be the case ;
For never since that windy Pentecost
In which we thought we saw the top and turn
To this delirium of delusion touched,
Never, I say, till now were seen so many
New perverts to the Nazarene as seems

You two, between you, you and Stephen, Saul,
Managed, that memorable day, to make.
It is a pity, and I grieve with you.
Still, Saul, let us consider that your case,
Undoubtedly unfortunate, presents
This one alleviating circumstance,
At least, that your defeat demonstrates past
Gainsaying what an arduous attempt
Yours was, and thereby glorifies the more
That admirable headiness of yours
Which egged you on to venture unadvised.
For my own part, I like prodigiously
To see your young man overflow with spirit ;
Age will bring wisdom fast enough ; but spirit,
Like yours, Saul, comes, when come it does at all,
Born with the man.   Never regret that you
Dared nobly ; rather hug yourself for that
With pride ; pride greater, since, through proof, aware
You really dared more nobly than you knew.

  " Some increment too of wisdom you have won
From your experience ; not to be despised,
Though ornament rather of age than youth.
I may presume you now less indisposed

Than late you were, to reinforce, support,
And supplement mere obstinacy — fine,
Of course, as I have said, yet attribute
Common to man with beast — by counsel ripe
And scheme of well-considered policy,
Adapted to secure your end with ease.
Economy of effort well befits
Man, the express image and counterpart
Of God, who always works with parsimony,
Compassing greatest ends with smallest means,
To waste no particle of omnipotence.

" Count now that you have rendered plain enough
What single-eyed, straightforward stubbornness
Can, and cannot, effect in this behalf;
So much is gained ; now be our conscience clear
To cast about and find some other means,
Than mere main strength in public controversy,
Of dealing with these raw recalcitrants.
They lacked the grace to be discomfited
In honorable combat fairly joined,
Let them now look to it how much their gross
Effrontery in overthrowing you
Shall profit them at last.　I have a scheme " —

"Your scheme," — so, from the depths of his chagrin
And anguish at the contact of the man,
Spoke Saul, unwilling longer to endure
The friction and abrasion of his words —
"Your scheme, whatever it may be, cannot
Concern my knowing ; nothing you should plan
Were likely to conciliate in me
Either my judgment, or my taste, or please
My sense of what becoming is and right.
I pray you spare yourself the pains to unfold
Further to me your thought ; your work were waste.'

But Shimei, naught abashed, but rather more
Set on, imagining that he touched in Saul
The quick of suffering sensibility
Replied :
            " Yea, brother Saul, I did not fail
In our late session to observe what you
Hinted of your unreadiness to accord
Your valuable support to my advice,
Advanced on that occasion loyally
However far outrunning what the most
Were then prepared frankly to act upon.
We weaker, Saul, who may not hope to be

Athletes like you, whose sole resource must lie
In studying more profoundly than the rest,
Are liable to be misunderstood
Not seldom, when, through meditation deep
And painful, we arrive to see somewhat
Beyond the common, and propound advice
Startling, because some stages in advance
Of the conclusions less laborious minds
Reach and stop at contented — for a while,
But which mere halting-places on the road
Prove in the end, and not the final goal.
You probably remember, when I told
The council that some good judicious guile
Was what was needed, not one voice spoke up
To second my suggestion. Very well,
The lagging rear of wisdom has since then
Moved bravely up to step with me, and now
We walk along abreast harmoniously
Upon the very road I pointed out;
'Guile' is the word with all the Sanhedrim.

  " But stay, you may perhaps not be apprised
Exactly of the current state of things —
You have kept yourself, you know, a bit retired

These few days past, a natural thing to do,
Under the circumstances, all admit —
Well, we have made some progress; I myself,
To imitate your lack of modesty
And don the egotistic, I myself
Have not been idle; all in fact is now
Adjusted on a plan of compromise,
My own invention, everybody pleased.
We shall dispose of Stephen for you, Saul:
Council; Stephen arrested and arraigned;
Production of effective testimony;
A hearing of the accused; commotion raised,
While he is speaking, to help on his zeal;
Then, at the proper point, some heated phrase
Of his let slip, a sudden rush of all
Upon him with a cry of 'Blasphemy!' —
Impulse of passionate enthusiasm,
You know, premeditated with much care —
And he is stoned; which makes an end of *him.*
Such is the outline; not precisely what
I could have wished, a little too much noise,
The Mattathias tinge in it too strong —
Still, everything considered, fairly good.
The moment favors; for the very fume

And fury of the popular caprice
Has put it out of breath ; nay, for the nonce,
The wind sits, such at least my hope is, veered
And shifted points enough about to bear
A touch of generous violence from us ;
Then, as for those our rulers, they connive.

  "You see I have been open to admit
Ideas the very opposite of my own.
I am not one to haggle for a point
Simply because it happened to be mine.
The end, the end, is what we seek ; the means
Signifies nothing to the wise.   'Let us
Be wise,' as our friend Nicodemus said,
That day, with so much gnomic wisdom couched
In affable cohortative, as who
Should say encouragingly, 'Go to, good friends,
Let us be gods' ; wisdom and godship come,
As everybody knows, with equal ease
Indifferently, through simple conative,
'Let us,' and so forth, and the thing is done."

  This voluble and festive cynicism,
Taking fresh head again and yet again,
At intervals, to flow an endless stream,

From Shimei's mouth, of bitter pleasantry;
His vulgarly-presumed familiar airs
And leer of mutual understanding, felt
Rather than seen, upon his countenance;
The gurgling glee of self-complacency
That purred, one long susurrus, through his talk;
The insufferable assumption tacitly
Implied that human virtue was a jest
At which the wise between themselves might grin
Nor hide their grin with a decorous veil;
These things in his unwelcome guest, traits all
Inseparably adhering to the man,
Or fibre of his nature, Saul recoiled
From, and revolted at, habitually:
They rendered Shimei's very neighborhood
An insupportable disgust to him.
Still did some fascination Shimei owned,
Perhaps a show of wit in mockery,
Playing upon a momentary mood
Of uncharacteristic helplessness in Saul
(A humor too of wilfulness and spite
Against himself displacent with himself
That made him hold his sore and quivering pride
Hard to the goad that hurt it) keep him mute,

If listless, while thus Shimei streamed on :

"Well, as I said, friend Saul, I had no pride
To carry an opinion of my own ;
The scheme I brooded was a compromise.
I plume myself upon a certain skill
I have, knack I should call it, in this line.
I like a pretty piece of joinery
In plot, such match of motley odds and ends
As tickles you with sense of happy hit,
And here you have it.   See, I take a bit
Of magisterial statesmanship to start
With — go to Rome, as Caiaphas advised,
Though not quite on his errand ; Rome agrees
To wink, while we indulge ourselves in what
To us will be self-rule resumed, to her,
A spasm of our Judæan savagery.
Thus is the way made eligibly clear
For brother Mattathias with those stones
He raves about on all occasions — rubbed
Smooth, they must be, as David's from the brook,
With constant wear in Mattathias' hands !
Was it not grim to hear him talk that day ?
His dream of Maccabæan blood aboil

Within his veins has been too much for him,
Made him a monomaniac on this point;
He sees before him visionary stones,
Imponderable stones torment his hands;
Give him his chance, have him at last let fly
A real stone, a hard one, at somebody,
Who knows? it might bring Mattathias round.
Stephen at any rate shall be his man,
His *corpus vile*, as our masters say —
Fair game of turn and turn about for him,
Dog, to have handled you so roughly, Saul!
Trick of Beelzebub, no manner of doubt.

" But here I loiter, while you burn of course
To hear what figure you yourself may cut
In my brave patchwork scheme of compromise.
I modestly adjoin myself to Saul,
And so we two go in together, paired—
A little of your logic let into
A little of my guile, and a fine fit."

Shimei had counted for a master stroke
Of disagreeable humor sure to tell
On Saul, the piecing of himself on him
In plan, conscious of Saul's antipathy.

But Shimei still misapprehended Saul,
Lacking the standard in himself wherewith
To measure or assay the sentiment
Of such as Saul for such as Shimei.
Saul simply and serenely so despised
Shimei, that nothing he should do or say
Could change Saul's sentiment to more, or less,
Or other, than it constantly abode,
The absolute zero of indifference.
Half absently, through fits of alien thought,
And half with unconfessed concern to know
What passed among his fellow-councillors
Abroad, a little curious too withal
Wondering how any artifice of fraud
Could Saul with Shimei combine, to make
Such twain seem partners of one policy —
So minded, Saul gave ear, while Shimei thus
The acrid juices of his humor spilled :

" Here is the method of the joinery.
You know you put it strongly that the end
Of that pretended gospel which they preach,
Would be to overturn the Jewish state,
Abolishing Moses, and extinguishing

The glory of the temple, and all that —
Really sonorous rhetoric it was,
That passage, Saul, and it deserved to win ;
But who can win against Beelzebub ?
Logic turned rhetoric is my idea
Of eloquence, and my idea you
Realized ; but Stephen, without eloquence,
Bore off from you the fruit of eloquence :
Never mind, Saul, it was Beelzebub.
Let rhetoric now go back to logic ; you
Demonstrated so inexpugnably
The necessary inference contained
In Stephen's doctrine, hardly were it guile —
Though doubtless you will call it such, you have
Your sublimated notions on these points —
To say outright that Stephen taught the things
You proved implicit in the things he taught ;
At all events, guile or no guile — in fact,
Guile *and* no guile it is, if closely scanned —
Here is the scheme : — We find some blunderheads,
Who, primed with method for their blundering,
Will misremember and transfer from you
To Stephen what you stated on this point.
These worthies then shall roundly testify

Before our honorable body met
To give the fellow his fair hearing ere
His sentence — said fair hearing not of course
Eventually to affect said sentence due —
Shall, I say, swear that they distinctly heard
Stephen set forth that Jesus Nazarene
Was going to destroy this place and change
The customs Moses gave us; bring about
In brief precisely what, with so much force,
You showed would surely happen " —

                     " Shimei —

Saul interrupted Shimei again,
Surprised into expression by the shock
To hear himself mixed up in any way,
Of indirection even, in fraud like this —
" Shimei, I thought that nothing you could say
Would further tempt me into speech to you ;
But you have broken my bond of self-restraint.
Suborning perjury !   That well accords
With what you slanted at in council once,
And what I trusted I had then and there
Made clear my scorn of.   Shimei, hear — I set
My heel upon this thing and once for all
Grind it into the dust. "

                    " In figure, of course,"
Promptly leered Shimei, interrupting Saul ;
" The thing goes forward just the same ; you set
It under foot — in your rhetorical way ;
I, in my practical way, set it on foot ;
No mutual interference, each well pleased.

  " But, seriously, Saul, you overwork
The idea of conscience.   What is conscience ?   Mere
Self-will assuming virtuous airs.   A term
Cajoles you into making it a point
Of moral obligation to be stiff.
Limber up, Saul, and be adjustable.
Capacity of taking several points
Of view at will is good.   For instance, now,
Probably Stephen may, at various times,
Himself have stated quite explicitly
What your rhetorical logic showed to be
Inextricably held as inference
In his harangues.   Take it so, Saul, if so
Render your conscience easier ; I myself
Highly enjoy my easy conscience.   Still,
Nothing could be more natural than that some,
Hearers non-critical, you know, should mix

What you said with what Stephen said, and so
Quite honestly swear falsely — to the gain
Of truth.   And to whose loss ?   Stephen's, perhaps,
But other's, none.   So, salve your conscience, Saul —
Which somehow you must learn, and soon, to do ;
Unless you mean to play obstructionist,
Instead of coadjutor, in the work
You, with good motive, but with scurvy luck,
Set about doing late so lustily.
Conscience itself is to be sacrificed,
At need, to serve the cause of righteousness.
What is it but egregious egotism
To obtrude, forsooth, a point of conscience, when
You jeopard general interests thereby ?
One's conscience is a private matter ; let
Your conscience wince a little, if need be,
In order that the public good be served.
That is true generosity.   ' Let us
Be just,' said Nicodemus ; good, say I,
But in this matter of our consciences,
Let us go further and be generous. "

    As one who turns a stopcock and arrests
A flow of water that need never cease,

So Shimei left off speaking, not less full
Of matter than at first that might be speech.
With indescribable smirk, and cynic sneer
Conveyed, sirocco breath of blight to faith
In virtue and in good, he went away,
Cheering himself that he had somewhat chilled
Within the breast of that young Pharisee
The ardor of conviction, and of hope
Fed by conviction, — but still more that he
Had probed and hurt the festering wounds of pride.

Saul's first relief to be alone again,
Rid of that nauseous presence, presently
Was followed by depression and relapse
From his instinctive tension to resist
The unnerving spell of Shimei's influence.
Saul found that in the teeth of his contempt
For Shimei, absolute in measure, nay,
By reason of that contempt, he had conceived
Shame and chagrin beyond his strength to bear.
That Shimei, such as Shimei, should have dared
To visit Saul, and drill and drill his ears,
With indefatigable screw of tongue
Sinking a shaft through which to drench and drown

His soul with spew from out a source so vile —
This argued fall indeed for him from what
He lately was, from what he hoped to be,
Far more, in popular repute.   The sting
That Shimei purposed subtly to infix,
With that malicious irony and taunt
Recurrent, the intentional affront,
All of it, failed, blunted and turned in point
Against the safe impenetrable mail
Of Saul's contempt for Shimei.   But that
Which Shimei meant not, nor dreamed, but was,
Went through and through Saul's double panoply,
Found permeable now, of pride and scorn,
And wilted him with self-disparagement.

He marvelled at himself how he had not,
At first forthputting of that impudence,
Stormed the wretch dumb, with hurricane outburst
Of passionate scorn ; a quick revulsion then,
And Saul was chafing that he had so far
Grace of rebuff vouchsafed, and honest heat,
To creature lacking natural sense to feel
Repudiation.   Comfort none he found,
No refuge from the persecuting thought

Of his own fall.   He tried to brace himself
With thinking, " If I failed, I failed at least
Not for myself, but God ; I strove for God. "
But, ceaselessly, the image of himself,
Humiliated, swam between to blur
His vision of God.   He could not cease to see
Saul ever, in the mirror of his mind,
And ever Stephen shadowing Saul's fair fame.

BOOK VI.
SAUL AND RACHEL.

To Saul, wrapt in his gloomy contemplations, Rachel unobtrusively presents herself. Conversation ensues between
them, and Saul confides to his sister his own most secret
purposes and hopes, dashed now so cruelly. The fact, however, at length comes out that Rachel was herself converted
to Christianity as a result of Stephen's reply to Saul. Saul
instantly hereon experiences a violent revulsion of feeling.
He breaks away from Rachel, spurning her, and breathing
out threatening and slaughter against the Christian church.

SAUL AND RACHEL.

Saul thus forlorn, a voice smote on his ear,
Voice other than of Shimei, clear and sweet ;
The very sound was balsam to his pain.
Rachel's the voice was, who, with deep distaste,
As jealous for her brother, had perceived
The entering in to Saul of his late guest
Ill-favored, and through all his stay had still,
Impatiently awaiting, wished him sped.
He now some moments gone, she issued forth
From out her curtained chamber glimpsing gay
Behind her, through the hangings, as she passed,
With color — stuff of scarlet, linen fine
Embroidered, weft of purple tapestry,
Her handiwork — and sending after her
Sweet scent of herb and flower, her husbandry —
Forth issued, and across the inner court
Open to heaven — small close of paradise,

A tall palm by a fountain, bloomy shrubs,
And vines that clad with green the enclosing walls —
Stepped lightly to Saul's side.   Saul sat beneath
A tent-cloth canopy outspread, his own
Tent-making skill — the high noon of the sun
To fend, if place perchance one then might wish
In which free air to breathe safe from the heat —
There sat relapsed, deep brooding gloomy thoughts,
Wnen now his sister pausing stood by him.
A lovely vision !   Moving, or at rest,
Ever a rapture Rachel seemed of grace
Which but that moment that felicity
Of posture or of gesture had attained,
By accident, yet kept it, through all change,
Inalienably hers, by right divine
Of inward rhythm that swayed her heart in tune.

   The sister had, with love's observance, watched
Some days the phases of her brother's mood,
Biding her time to speak ; and now she spoke.
" Brother," she murmured softly, " thou art sad.
Thy brow is written over like a scroll
With lines of trouble that I try to read.
Unbind thy heart, I pray, to me, who grieve

To see thee grieve, and fain at least would share
Such brother's sorrow as I may not soothe."

This suave appeal of sister's sympathy
Won upon Saul to wean him from himself—
A moment, and that moment he partook
Comfort of love, nepenthe to his pain,
While thus he answered Rachel :

　　　　　　　　　　" Nay, but thou.
My sister, thou thyself art to me rest
And solace.　Sit thee down, I pray, beside
Thy brother.　But to have thee nigh as now
Refreshes like the dew.　I bathe my heart
In thee as in a fountain.　Ask me not
To ease its aching otherwise than so.
Pillow me on thy love and let me rest
In silence from the sound of my own voice.
I hate myself, Rachel."

　　　　　　　　　" But I love thee,
My own dear, noble brother," Rachel said ;
" I love thee, and I will not let thee hate
Thyself.　Brother and sister should be one
In love and hate.　Hate what I hate, and what
I love, love thou — that is true brotherhood."

"Safe law of brotherhood indeed for me,
With thee for sister, Rachel," Saul replied,
With fondness and self-pity, as he kissed
The pure young brow upturned toward him; "but me,
Thou dost not know me as I know myself."

"O nay, but better, brother," Rachel said;
"Right hate is good, as good as love.   So, hate,
But not thyself, Saul.   Shall I tell thee one
To hate?   I hate him, and I counsel thee,
Hate, Saul, that evil man I saw but now
Steal from his too long privilege at thine ear."

"Him, Rachel," Saul replied, "I cannot hate;
Hatred is made impossible by scorn."

"Thou scornest him," she said, "but not too much
To have been disturbed by him.   The cloudy brow,
So unlike my brother — I have brought it back,
I see, dear Saul, by only mentioning him.
Hate him well, Saul, and be at peace again.
To hate is safer, better, than to scorn.
We scorn with pride, we must with conscience hate,
Such hating as I mean.   Thou art too proud, Saul."

Saul answered, "For my pride I hate myself."

But she : " Were it not wiselier done to hate
One's pride, than for one's pride to hate one's self ?
Whoever hates himself for his own pride
Still keeps the pride for which he hates himself.
Hate and abjure thy pride, and love thyself."

" Easy to say, O Rachel, hard to do,"
Sighed Saul,—" at least for such as I, who am
Too proud, too proud !   Thou seest that after all
Thou and myself know Saul alike, too proud,
Albeit the too proud man we treat unlike,
Thou loving and I hating him."

                              "O Saul,"
Thus spoke she, gazing steadfastly at him,
But sudden-starting tears swam in her eyes,
"O Saul, Saul, Saul, my brother, whence is this?
Thou wert not wont to talk thus.   Changed art thou
Since when I heard thee speak in that dispute
With Stephen—"

                  "Thou heard'st me ?" asked Saul.

                              "Yea, Saul,"
Rachel replied, "I heard both thee and him."
(Saul proudly hid an answering hurt of pride.)

" I heard thee, brother, and was proud for thee ;
I never knew more masterful high speech
Fall from thy lips.   My heart leaped up for joy
To listen.   When those men of Israel
Shouted, I shouted with them, silently,
Louder than all.   God heard the secret noise,
Like thunder, of the beating of my heart
In sister's pride for brother's victory.
I crowned thee, I anointed thee my king,
So glorious wast thou in thy conquering might !
And that effulgent pride upon thy brow ! "

  " But when, " said Saul, forestalling ruefully
The expected and the dreaded change and fall
From such a chanted pæan to his praise —
" But when " —

            " But when, O Saul," she said, " when he,
Stephen, stood forth to answer thee, there was —
Didst thou not feel it ? — "

                " Sister, yea, I felt,
More than my sister even could feel, that I
Was baffled, put to shame. "

                " Nay, nay," she said ;
" Not that, O Saul, dear Saul, it was not that. "

"What, then ?   For I felt nothing else," said Saul ;
" That feeling filled me, as sometimes the sound
And stir of whirlwind fill the firmament.
My mind was one mad vortex swallowing up
All other thought than this, ' Saul, thou art shamed ! ' "

" Why, Saul," cried she, " what canst thou mean ?
          Thou shamed ?
How shamed ? "

                    " Rachel, I lost, and Stephen won."

" What didst thou lose ? " said Rachel, wonderingly ;
" And what did Stephen win, that also thou
Won'st not ?   I cannot understand thee, Saul. "

Such crystal clearness of simplicity
Became a mirror, wherein gazing, Saul
Beheld himself a double-minded man.
How should he deal with questioner like this ?

" Why, Rachel, canst thou then not understand,"
He said, " how I should wish to conquer ? "

                              " Yea,"
Said she, " for truth's sake, Saul.   And still, if truth
Conquered, though not by thee, thou wouldst be glad,

Wouldst thou not, Saul?   Here sad I see thee now,
As if truth's cause were fallen — which could not be,
Since truth is God's — and yet thou sayest not that,
But, ' Saul is shamed ! ' and, ' Saul has lost ! ' Not truth,
But Saul.   I cannot understand.   Thou hadst
Perhaps, unknown to me, some other end
Than only truth, which also thou wouldst gain ? "

   It was his sister's single-heartedness
That helped her see so true and aim so fair.
Saul was too noble not to meet her trust
In him with trust in her as absolute.

   " Rachel, " he said, his reverence almost awe,
" Never did burnished metal give me back
Myself more truly, outer face and form,
Than the pure tranquil mirror of thy soul
Shows me the image of my inner self.
The truth I see by thee is justly thine,
And thou likewise shalt see it all in all.

   "The law of God was ever my delight,
As thou knowest, sister, who hast seen me pore
Daily from boyhood on the sacred scroll
Of Scripture, eager to transfer it whole
Unto the living tablets of my heart.

And I have sought, how earnestly thou knowest
To make my life a copy of the law.
No jot or tittle of it was too small
For me to heed with scruple and obey.
With all my heart was I a Pharisee,
Born such, bred such, and such by deep belief.

  " But more, my sister.   Musing on the world,
I saw one nation among nations, one
Alone, no fellow, worshipper of God,
The True, the Only, and by Him elect
To be His people and receive His law ;
That nation was my nation.   My heart burned,
Beholding in the visions of my head,
The glory that should be, and was not, ours.
Think of it, sister, God Himself our King,
And bondmen we of the uncircumcised !
I brooded on the shame and mystery
With anguish in the silences of night.
I saw the image of a mighty state
Loom possible before me.   Her august
And beautiful proportions, builded tall
And noble, rested on foundation-stones
Of sapphire, and in colors fair they rose ;

Her pinnacles were rubies, and her gates
Carbuncles — I beheld Jerusalem,
The city of Isaiah's prophecy ;
Her borders round about were pleasant stones.
She sat the queen and empress of the earth ;
The tributary nations, of their store,
Poured wealth into her lap, and vassal kings
Hasted in long procession to her feet.
The throne and majesty of God in her
Held capital seat, or his vicegerent Christ
Reigned with reflected splendor scarce less bright.
Such, sister, was the dream in which I lived,
Dream call it, but it is the will of God,
More solid than the pillared firmament.

" Was it a fault of foolish pride in me,
Did I aspire audaciously, to hope
That I, by doing and by daring much,
Beyond my equals, might beyond them share
Fulfilments such as these ?   I heard a voice
Saying, ' Prepare the Lord His way.'   I thought
The Lord was near, and what I could, I would
Do to make wide and smooth and straight His way
Before Him, ere He came.   I trusted Him

That, when He came, He in His hands would bring
Large recompense for servants faithful found,
And not forget even Saul, should haply Saul
Not utterly in vain prove to have striven,
Removing from the path of His approach
The stone of stumbling.

              " Sister, these are thoughts
Such as men have, but cherish secretly,
Even from themselves, and never speak aloud
To any ; I have now not spoken these
To thee ; thou hast but heard a few heart-beats
Rendered articulate breath by grace of right
Thine own to know the truth, who hast the truth
Revealed to me.

             " O other conscience mine,
Wherein have I gone wrong ?   I felt the power,
Asleep within me, stirring half awake,
To take possession of the minds of men
And sway their wills ; the world was not too wide
To be the empire I could rule aright,
As chiefest minister, were such His will,
Of God's Messiah.   Some one needs must sit
At His right hand to hear and execute
His pleasure — why not Saul ?   Who worthier ?

But now, alas ! less worthy who, or who
Less likely ?   I am fallen, am shamed — past hope,
Past hope !   I who aspired to greatest things
Am to least things by proof unequal found !
How shall I *not* hate Stephen, who has wrought
On me this great despite — besides what he
Wrought on the suffering cause of truth divine ? "

Rachel's heart heaved, but in what words to speak
She did not find.   Saul into his dark mood
Retired, and sat in silence for a while.
Returning, then, for torture of himself,
To that which Rachel brokenly began
To say, and left unsaid, Saul asked of her :
" What was it, sister, thou beganst to tell,
When, not thy brother, but thy brother's spleen,
Broke thy words off with interruption rude ?
Something it seemed of how, at Stephen's words,
A change fell on thee, from thy first applause
Of me — "

" O Saul !   A chasm of difference, "
So to her brother, Rachel sad burst forth,
" Yawns betwixt thee and me this day, how wide,
How wide !   I feel the bond of sisterhood,

Stretching across, not strained to break — for that
Shall never, never be, in any world,
O brother, truest, noblest, best beloved ! —
But strained to draw thee to me where I am
From where thou art, far off, albeit so near ! "

" A tragic riddle which I fail to read,
Rachel," said Saul, perplexed ; " solve thou it me."

" Brother, I fear I cannot," Rachel said ;
" But loyally I will try.   When Stephen stood
To answer thee that day, a power not he
Oppressed my spirit with a sense of weight,
Gentle but insupportable, which grew
Instantly greater and greater, until it seemed
Ready to crush, unless I yielded ; Saul,
I yielded, and that weight became as might
Which passed to underneath me and upbore."

" Rachel, be simpler," Saul severely said ;
" My soul refuses to be teased with words.
Meanest thou this, that Stephen mastered thee ? "

" Nay, Saul, my brother," meekly Rachel said,
Meekly and firmly ; " Stephen not, but God.
No man could master me away from Saul.

Proudly I was thy vassal sister, Saul,
Until God summoned me with voice that I
Might not resist; God's vassal am I now,
But sister still to thee, and loyal, Saul,
Beyond all measure of that loyalty
I held before, which made me proud of thee,
And glad of thee, and spurred me on to praise
My brother as the paragon of men.
O Saul—"

       "Nay, Rachel," Saul said, with a tone
Repressive more than the repressive words,
" I will not hear thee further in this vein.
Thou art a woman, and I must not blame
Thy weakness; sister too to me thou art,
And I will not misdoubt thy love; but thou
Hast added the last drop of bitterness
To the crowned cup of grief and shame poured out
For me to drink. Go, Rachel, muse on this:
A brother leaned an aching, aching heart
Upon a sister's bosom to be eased,
And that one pillow out of all the world
To me, that trusted downy softness, hid
The cruelest subtle unsuspected thorn.

Saul's sister a disciple and a dupe
Of those that preach the son of Joseph, Christ!
And this, forsooth, the fruit that was to be
Of Saul's aspiring trust to strike the stroke
That in one day should crush the wretched creed!
Rachel, methinks thou mightst have spared me this!
But nay, my sister, better is it so.
Haply no barb less keen had stung me back
To my old self and made me Saul again—
The weakling that I was, to pule and weep,
As if the cause were lost and all were lost!
I thank thee, sister, thou hast done me good,
Like medicine — like bitter medicine!
Tell me true, Rachel, thou didst feign me this,
To rouse me from my late unmanly swoon.
That is past now; I rise refreshed and strong,
I see my path before me, stretching straight,
I enter it to tread it to the end.
Doubt not but I shall feel the wholesome hurt
Of the shrewd-spur my sister, with wise heart
Of hardness, plunged full deep into my side
Betimes, when I was drooping nigh to sink.
Peace to thee, sister, cheer thee with this thought,
'I saved my brother from the last disgrace

By a disgrace next to the last — it was
A hard way, but the only, and it sped!'"

    Such cruel irony from her brother cut
The tender heart of Rachel like a knife.
But more for Saul she grieved than for herself;
She knew that naught but anguish of chagrin
The sharpest could have tortured out from him,
So noble and so gentle, any taunt.
From sheer compassion of his misery,
She wept, and said:

           "O Saul, Saul, Saul—"

                              But he:
"Rachel, no more; already deep enough,
I judge, for present use, the iron has gone;
I shall not falter; thou mayst safely spare
To drive it deeper now — it rankles home.
And surely, if hereafter I should feel,
At some weak woman's moment, any touch
Of foolish tenderness to make me pause
Relaxing and relenting from my course —
A sad course, Rachel, traced in blood and tears! —
Should ever such a softness steal on me,
Surely I should but need remember thee,

Thou younger playmate of my boyhood! thee,
Mirror, that was, of saintly sisterhood!
Loveliest among the daughters of thy race
Once, to thy brother! fountain flowing free
Of gladness, never sadness, unto him!—
Never of sadness until now, but now —
O Rachel, Rachel, sister, changed this day
From all thou wert to what I will not name —
Surely I shall but need bring back this hour,
And let the image of my sister pass —
O broken image of all loveliness,
Distained and broken!— pass before my eyes,
As here I see her, separate from me
Forever, and outcast from God — that thought,
That image, shall make brass the heart of Saul,
And his nerve iron, to smite and smite again,
Until no wily Stephen shall remain
For any silly Rachel to obey!"

    Fierce so outbreathing threat and slaughter, Saul
In bitterness of spirit broke away.

BOOK VII.

STEPHEN AND RUTH.

RACHEL in dismay soliloquizes. She at length resolves on conveying to Stephen, through Ruth, his wife, a warning of his danger. Ruth, not a Christian, expostulates with her husband, attempting to dissuade him from his course — a course certain, she says, to end fatally for him. After a gentle, long, anguished effort on his part to bring Ruth to sympathy with himself in his Christian faith, Stephen parts from her with presentiment that it is never to return. Under the power of the Holy Spirit, he takes his way from Bethany, where his home is, to Jerusalem. His friends Martha and Mary, with their brother Lazarus, see him going, and follow.

STEPHEN AND RUTH.

RUDELY thus parted from his sister, Saul
Straightway sought certain of his synagogue —
The synagogue of the Cilicians — men
Less alien from himself than Shimei was
In spirit, while compatriot too by birth
As was not Shimei, an Asian he —
And these made privy to his changed resolve.
They, glad of such adhesion, opened free
Their counsel to him, telling, with grimace
Added, and shrug of shoulder, to attest
Their scorn of Shimei, Shimei's scheme, which they
Sourly, as from compulsion, now took up.
Saul, swallowing a great throe of innermost
Revolt that well-nigh mastered him, subscribed
Himself, by silence, partner of their deed.

Rachel, spurned from him by her brother, sat
Moveless a while, the image of dismay,

Her two ears caves of roaring sound, her mind
A whirling void of sheer astonishment.
When presently the storm a little calmed
Within her, and she knew herself once more,
She cleared her thought by settling it in words—
Words which through fluent mood and mood changed swift
From passionate soliloquy to prayer,
And from prayer back to soft soliloquy:
" My brother shall not excommunicate
His sister!   While I love him he is mine,
And I shall *not* be 'separate' from him
'Forever'—let him hate me as he will,
Who hates himself, and otherwise amiss
Hates liberally.   Why did I let him go?
I should have held him, should have told him I
Am of one blood with him, as high as he
In spirit ; though a ' woman,' not to be
Put down ; he gave me right, with speech like that,
To equal him in stinging word for word.
I could have done it.   Woman am I?   Yea,
And Deborah was a woman, Miriam too.
I feel my blood a-tingle in my veins
With lust to have him back, and make him know

The lion with the lamb lies down in me
Together; and I showed him but the lamb!
The lion rouses late, occasion gone!
Did he cow me?   So tamely I endured
His contumely!   Anger none till now,
Nor shame not to be angry at such speech
From him; but now — anger with burning shame
Turns inward and incenses me like fire.
I scorn myself for that, reed-like, my head
I bowed before the tempest of his scorn,
When blast for blast I should have blown him back
His tempest."

   Rachel's indignation so
Like a sea wrought and was tempestuous.
But the recoil of her own violent speech
First gave her pause, then pierced her with remorse.
Daily, from when she, hearing Stephen speak,
Heard God through Stephen speaking, and obeyed,
Rachel, first having in baptism testified
Her death to sin, her birth to righteousness —
Never her absent brother dreaming it —
Gladsome had broken bread of fellowship
With the disciples of the Lord, and learned,

Both from their lips and from their lives beheld,
Deep lessons in the lore of Jesus, apt
By the tuition of the Holy Ghost.
The better spirit, for a moment lost,
So lately made her own, came back to her.
Sadly she mused, recalling her hot words
Of passion :

    "'Tempest'?   Tempest sure just now
Hummed in me. 'Scorn myself'? What word was
  that ?
Rachel forsooth forbade Saul saying, ' I hate
Myself' — and scorn herself does she, yea, here
Sit impotently brooding scorn for scorn
To rival him ?   Surely I missed my way.
' Scorn,' ' hate,' one spirit both these speak, such scorn
Such hate, in him, in me.   One spirit both,
And that the spirit of this world, not His,
Not Christ's, no spirit of Thine, O Crucified,
Thou meek and lowly holy Lamb of God !
Forgive, forgive me, from Thy cross of shame
And passion, O Thou suffering Son of God !
Once prayedst Thou thence for those that murdered
  Thee,
' Father, forgive them, for they know not what

They do.'   I knew not what I did when so
I crucified Thee afresh through shameful pride.
My heart breaks with my sorrow for my sin,
A broken and a contrite heart, O Lord,
Thou never wilt despise.

                    " And now yet more
My heart breaks with forgiveness poured on me.
O sweet and blessed flood, pour on me still !
Deliciously I tremble and rejoice.
To be thus broken is bliss more to me
Than to be whole.   I love to lie dissolved,
Dissolving, under this soft fall of peace
Distilled like dew from out Thy bleeding heart !
Lo, here I wholly, wholly, wholly yield
To Thee, O Christ, am fluid utterly,
To take whatever shape Thee best may please.
Remake me after Thine own image, Lord !

" I pray Thee for my brother.   Suffer not
That he act out his purposed madness.   Save,
O save him from that dreadful sin he means
Against Thee and against Thy holy cause.
I cannot bear it, that my brother rage
Against Thee like the heathen.   Thou art strong,

O Christ!   I pray Thee — Thee I pray, O Christ,
Thee only, for none other can — meet Thou
And master Saul!   His sister pleads with Thee;
I plead for his sake, he being dear to me,
But more for Thine own name and glory's sake,
And for Thy suffering cause!

                    I thank Thee, Lord,
With joyful tears, I thank Thee, gracious Lord,
That Thou restrainedst me dumb with silence then
When Saul spake evil of me — for Thy sake.
Through Thee, Who, when reviled, reviledst not
Again, through Thee, through Thee, I, also I,
Proud foolish Rachel, then refrained from words!
No taunt retorted, no reproach, no blame,
Stung him from me to sin; I thank Thee, Lord,
For that!

                    " Now is there naught that I may do?
May I not warn that prophet Stephen?   Saul
Wildly foreshadowed harm himself might wreak
On him; and what meant Shimei's visit here?
Mischief, no doubt of that; collusion strange,
Incredible, impossible, such twain,
That Shimei and my brother!   I will go
And talk with Stephen's wife, her, what I can,

Without disloyalty to Saul, stir up
To fear for Stephen's safety ; he need not,
Surely, dauntless high prophet of the Lord
Although he be, still ready-girt to die,
Rush blindfold into danger unforewarned."

  So to the house of Stephen Rachel went
With haste, and there, in darkened words to Ruth,
Perturbed her woman's breast with vague alarms :
' Her husband must of stratagem beware,
And even of violence, aimed against his life.'
Stephen, by Ruth his wife, of all advised,
Armed him his heart to face what must befall.

  Ruth shook him to the centre of his soul
With storms of wife's complaints and love and tears :
" Nay, Stephen, many a time, bear witness thou,
My heart before she came misgave me sore ;
But now, since Rachel's words, no peace I find
Concerning thee, in this thy wilful way
Wherein thou goest — whither, I know not, whence,
Too well I know, for from a home thou goest
Once happy, ere this madness came on thee !"
Sharply so Stephen's wife upbraided him.
Gravely and gently he admonished her:

" Name it not madness, woman, lest thereby
Thou sin that sin against the Holy Ghost.
No madness is it when the soul of man
Is sovereignly usurped by the Most High
To be the organ of Almighty Will.
I yield myself, nay, Ruth, I join myself,
To God — no blind unsharing instrument,
But joyful partner of His purposes. "

    Solemnly chided so, Ruth quick replied :
" And what if of His purposes one be
To let thee plunge, as headstrong, so headlong,
Thy way to bloody death, thou stiff-necked man ?
Thou hearest what Rachel brings us, doubtful hint
Indeed, but therefore in itself to me
Only more fearful ; and how fearful joined
To what thyself confessest thou of late,
With thine own ears, hast, from the public mouth,
Heard — instigated whisper, Shimei's brew,
Accusing thee of treason to the hope
Of Israel, and purpose to destroy
The temple, and the customs do away
Which Moses left us !   Stephen, all these signs
Singly, much more together, point one way —

They threaten death to thee, if thou persist
To preach things hateful to the wise and good."

Ruth intermitted, and her husband said :
" The danger, Ruth, I know, but I must not,
For danger, slack obedience to my Lord."

Then Ruth said :

                    " But I only ask that thou
Now, for a little, prudently abide
In hiding till this storm be overpast."

He, with a glance of irony, replied :
" And always run to covert at the first
Bluster of opposition ?   Yea, to some
That is permitted ; but to other some,
Whereof am I, only to stand foursquare
And take the buffet of whatever storm.
And the best prudence is obeying, Ruth."

High answered Stephen thus, but Ruth rejoined :
" Stephen, thou ever wert a stubborn will,
And overweening of the wisdom thine,
Hard-hearted and unloving never yet,
Never, till now.   How canst thou bide thus calm,
And I, thine erst loved wife, beheld by thee

So tossed with tempest and not comforted ?"

Wherewith self-pity broke her words to sobs :
She fell on Stephen's neck and wept aloud.
With both his arms he folded her about,
While his heart, hugely swelling in his breast,
Forced to his eye the slow, large, rounding tear.
It was as if a cloud that wished to rain
Strongly held back its drooping weight of shower.
His melting voice at last he fixed in words :
" What meanest thou to weep and break my heart,
O thou, mine own, most loving and most loved
Of women ?   Flesh cries out to flesh in me
Against the purpose of my spirit set
To crucify the flesh with its desires !"

Ruth caught her sobs and held them while she spoke :
" Flesh of thy flesh am I; thou slayest me
In slaying thyself; I will not have it so.
Not ready yet am I to die in thee ;
And thee God surely needs alive, not dead :
The dead cannot praise God nor serve His cause.
Who will so preach that gospel that thou lovest
When thou art gone ?   Who then will silence Saul ?
I tell thee, Stephen, this is Satan's guile —

To get thee slain — and overmatch mightst thou
The arch-deceiver, easily, if thou wouldst,
So easily — only live."

                    Conclusive seemed
Her argument to Ruth and stanched her tears.
She gently disengaged the fond embrace
That held her to her husband's heart, and, drawn
A little backward from his face her face,
She smiled on him like sunshine after rain.
Smiling pathetically back, he kissed,
With kisses that she felt like sacraments,
Then, and forever after till she died,
His wife's brow beautiful with hope, and said:
" Ruth, thou hast said; it is, be sure, his guile,
Satan's, whereby I presently shall die;
If so to die indeed be mine, who feel
Too young still, and too strong, too full of hope,
Too full of — shall I name it, Ruth ? — too full
Of God Himself, the Holy Ghost, to die !
For He within me lives such life and power,
Death seems impossible, all weakness seems
Far off, an alien thing, and not for me ;
I am immortal and omnipotent.

That, Ruth, is when I stand to speak for God,
Preaching to men the gospel of His Son.

  " But when, as now, I sit with thee and talk,
Or when my children cluster round my knees,
And I hear husband, father, from fond lips
Pressed to these lips so oft, and with such joy,
When all the dearness that is meant by home,
And all the drawing lodged in kindred blood,
And all that sense, unutterably deep,
Of oneness, soul in soul, with those we love —
O Ruth !— but, Ruth, our tears commingled flow,
'Tis our hearts flow together in those tears !
O wife and life, when all that I have said,
And that far more which never tongue could say,
Surges upon me, surge on surge of thought
And feeling, like an overflowing flood,
Belovéd, then, how weak I am, how frail,
How low and like to. die !   I lean toward thee,
As if the oak should lean upon his vine."

  Ruth took his word from him and made reply :
" So lean on me, my love, and be at rest ;
Lean, and make proof how vines at need are strong.
In me no faltering purpose weakens will.

Thou speakest of flesh within thee crying out
To flesh against the spirit — warfare strange
Of elements that dwell in me at one.
My nature moves straightforward all one way.
Rebellion none, no mutiny, I find
Only resolve to thwart thy mad resolve,
Thy half resolve, say rather, half and mad —
So proved by these compunctious visitings
Thou hast, these gracious sweet remorses wise,
Relentings toward thy children and toward me ;
Divine presages, Stephen, scorn them not,
Sent to forewarn thee ere it be too late !

  " Bethink thee, Stephen, when didst thou before,
Ever, thus will and straight unwill, thus halt,
Thus parley with thyself, thus stand in doubt
Like a reed shaken with the wind, as now
I see thee here ? Thou art not like thyself ;
Not like that Stephen, ready, combative,
Thy stature still elastically tall
To tower and overtop and overfrown
Whatever front of menace challenged thee.
By thy changed state, I pray thee, be advised.
God teaches thee hereby. He does not wish

Thy will with thy desire to be at war.
Give up thy heady will, and let desire,
Divinely wise, the wisdom of the heart,
Guide thee ; her ways are ways of pleasantness,
And all her paths are peace."

                              Again well pleased
With her own argument, Ruth tearful smiled
A smile that, tenfold tender through those tears,
Was argument to Stephen more than words.
From deep within he heaved a sigh and said :
"Oh ! Woman ! Woman !   Ruth, thou teachest me
How Adam could, by Eve's enticement drawn,
Be even beguiled to die.   And now, to live,
Not die, my Eve entices me.   O Ruth,
I feel, I feel, doubt not but that I feel,
The sweet, the subtly sweet, dissolving spell
Of wish infused by thee, with thee to live,
With thee and for thee, nay, in thee, as thou
In me — this twain one life, how dear, how dear !
O wife, what is there that I could not bear
And dare of hard and high, wert thou, with smiles
And tears and love, for Christ but eloquent,
As all too well I feel thee eloquent

For our sweet selves?"

              Ruth's heart sank, but she said:
" O Stephen, for our children!"   Then she threw
Her head upon his bosom, there in tears,
With passionate sobs and throbs, poured out her heart.

    He mightily a mighty swell that yearned
To be a storm within him, ruled, and said:
" Nay, **Ruth**, but we forget.   Life beyond life
Remains to us and to our children.   We,
Forgetfully, desire and hope and fear
As if death bounded all.   A little while
And Christ will come again.   Then they that sleep
In Him will wake to Him, and they that still
Wake when He comes, but love Him, will, with those
Late sleeping in Him now awake, ascend
To meet the Lord descending, in the air :
Thenceforward all that love Him, loved of Him,
Will be forever with Him where He is,
Beholding there His glory.   Blessed state !
No tears, no fears, no hearts that break, no hearts
That will not break, although they ache the more,
Perhaps, God knows, not breaking — naught of these,
And naught of any ill, but only peace,

Joy, love, security of peace and joy
And love, and fellowship in peace and joy
And love, forever, perfect, more and more,
With vision beatific still of Him
Who washed us in His blood and made us kings
And priests to God.   Ruth, here is hope indeed
For us that will not make ashamed."

          But Ruth
Unhearing heard and was not comforted.
She raised her head from Stephen's breast, with act
As if to part herself in hope from him,
And, with regard made almost alien, said:
" Hug thou thy hope, thy hope is not for me.
He could not save himself, thy Christ, but died
As the fool dieth — and as die wilt thou,
If thou despise my counsel!   Stephen, I
Would rather take my lot a little less,
Less large, less perfect, and less durable,
Than that thou figurest in thy fantasy,
So I might have it something different
From that, real, substantial, palpable
To sense, something whereof one could be sure.
I am no visionary.   Take, say I,

With thanks the good God gives us now and here ;
Not spurn His bounty back into His face,
And reach out emptied hands of wanton greed
To grasp at more He has not offered us.
We have no right to throw our life away !—
In hope of life hereafter, only ours
Then when with patience our appointed time—
'*All*' our appointed time, Stephen — we wait,
Till our change come."

                Ruth's chill repellent tone,
Her mask of manner hard, could not deceive
Her husband, who, through such disguise with pain
Put on, well recognized a new device
Of wife's love, versatile as resolute,
Constraining tenderness to play severe.
Yet not the less for that, more rather, he
Felt at her words a dull weight of despair
Oppress his spirit; he could only pray,
In silent sorrow not to be expressed,
" O Holy Ghost of God, pity and save !"
A hundred times so praying for his wife,
In anguished iteration o'er and o'er,
Stephen not speaking sat, and speechless she.

At last, as if one bound with green withes rose
Rending the withes to rise, rose Stephen, sweat
Of supreme agony victorious
At dreadful cost dewing his brow ; he took
His wife's hand solemnly and tenderly,
His port majestical compelling awe,
And, with tense speech, in tones that strangely mixed
The husband with the prophet, slowly said :
" Farewell, Ruth, for the hour is fully come
That I must hence.   The burden of the Lord
Is instant and oppresses me.   I go,
Whither I know not, but He knows, to bear
Witness once more to His most worthy name.
I thought that I should never preach again
His gospel in those temple courts, but now
Perhaps He wills even that ; whatever be
His purpose, unforeshown, I welcome it.

" Lo, Ruth, this is the last time, for full well
I know I never shall come back to thee !
Come thou to me, I charge thee that, and bring
Our children to their father.   Always think
Hereafter, ' He, that last time, charged me that ! '
I think my God in this has heard my prayer,

And I go hence in comfort of some hope.
Our children! Oh! My children! God in heaven,
Have mercy! How a father pitieth
His children, think of that, and pity me!
A father lays them on a Father's heart;
Father, I charge Thee, by Thy father's-heart,
Not one be plucked from out His Father's hand!
Lord Christ, see Thou to this, in session there
Forever, interceding for Thine own!

" Ruth, give their father's blessing to our babes;
I trust that they will cheer their mother well,
When I am gone, and cheer thee to the end.
Their sweet unconscious voices now I hear
In laugh and prattle of pathetic glee!
I fain would see their faces once again,
Kiss them once more, and take a last caress!
But nay, I spare myself one pang; sweet babes,
They are too young to know! But by and by,
When they are older and will understand,
Then tell them thou what I now cannot, say,
'Your father loved you, loves you, and will love
Forever — that was his last word to me
For you.' So, Ruth, farewell!"

                          With first his hands,
Both, placed in solemn blessing on her head,
She kneeling by his knees, forth from his house
Therewith went Stephen all as in a trance.
With open eyes that saw not, yet with steps
Guided — how, he well knew, but whither not —
In simple rapt obedience, he his way
Took absently like one that walks in sleep.

  Stephen his home had fixed in Bethany —
Sequestered hamlet on the slope behind
The Mount of Olives from Jerusalem.
Mary and Martha, here, and Lazarus,
He knew and loved; and with them oft, their guest,
Held converse sweet of what He said and did,
And was, the Friend Who wept when Lazarus died,
The Lord of life through Whom he lived again :
But Ruth, self-sundered from this fellowship,
Abode apart, or only with them bound
In bonds of kindly common neighborhood.
These marked when Stephen, marking not, passed by,
That day, steps toward the holy city bent,
And to each other said : ‘ He goes once more
Bound in the spirit to Jerusalem

To preach the gospel of the grace of God.
Behold the lit look on the forward face !
Behold the gait half-buoyed as if with wings !
It is like Jesus hastening to His cross !
Lo, let us follow !' and they followed him.
But he went ever onward, slacking not
His steps, nor heeding when the brow he reached
Of Olivet and thence, across the deep
Ravine of Kedron worn with rushing floods,
Before him and beneath him saw outspread
The city of David with its palaces.

BOOK VIII.
STEPHEN MARTYR.

As Stephen approaches the temple, he is suddenly arrested and brought before the Sanhedrim. There making his defence, he is interrupted with hostile demonstrations, instigated by Shimei. On this, he bursts out with noble indignation, which furnishes the desired occasion for a cry against him of "Blasphemy!" from all, and for a violent hurrying forth of the prisoner without the walls to be stoned. A file of Roman soldiers confronts and stays the tumultuous crowd ; but, after parley conducted by Shimei with the centurion, their leader, the rout is suffered to proceed. Meantime, however, a little company of sympathizing Christians, including Rachel with the three from Bethany, have gathered round Stephen and listened to cheerful, tranquillizing words from him. After the stoning, these friends carry the body of Stephen for laving to the pool of Siloam, whence by moonlight up Olivet to Bethany. Here they lay it in a room of Martha and Mary's house until morning.

STEPHEN MARTYR.

The sun of Syrian afternoon, declined
Half-way betwixt the zenith and the west,
Burned blinding in the cloudless blue of heaven
And fired a conflagration in the copes
Of beaten gold hung over the august
House of Jehovah, whither Stephen now
Tended unconsciously with wonted feet.
That spectacle of splendor he, agaze
With holden unbeholding eyes, saw not,
Or, as but with his heart beholding, saw
Only as goal of his obedience due.
Down the abrupt declivity with speed,
The westward-slanting slope of Olivet,
Descending by a path stony and steep —
The same whereon full often to and fro
Had fared the Blessed Feet, between the dust
And din and fever of Jerusalem,
And the sweet purity and peace, the cool,

The quiet, of that home in Bethany,
His refuge !—so descending, Stephen passed
On his right hand Gethsemane, that moved
Muse of the Master's agony for men,
Crossed Kedron, and thence upward pressing gained
Gate Susan, whence the temple nigh in view.
'Perhaps,' thought he, 'perhaps, once more, against
My expectation, I am thither brought
To preach as when I answered Saul that day.
The Lord will show me, in full time, alike
What I must speak, and when, and where.'

                                        So wrapt
In welcome of the will unknown of God,
And full of faith and of the Holy Ghost,
Stephen with no amazement was afraid
When, suddenly and rudely, in the street,
A band in service of the Sanhedrim
Set on him, and, by their authority,
Seized him and brought him prisoner accused
Of blasphemy before their council, there
To be examined for his words and deeds.
Captive in body, he in soul was free,
Exulting in that glorious liberty,

The sense of sonship to Almighty God.

False witnesses, by Shimei suborned,
And well their lesson taught by Shimei,
Stood forth, who, to the teeth of Stephen, swore:
"This person never ceases speaking words
Against this holy place and Moses' law ;
We heard him say that Jesus Nazarene
Is going to destroy this place, and change
The customs Moses handed down to us."

All the assessors in the Sanhedrim,
Fastening their eyes on Stephen, saw his face,
As it had been an angel's, kindling shine.
Saul marked it, and remembered how that day
The lightning of that face had blinded him!

The high priest now, accosting Stephen, asked,
"Are these things so ?" and Stephen thus replied:
"Brethren and fathers, hearken to my words.
With ears that tingle to the echoes yet,
Perchance, of that high passionate harangue
Which late from Saul ye heard concerning wounds
Intended to this Jewish commonwealth,
Ye now have heard forsooth again from these —
How temple, law, and well-belovéd ways

Bequeathed us by our fathers from of old
Are threatened in the message that I preach.

" But, brethren, he mistakes who deems that God
Is to one place, one race, one time, one clime,
One mode of showing forth Himself, shut up.
Consider through what phases manifold
Has passed already heretofore God's way
With men; thence learn how lightly reckons God
Of place or method.
                              " Unto Abraham first
Before he came to Charan, while he yet
Dwelt in the land between the rivers, God
Appeared.   Nor in a place thus holy made,
And glorious, by theophany, was he,
Our father, suffered to abide.   ' Arise,'
Jehovah said, ' and get thee hence and come
Into the land which I will show thee.'   Then
To Charan that obedient pilgrim passed.
Nor there found he a settled rest.   Again
He journeyed and in Canaan, this fair land
Wherein ye dwell, a sojourner became ;
For here God gave him no inheritance,
Promising only that in after times

That childless father's children here should dwell.

" Meanwhile another change, and now what seems
A long postponement of the purposed grace.
Four hundred years should Abraham's seed sojourn
As strangers in an alien land where they
Should suffer bondage and an evil lot :
Delivered thence with judgment on their foes,
They then should hither come and here serve God.

"Yet when the ripeness of the time was full,
And Moses offered to deliver them,
Our fathers doubted and refused his hand :
But Moses notwithstanding led them out.
And that same Moses prophesied of One
To follow him as Prophet Whom must all
Obey.   Yet Moses, mouth of God to men,
Obeyed our fathers not, but, in their hearts
Gone back to Egypt, spurned him far aloof
From them.   Then followed that apostasy
To idols, by Jehovah God chastised,
On those offending, with captivity
Which beyond Babylon carried them away.

"Albeit Jehovah gave to Moses such

Honor as never yet to man was given,
Still much that Moses wrought was cast aside.
That tabernacle, made by him express
As God Himself had shown him in the mount,
And so inwove with Hebrew history,
God suffered this to pass, and in its place
Preferred the temple built by Solomon.

" Yet not in houses built with human hands
Dwells the Most High ; as, by His prophet, God
Says, ' On the heaven sit I as on a throne,
And the earth make a footstool for My feet. '
' What house will ye build Me, ' the Lord inquires,
' Or what shall be the place of Mine abode ? ' "

So far a loth penurious decent heed
The council had grudged out to Stephen ; here
The scowl of curious incredulity,
Wherewith they listened while as yet in doubt
Whither might tend his drift of argument,
Changed to a frown of deadly hate, as they
Conclusion from his use of Scripture drew
That Stephen glanced at overthrow indeed
Meant for the temple.   Instantly, alert
To seize occasion, Shimei the sign

Gave to prepared conspirators, who now
Obediently framed a menace grim
Of gesture to denounce the speaker's aim ;
And all the council, as one man, astir
With insurrection, frowned a vehement
Refusal to receive the word of God.

  Stephen beheld their aspect, and his soul,
Dilating to a seraph's measure, filled
With sudden prophet's zeal aflame for God.
He forged his indignation into words
Which, like bolts kindling, now he launched at them.
He said:
          "Stiff-necked ye, and uncircumcised
In heart and ears ! Always do ye resist
The Holy Ghost ; as did your fathers, so
Do ye.   Which of the prophets did they not,
Your fathers, persecute ? Who showed before
The coming of the Just One, those they slew ;
And of Him now have ye betrayers been
And murderers.   Ye who the law, received
At angels' disposition, have not kept !"

  Cut to the heart at this, those councillors

Gnashed with their teeth on Stephen.

                                     But that sight
Stephen, his eyes rapt elsewhere, did not see.
Full of the Holy Ghost, his face he raised,
Gazing with sense undazzled into heaven,
And saw the glory of God, and Jesus there,
Not sitting, as at ease, but, as in act
To help, standing, on the right hand of God.
He testified that vision thus to men :
"Opened see I the heavens and standing there
The Son of Man on the right hand of God."

    Thereat a loud acclaim of hatred forth
Burst in one voice from all the Sanhedrim.
Full come was Shimei's opportunity.
As started Mattathias to his feet
In honest wrath instinctive, Shimei too
Rose, counterfeiting wrath, sign understood
By his complotters, who now likewise rose
In simultaneous second and support,
Setting the council in a wild turmoil.
They stopped their ears, and all together ran
On Stephen with tumultuary rage
To thrust him forth without the city walls.

The rush of such commotion through the streets,
A torrent madness raging on its way,
Raging and roaring, every moment more,
Roused a wide wind of rumor and surmise
Troubling the air of all Jerusalem.
Tremor of this reached Rachel's jealous sense,
On edge — she knowing that the Sanhedrim
Would that day summon Stephen to its' bar —
To fear the worst for Stephen and for Saul.
But Ruth, her home more distant, she at home
Urged by importunate cares which for her wrought
Some present respite from the strain and pain
Of that farewell with Stephen — vexing thought !
Too certain to return insistently,
In waking and in sleeping vision, soon,
At night upon her bed, unbidden guest,
And haunt her bosom with sad memories,
And vague, unhappy, beckoning shapes of fears !—
Ruth, so precluded, nothing knew of all.

Rachel, with other women of the Way
Like-minded with herself, pathetic group !
Drew timorous nigh the ragged rushing rim
Of that confusion pouring toward the gate
Which northward opened on Damascus road.

The self-same path it was whereby had walked
A little while before, bearing His cross,
The Saviour of mankind toward Calvary.
Stephen remembered, and, remembering, went
Both meekly more, and more triumphantly,
To suffer like his Lord without the gate.
He said within himself, 'I follow Him;
I feel His footprints underneath my feet.'
Those women watched the martyr every step,
And with hands waved signalled him sympathy.
Such helpless help was help the more to him —
Who had no need, but gave them back again
Their sympathy in looks of strength and cheer
Which bade them too be faithful unto death,
As they saw him that day.   The peace of God,
Lodged in his heart—a trust from Christ, Whose word
Was, " Peace I leave with you, My peace to you
I give; not as the world gives give I you:
Let not your heart be troubled, neither let
It be afraid " — that peace steadfast he bore
Amid the tumult round him, the one thing
Not shaken in a shaken universe,
Like the earth's axle sleeping and the earth
Whirling from centre to circumference !

Not yet the rout had reached the city gate,
When, lo ! a sudden halt, a sudden hush,
Arrested and becalmed the multitude.
A file of Roman soldiers from the fort,
With swift, straight, sure lock-step, steel-clad, that
        clanged,
Flowed like a rill of flowing mercury,
Heavy yet nimble, through a street that crossed
The course of that mad progress, and, athwart
Its head abutting, stayed; the clang of pause
Rang sharper than the clang of the advance.
The leader, a centurion, sternly spoke :
"What means this uproar?   Seek ye to provoke
Your rulers?   Love ye, then, your yoke so well
Ye fain would feel it heavier on your necks ?
Sedition into insurrection grows
Full easily, and this sedition seems.
Speak, who can tell, and say, What would ye ?"
                                        Prompt,
Then, Shimei, of the foremost, stepping forth
Said :

        " This is no sedition as might seem ;
A crushing of sedition rather.   We,
The Sanhedrim "—wherewith a smirk and bow

From Shimei, with wave of hand swept round
Upon his colleagues in their sorry plight
Dishevelled, seemed, in sneering cynic sort,
To introduce them with mock dignity—
"We Sanhedrim this fellow caught employed
In stirring up sedition, and our zeal
For peace and order under Roman rule
Inflamed us, following our forefathers' way,
To visit death on him without the gate.
We beg you will allow us to proceed
And put to proof of act our loyalty "—
Hot breath, half hiss, from Mattathias here —
" This script perhaps will help determine you."

   And Shimei handed up a tablet writ.
The Roman read :

           " Let this disorder pass;
It may be useful.   Watch it well."

                 The seal
Once more with care examined, parley had
With Shimei, whose crafty answers meet
Each wary scruple of the officer,
And sign is given to let the rout proceed.

   Meantime a different scene has quietly

Been passing unperceived. That company
Of ministering women Rachel found,
Salomé, and the Marys, blessed name!
With others who had followed and bewailed
When Jesus suffered — these, joined now by those
From Bethany, with Lazarus, prevailed
To edge their way ungrudged through the close ranks
Of idle gazers round not undisposed
Themselves to sympathize, until they stood
Nigh Stephen, and in undertones could speak
With him, and hear his words.

                             " Weep not for me, "
He said, " ye blesséd! I am well content.
I think how short the way is, not how sharp,
To Jesus where just now I saw Him. There
He stood in heaven on the right hand of God.
He seemed to lean toward me with arms outstretched
As if at once to take me to Himself!
I spring toward Him with joy unutterable.
I shall not feel the pain, which will but speed
Me thither. He hath overcome the world.
Be of good cheer, belovéd, ye who wait
A little longer to behold His face.
For you too He hath overcome the world.

Be strong, be faithful, be obedient,
A little while — and we shall meet again
Safe, happy, in the New Jerusalem,
Forever and forever with the Lord.

" But Ruth, my wife, yet unbelieving — care
For her and for my children !   God will give
All to our prayers.   And Husband He will be
To her, and Father to the fatherless. "

Rachel to Lazarus whispered :

"Tell him I,
Rachel, Saul's sister, would do something.   Ask
What I may do for Ruth, to testify
A sister's sorrow for a brother's fault.
And let him not think hardly, not too hardly,
Of Saul who wrongs him so ! "

And Lazarus
Told Stephen, who, with look benign addressed
To Rachel, said :

" Thou, Rachel, thou thyself,
No other, shalt to Ruth my wife convey
Her husband's very last farewell ; good-night
Call it, and bid her meet me there to say
Good-morning.   Comfort her with words.   To Saul

Say -- when the time comes he will hear, not now —
That all is well, is wholly well.   I go —
And that is well — perhaps in part through him,
Which seems not well, but is, by grace of Christ,
Who thus, in part through me — and surely that
Likewise is well — erelong will make of Saul,
In Stephen's room, a more than Stephen both
To preach and suffer for His name.   This hope
Be thine, Rachel, and God be with thee, child ! "

Martha, her hand as ready as her heart,
Had other cheer provided than of words.
'The willing spirit, if the flesh be weak,
May faint,' she thought, 'and angels strengthening
     Him
Brought Jesus succor in Gethsemane.
May I not be his angel, Stephen's, now,
And his flesh brace to bear his agony ?'
She said to Stephen :

                    " I have brought thee here
A cake of barley and a honeycomb.
I pray thee eat and cheer therewith thy heart."
" God bless thee, Martha, for thy loving thought ! "
Said Stephen ; and he took the food from her

And ate it, giving thanks before them all.
And all with him gave thanks, for nothing else
Could so have cheered them in their sad estate
As thus to see their friend at such an hour
Cheering himself with food, his appetite
Not troubled by least trouble of the mind,
And he approved superior to his lot,
Not by a strain of high heroic pride,
Not by access of transient ecstasy,
But simply by the sober confidence,
Well-grounded, of the soul enduring all
As seeing Him Who is invisible.
Besides, had any deemed that Martha erred,
Inopportunely ministering to the flesh,
When spirit unsupported by the flesh
As well had conquered, and more gloriously,
Haply, too, letting this their thought escape,
Unmeant, in look or gesture, to her pain —
Such might, in Stephen's gracious act, have heard
As if a silent echo of those words —
Ineffably persuasive sweet reproof
At once and soft assuagement of unease —
" Why trouble ye the woman ?   She hath wrought
A good work for Me."

       But the Sanhedrim,
Permitted by the Roman to resume
Their way with Stephen, now to him once more
Their notice turned.	Within their heart enraged,
First, to have met with such a check, and then,
Scarce less, *so* to have had the check removed —
Both this and that their sense of bondage chafed —
Ill brooked it they to see what now they saw,
Their prisoner in calm converse with his friends.

  " Begone!" to these they cried.	" For shame to
    show
Untimely softness thus to whom ye see
Your rulers judge worthy of death.	Begone !"

  One churl among those councillors was found,
When Stephen gently bade his friends give way,
Even for his own sake, who could least endure
To see them suffer roughness, most unmeet
For such as they — one graceless churl was found
To raise his hand at Stephen speaking so
And smite him on the mouth.	A wail at this
Broke from those women, and their hair they tore
In passion of compassion and of wrath

Holy as love.   But Stephen was most meek,
And only in a shadowed look expressed
Pain at such painful sympathy with pain.
This seen by those, they soon responsively
Resumed composure like his own, and walked,
Following, molested not, at small remove
From the belovéd martyr, cheering him,
And cheered, with sense of some society.

 So, on, with going less precipitate,
And less vociferous rage, but not less fell,
Moved the infatuate multitude, repressed
And maddened, both at once, to feel themselves
Only by sufferance masters of the fate
Of Stephen, and their very footsteps timed
To regular and slow behind those few
Austere, impassive, automatic men
Armed, who, though few they might be, yet meant
     Rome.

 Arrived at length at the acccurséd spot,
They stay.   The ground about was strewn with stones,
Rejected fragments from the quarry cleft,
Flakes from the mason's chisel, interspersed
Dilapidations from the city walls

Twice overthrown and razed, or missiles thence
Once by defenders on assailants hurled.
They stay, and, Stephen stationed in the midst
Where, first, a circle of spectators round
Was ordered in disorderly array,
Prepare to act their dreadful blasphemy.

Within, opposed to Stephen, Saul stood, pale,
Blanched with resolve, anguished, and tremulous,
But in nerve shaken, not in will, to take
His part.   Saul's part was only to consent.
Perhaps the eyes, the beautiful sad eyes,
Of Rachel, dark and liquid ever, now
Unfathomably deep with unshed tears —
Perhaps such eyes, his sister's, fixed on him,
He seeing not because he would not see,
Wrought yet some holy spell that charmed him back
Insensibly from part more active there.
But his consent Saul testified with sign
Open to all to see, and understood.
He held the outer robes thrown off of those
Who, disencumbered so, might, with main strength,
And aim made sure, the better speed to fling
At that meek heavenly man the murderous stone.

Those witnesses malign who had forsworn
Stephen to this, were first to cast at him
The stone to slay.   There Stephen stood, his face,
His glory-smitten face, upturned to heaven,
And his arms thither raised as if to meet
The down-stretched arms of Jesus from on high.
It was a sight both beautiful to see
And piteous.   The angels might have wept,
Who saw it, but that they more deeply saw,
And saw the pity in the beauty lost,
Like a few drops of water on a fire
That only serve to feed the flames more bright.

At the first shower of stones at him with cry
Of self-exciting execration flung,
Stephen, with answering cry, as if of one
Running to refuge and to sanctuary,
Betook him to the covert of the Wings
That trembled with desire to be outstretched
Once over doomed Jerusalem unfain,
And, " Jesus, Lord, receive my spirit!" said.
That his friends heard and echoing said "Amen!"
But they the flying stones saw not, nor saw
Alight the flying stones upon their friend ;

For they too turned their faces upward all,
And, gazing unimaginable depths
Beyond the seen, beheld the glory there,
Wherein the scandal and the mystery
Of visible things vanished, like shadows plunged
In the exceeding brightness of the sun,
Or were transformed to make the glory more,
Like discords conquered heightening harmony.

    With the next flight of stones, unwatched likewise,
Stephen, raised far above the fierce effect,
Stinging or stunning, of the cruel blows,
Spoke heavenward once again, not for himself
Petitioning now, but pleading for his foes.
His foes already had prevailed to bring
The martyr to his knees, and, on his knees,
With loud last voice from lips inviolate yet —
As if that angel chant at Bethlehem
Still sounded, " Peace on earth, good will to men,"
Or that diviner tone from Calvary,
" Forgive them, for they know not what they do " —
One ransomed pure and perfect human note
Threading the dissonant noise with melody —
He prayed, " Lord Jesus, lay not Thou this sin

To their account." Therewith he fell asleep.
That holy prayer exhaled his breath away,
And on his breath exhaled to heaven in prayer
His spirit thither aspired and was with Christ.

As Stephen fell asleep, the sun went down ;
But over Olivet the great full moon
Rose brightening. ' So,' thought Stephen's friends of
          him,
' His life has been extinguished to our eyes,
Only elsewhere to shine, but while we wait
For the new day to dawn that lingers, lo,
His memory instead shall give us light,
Not splendid like the sun, yet like the moon
Lovely !'
          Thus comforting themselves, they saw
The murderers of their friend above his corse
Build roughly of the stones that smote him dead
A kind of cairn in mockery of a tomb.
Melted away meanwhile the multitude
In silence, and, soon after, all were gone
Save the true lovers of the man. Then these
Gathered together round the accurséd spot,
Now hallowed, where he stood to suffer, where

He prayed, and where he fell, and whence he rose
Deathless, leaving the sacred body there,
Dead, desolate of the spirit, but still dear,
Most dear to them.   And so, with many tears
Fast falling that nigh blinded them, they took
From off the body, one by one, the stones —
Almost as if they loved them, with such care ! —
Until his face, his fair disfeatured face,
And his form marred and broken, open lay
To the mild moon that seemed to sympathize,
And touched and softened all with healing beams.

" Let us bear hence the sacred clay," they said,
" And wash it from the pool of Siloam."
Then Lazarus, with three fellow-helpers more —
Nathanael, Israelite indeed, was there,
Joseph of Arimathæa too had come,
Later, and Nicodemus, by nightfall,
These were the chosen four, with Lazarus —
Making a litter of their robes, took up
The noble form that lately Stephen wore,
And gently carried it to Siloam.
With soft lustration there at loving hands,
The dust and blood were wholly washed away ;

The hair and beard then decently arranged,
With skill that hid the wounds on cheek or brow,
The eyelids closed on eyes that saw no more,
The scarce cold palms folded upon the breast,
Stephen it seemed indeed just fallen asleep.
Then they were glad that Ruth would see him so,
So peaceful and so beautiful asleep,
Expecting soon to waken satisfied !
" To-morrow will be time enough," they said,
" To tell Ruth—let her sleep to-night."   But Ruth
Slept not, or if she slept, slept but to dream
Of Stephen and his last hands on her head.

   Under the balmy moon, up Olivet
To Bethany they bore the holy dust,
And there, beneath the roof that sheltered oft
The Man who had not where to rest His head,
They laid the body down to dreamless sleep ;
And slept themselves until the morrow morn.

BOOK IX.
RUTH AND RACHEL.

VERY early in the morning, Rachel, charged with this office by Stephen, breaks to Ruth the news of her husband's death. The two then go together to the place where the body of Stephen is laid. There, Ruth, kneeling in prayer beside her martyred husband, repentantly accepts his Lord for hers, becoming a Christian. Rachel, having hastily visited her home, to find Saul gone thence with purpose not to return, leaves the house in her maid's care and goes back to Ruth, to whom, being requested to do so, she tells the story of Stephen's stoning. Then the funeral of Stephen takes place, with a memorial discourse pronounced, and an elegy recited, at the tomb.

RUTH AND RACHEL.

THE morrow morn broke fair in Bethany,
And Ruth rose early from unquiet sleep ;
Rachel likewise, who slept in Mary's house.
The sun had not yet risen, but in the west
The moon hung whitening opposite the dawn,
When Ruth, her children left asleep, went forth
To feel the freshness of the morning air
Without, and water from the village well
To draw, both for the slaking of her thirst
And for the cooling of her brow that burned
And of her throbbing temples. At the well
Rachel she met who earlier still was forth
On the like errand. The two women hailed
And kissed each other. Ruth to Rachel then
Said : " Thou art not, I trow, this morning come
Hither the long way from Jerusalem ? "

" Nay, Ruth," said Rachel, " here the yesternight
With Mary and Martha I abode a guest. "

" How fresh the wind is," Ruth said, " hither blown
From off the western sea !   Us, underneath
The crest of Olivet, it lights upon
Descending, broken, like a breath from heaven.
What a delicious balm !"

                         " About my brow,"
Said Rachel, " gratefully I feel the air,
Attempered so, soft flowing, as if one
That loved me like a mother gently stroked
My temples to undo a band of pain
Bound round them."

                         "And, in sooth," the other said,
Now looking narrowly at Rachel's face,
" Thou seemest sad of favor, Rachel.   Thou,
Thou too, so young, hast then thy cause to grieve !
It is a sad world and a weary.   But —
Forgive me if such quick instinctive fears
Be selfish, I am wife and mother — aught
Of evil tidings bringest thou me?   Spare not
To speak.   Thou wilt but answer to the dreams
I had this night, portending nameless ill.
Stephen — I fear for him.   He yesterday
Left me beyond his wont oppressed in spirit,
And has not since returned. Strange — yet not strange ;

Sometimes the livelong night he spends in prayer
Alone upon the top of Olivet
Or in the shadows of Gethsemane."

"Ruth," Rachel said, "the Angel of the Lord
Round His belovéd, like the mountains round
Jerusalem, encampeth ever ; he
Of God's belovéd is, and guarded well !"

But Ruth scarce listened; she insisting said :
"Perhaps of Stephen some report thou bringest,
Hint doubtless of new danger threatening him !"

"Nay, Ruth, no longer danger threatens now
Thy husband ; that is past, and he is safe."

"Thank God," said Ruth ; "but stay, I dare not yet
Thank God.   Tell me, have then our rulers ceased
To frown on Stephen preaching Jesus Christ ?
Or Stephen, will he cease and preach no more ?
This cannot be, for Stephen is such stuff
As never yet did bend to mortal beck ;
And that — our rulers surely have not changed
Thus suddenly their mind.   Thou art deceived,
They have deceived thee — Stephen is not safe ;
It is their guile to make us think him safe,

He off his guard will fall an easier prey
Into their hands.   Rachel, it was not kind,
Not faithful in thee so to be deceived.
More love had made thee more suspicious.   I
Suspect forever everybody; thee
Now I suspect.   Thou keepest something back,
Or haply palterest with a double sense.
Rachel, I charge thee, I adjure thee, speak
And tell me all.   Stephen is dead!   Say that —
Is dead!   Thou meantest that by, ' He is safe.'
They have stoned him, stoned my husband, stoned
      the man
That was the truest Hebrew of them all!"

  Though by her words Ruth challenged frank reply,
Yet by her tones and by her eager looks
She deprecated more what she invoked.
This Rachel saw, and answered not a word.
Then Ruth gainsaid what Rachel would not say :
" They have not done it, could not do it, he —
Rachel, it is not true, unsay it, quick,
It was a cruel jest to tease me so,
Thou art not a wife, thou art not a mother, else
Thou never hadst conceived so ill a jest!"

Rachel was tortured, but she could not speak,
And Ruth, secure in sense of respite yet,
Went on invoking what she would not hear:
" Why art thou silent ?   Speak, and keep not back
The truth, whatever it may be ; there's naught
So soothing and so healing as the truth.
But I will not believe that he is dead.
Thou didst not know my husband. Dead ! dead ! dead !
I tell thee, Rachel, *that* is something past
Imagining dreadful, hopeless.   To be dead
Is — not to love, and not to speak to those
Who loved and love thee, not to hear them speak,
Saying they loved and love thee and lament
They ever gave thee cause of grief and now
Are different and would die a thousand deaths
To   have   been   different   then   when   thou   couldst
      know —
Death, Rachel, — but of death what canst thou learn,
For thou art but a child and never wast,
Never, to such a husband such a wife —
To vex the noblest heart that ever broke !"

Rachel at first had listened with dismay,
And nothing found to answer to Ruth's words,

Whose words indeed flowed on and made no pause
For answer, as if she in truest truth
Sought not the answer that she seemed to seek,
Would fain postpone it rather, or avert.
But when at length the utterance of Ruth's thought
From converse passed into soliloquy
And the deep secret of her soul revealed,
Then Rachel caught a welcome gleam of hope.
A sign of grace she saw or seemed to see
At work for Ruth within her heart of grief,
Transmuting human sorrow to divine
Repentance, and for pain preparing peace.

" Let us go in together," Rachel said,
For they by this were nigh to Ruth's abode,
" Let us go in where we may be withdrawn
From note of such as here might mark our speech
Or action ; I have word from him to thee."
Then they went in, and Ruth bestirred herself
To make a cheer of welcome for her guest.
That momentary truce to troubled thought
For Ruth, and interspace of quietness
From her own words which could not choose but flow
With helpless importunity till then,

Gave Rachel needed chance to speak.   She said :
" O Ruth, thy husband fell asleep last night,
And slept a sweeter sleep than thine or mine,
A deep sweet sleep, a happy sleep, a blest.
Thou wouldst not wake him thence for worlds on
     worlds.
He felt before he slept that he should sleep,
And me, whom God our Father let be nigh,
Stephen bade bear a last good-night to thee.
He did not think the night was very long
Before him for his sleeping, and his wish
Was thou shouldst meet him presently to say
Good-morning.   This was his true message, Ruth."

   The ineffably serene steadfast regard
Of Rachel's eyes, that, out of liquid depths
Unsounded, looked angelic love and truth,
With pity mingled, equal measure — tears
Orbing them large, shot through and through with
     light
Of heavenly hope for Ruth — but, more than all,
A subtly sweet insinuating tone,
Most musical, of softness in the voice,
That gently wound into the listener's heart —

These, with what else, who knows? of help from
      Heaven,
Wrought a bright miracle of change in Ruth.
She had been hard and dry, a desert rock ;
The rock was smitten now with Moses' rod.
Ruth gushed in gracious tears, she veiled herself
With weeping, as sometimes a precipice
Veils itself dim with mist of cataract.
And Rachel wept with Ruth, until Ruth said :
" But where is Stephen, Rachel?   It might be
They, meaning death, yet did not compass death.
Such things have been ; haste, let us go and see.
Monstrous it were, if he should need me — I
The while here sitting weeping idle tears!"

  " Come," Rachel said, and took her by the hand.
So hand in hand they went to Mary's house,
The elder guided as the younger led,
And neither speaking, stilled with solemn thought.
Mary and Martha met the twain, with mute,
Subdued, affectionate greeting, at the door,
And, understanding without word their wish,
Straight led them inward, with a quietude
Of gesture that spoke peace and peace infused,

To the place where in quietude reposed
That slumberer late so violently lulled
To this so placid sleep.   The room was flushed
With hue of gold in hangings round the walls
And rugs of russet muffling deep the floor,
That made a kind of inner light diffused,
Like sunshine without sun and shadowless.
A golden-curtained window opened east,
And east the upturned face of Stephen looked,
Lying there motionless in that fast sleep —
So lying that, had he his eyelids raised,
He without moving might have seen the morn.
The rest, with one accord not entering, stood
About the door without, silent, and saw
While the wife sole went to the husband's side.
That instant, lo, from out the breaking dawn
A level sunbeam through the curtain slipped
And touched the fair translucent face with light.
Ruth marked it and she testified and said,
Falling upon her knees beside the couch : •
" I take it as a token, Lord, from Thee ;
Even so send Thou Thy light into my heart !
Lo, by the side of him made beautiful
In death, of whom I was unworthy, here

I give myself — alas, that it should be
Too late for him to have known it ! — to his Lord.
I trust to be forgiven for my sin !
I thank Thee that I was not weight enough
Upon him to prevail against Thy might
Within him and prevent this sacrifice —
Accomplished all without my help, nay, all
In spite of my resistance!   O my God,
How hast Thou humbled me !   To have had no part,
Wife with her husband to have borne no part —
Save hindering what she could ! — when such a deed
Of martyrdom for Christ was possible !
Behold, O Lord, thus late I take my part !
This now is also mine, as well as his,
This sacrifice.   I have offered him to Thee !
And if my share be heavier even than his —
To live bereaved more grievous martyrdom
Than to have died — this too is my desert,
Accept the witness of my widowhood !"

    Ruth ceased, but rose not from her knees, still fixed
In posture as if grown a pillar of prayer.
Then those three women came and knelt with her
Beside her dead, a silent fellowship

Of sympathy in sacrifice; but soon
Rachel and Mary, one on either side
Of Ruth, borne by the self-same impulse each,
Each at the self-same instant borne, unto
The self-same beautiful appeal, pure love's
Pure touch, stole softly each a hand in hers.
Each plighting hand so proffered Ruth upraised
Slowly and solemnly as with a kind
Of consecrating gesture to her lips,
And kissing seemed to seal a sacrament.
Then she arose, and all arose with her,
When Martha, not forgotten, likewise shared,
She too, with Ruth the kiss of sisterhood.
So, never a word between them spoken, all
Went backward and withdrew, Ruth last, who saw
That sunshine glorifying Stephen's brow,
And bore it thence, Shekinah in her heart.
Her countenance thus illumined from within,
The mother to her orphan children went,
And moved, a light, about her household ways.
She knew that others would with holy heed
Prepare that holy dust for burial.

But Rachel was more comfortless than Ruth.

Rest in her spirit found she none — until,
First having broken fast, but sparingly,
She hastened with winged footsteps to her home.
There her maid told her Saul went early forth
Leaving this message for his sister: "Here
Bide, if thou wilt; this house be still thy home.
But I go hence, whither I cannot tell,
Nor yet for how long absence ; to what end —
Thou knowest.   Cheer thee well!"   The little maid
Looked rueful and perplexed, but nothing asked,
As nothing Rachel told her, save to say :
" Quick, bring thine elder sister, thou and she
Shall keep the house together for a time.
I also go, my little maid "— wherewith
Her little maid, now weeping, Rachel kissed—
" I also go, but weep not, I shall come
Again, I trust, in happier times.   Farewell!"
Then Rachel straight to Ruth's abode returned.

" Glad am I thou hast come once more," said Ruth,
" For I have wished to ask thee many things.
How came his dreadful chance of martyrdom
On Stephen ?   I can bear to hear it all,
Since all is done and past and — ' He is safe,'

As thou saidst, Rachel !"

     Tenderly Ruth smiled,
With tears behind her smiles that did not fall.
Then Rachel said :

     " I cannot tell thee all
As having all beheld, but this I heard,
That Stephen gave a noble testimony
Before the council who had cited him ;
That there his face shone like an angel's, God
Himself so swearing for His servant, while
Against him swore false witnesses suborned
By Shimei ; that his enemies could not bear
The fierceness of the love with which in wrath
He burned for God against their wickedness,
And so they rushed upon him violently
And thrust him forth without the city walls.
But God beheld their threatening, and He sent
His Romans to withstand them for a while.
Then we that loved and honored him drew nigh,
And would have spoken words of cheer to him,
But he — O Ruth, thou shouldst have seen him then !
I never can describe to thee how fair
Thy husband was to look upon, while he,
As steadfast as a star and as serene,

And not less lovely-luminous to our eyes,
Stood there amid the angry Sanhedrim
And to us spake such heavenly words of cheer !
He spake of thee, Ruth, and I think God gave
His spirit comfort in good hope for thee.
For, ' God will give all to our prayers,' said he,
And added, ' Husband He will be to her,
And Father to the fatherless.'"

        Thereat
Ruth's tears as from a fresh-oped fountain flowed,
And eased her aching heart, too full before
Of love, remorseful love, for perfect peace.
Rachel with Ruth wept tears of sympathy ;
But with the sweet and wholesome in her tears
Mixed salt and bitter, for she thought of Saul.
Ruth at length ceased to weep and yearning said :
" And then those Romans let them work their will !"

 " On Stephen's body, yea, Ruth," Rachel said,
" But on his spirit they could have no power."

 " The stones," said Ruth —

      " The stones, Ruth," Rachel said,
" God gave His angels charge concerning them —
So verily I believe — and strictly bade,

' Lo, let these slay, but see ye that they do
No harm unto My prophet.'   So the stones,
They slew, but hurt not.   God translated him;
He rose triumphant in meek majesty.
I should have told thee, Ruth, that while he stood
Before the council, he looked up and saw
Jesus in heaven on the right hand of God—
There standing; this he testified to all.
It was as if his faithful Lord had risen
To side with Stephen in his agony.
So, when they stoned him, Stephen upward spoke,
' Lord Jesus, take my spirit'; then once more,
' Lord, lay not Thou this sin unto their charge.'
This he said kneeling and so fell asleep."

The two some space sat musing silently;
Then Ruth:

          " I feel that thou hast told me all
Most truly, Rachel, as most tenderly.
Thus, then, God giveth His belovéd sleep,
Thus also!   And He doeth all things well!
Amen!"

          Silence once more, that seemed surcharged
With deepening inarticulate amen

From both, and Ruth, regarding Rachel, said:
" Even so!   But, Rachel, us not yet doth God
Will thus to sleep.   Still, otherwise to sleep —
For His belovéd are not also we? —
May be God's gift to us.   Thou surely needest,
Body and spirit, rest."

           And Rachel said:
" The words of Stephen leap unto my lips
For answering thee; and these were Stephen's words:
' God bless thee, Martha, for thy loving thought!'
And this makes me remember that one thing
Done yesterday I missed to tell thee of.
For Martha, faithful heart, forecasting well,
Brought food for Stephen that might hearten him
To bear whatever he had need to bear,
A cake of barley and a honeycomb.
' God bless thee, Martha, for thy loving thought!'
Said Stephen, and so took the food from her,
And ate it giving thanks before us all.
He ate it with such look of appetite,
It cheered us with a sense of freedom his
From any discomposure of the mind.
O Ruth, in His pavilion God did hide
Thy husband, and his soul had perfect peace!"

"Was it not done like Martha?" Ruth replied;
"And done like Stephen too.   For courtesy
Bloomed like a flower to grace his daily life.
I used to wonder at it — and I now
Wonder I did not see where such a flower,
Where, and where only, such a flower could find
Rooting to flourish in a world like this!
He always told me that the heart of Christ
Nourished what good in him, or beautiful,
I found — or fancied, as he smiled and said.
But I — Oh, holden heart! — I did not see.
And now it is too late, too late, for him
To have known !   It may be that he knows it, yea,
But now to know it is not wholly such
As to have known it then, to have known it then !
Alas, there is not any chance of hope
Behind us, Rachel ; hope is all before.
Let us look onward ; we in hope were saved,
So Stephen used to say, and, ' I go hence
In comfort of some hope,' were his last words,
Or of his last, to me — concerning me,
Spoken with a sad cheerfulness that now
Breaks me with such a surge of memory !
But this is endless, let it here have end.

Come, Rachel, see, the sun rides high, come thou,
And I will bring thee to a quiet room,
Safe from the sun, where thou shalt rest a while."

So Rachel followed Ruth, not ill content
To be alone for thought if not for sleep.
Her will was not to sleep; but weariness,
With youth and health, was stronger, and she slept.

Already, when she woke, the sun halfway
From his high noon had down the western slope
Of sky descended, and she hearkening heard
A rumorous noise without upon the ways,
The stir of movement, steps of many feet,
With sound, muffled, of many voices nigh,
That startled her from sweet forgetfulness
To sudden sad remembrance of the things
That had been, and that were, and were to be.
Instinctive up she sprang, for, " Lo," she said,
" They gather unto Stephen's funeral;
Behooves that I be ready with all speed."
Therewith upon her knees she sank and prayed
A prayer for Ruth and for Ruth's little ones,
Widowed and orphaned by so dear a death,
And for herself—and for her brother Saul !

Then her heart swelled to a capacious wish,
And, anguished in one swift vicarious throe
Of great desire for help and grace divine,
She embraced the total church of Jesus Christ—
Of such a guide, of such a stay, bereaved!
Then Rachel, with the Everlasting Arms
Invisibly, nigh visibly, around
Her to sustain her steps, came forth, as one
That meekly walks leaning on her beloved,
And begged of Ruth that she might sister be
To her, that day, and thenceforth ever, mourn
As sister with her in the eyes of all.
" For I am lonely, " Rachel said, " O Ruth,
As thou art; lonely let us be, we twain,
Together, widows both, and mix our tears.
For also I am widow, as thou art,
Yet not as thou—since me a heavier stroke
Makes widow, who have never been a wife!"

Ruth answered, though she did not understand,
And kissed her friend in plight of sisterhood.

So they two, clad alike from out Ruth's store
Of raiment, clad in sad attire alike,
As sisters walked together side by side—

Ruth's children with them, grieved, not knowing
    why —
To where, from Mary's house and Martha's borne,
With grievous lamentation, by good men
Devout, the flower and choice of Israel,
Was laid the sacred dust of Stephen down
And sealed within a rock-hewn sepulchre.

   Joseph of Arimathæa, he who sought
And gained from Pilate leave to take away
The body of Jesus crucified, had sent
To Bethany, betimes, before the hour
Of burial, rich spices, a great weight,
Aloes and myrrh, with linen pure and fine,
To wrap the body of Stephen for his tomb.
Mary, the mother of the Lord, with John
Beloved of Jesus, loving her as son,
Came to that feast of sorrow bringing tears,
To Ruth medicinal more than any, wept
By one who had so learned to weep. So there
With sackcloth worn and ashes on the head,
They wailed aloud, that Hebrew company,
Women and men, they beat the breast, they rent
Their raiment, until one stood forth who said :

" Enough already has to grief been given.

Us it befits not here, for Stephen dead,

To mourn as mourn others who have no hope.

He was a burning and a shining light,

And we a season in his beams were glad.

Glory to God who kindled him for us!

Glory to God who hath from us withdrawn

His shining, and now hides him in Himself!

We thought we could not spare him, but God knew.

Let all be as God wills Who knows.   Amen !"

" Amen !" they solemnly responded all,

And he who spake these things went on and said :

" The Lord anointed Stephen with the oil

Of gladness in the gift of speech above

His fellows.   How he flamed insufferably,

In words that leapt out of his mouth, like swords

Out of their sheaths, enkindled to devour

The wicked !   When he spoke, flew seraphim

And bore from off the altar living coals

Of God which, laid upon his lips, purged them

To utter those pure words that purified.

What zeal, what wisdom, what fixed faith, what power !

He stood our bulwark, he advanced our sword,

And single seemed an insupportable host.
Yet this puissant soldier of the truth,
To disobedience so implacable,
How gentle and how placable he was
To all obedience !   He was like his Lord,
That Lion of the tribe of Judah, named
Also the Lamb of God.   No words had he
Save words of vivid flame, sudden and swift
And deadly like the lightning, for God's foes ;
But for the little flock of Jesus, balm
His speech — into those lips such grace was poured !

" Nor less in him for mighty work than word
The Holy Ghost a fountain was of power.
From him or through him what a plenteous stream
Flowed like the river of God in miracle !
Signs, wonders, gifts of healing, heavenly powers,
Innumerable flocked about his hand,
Like doves unto their windows flying home,
Waiting there eager to perform his will.

" A prophet of the elder time, reborn
Into the spirit of this latter age,
Was Stephen.   Thanking God for him, let us
Together and steadfastly pray that He

Who made the great Elijah live again
In John the Baptist, give us Stephen back
In resurrection from his tomb with power.
Thus shall we pray as himself prophesied —
For Stephen, you remember, glanced at this
In prophecy; unless not prophecy
It were, but only generous hope, with wish
To comfort Rachel, when he spake to her
Of grace to come upon her brother yet —
We shall so seek what seems it he foresaw,
If we ask Jesus to make captive Saul!"

That speaker ceased, and then a prophetess
Among the women there took up a wail,
Which triumphed into gladness as it grew:

" Is fallen, is fallen, a prince in Israel!
Woe, while it yet was day, his sun went down!
Daughters of Judah, mourn for Stephen slain!

" Mourn for a candle of the Lord put out,
A torch of noble witness quenched in blood;
Wear sackcloth of thick darkness and bewail!

" Repent, O daughters of Jerusalem,
Repent, forsake your wickedness of woe;

Look up, look up, the quenched torch burns a star!

" Is risen, is risen ; behold, at the right hand
On high sits he of his ascended Lord ;
Rejoice, rejoice, for Stephen could not die!

" Comfort ye Ruth ; thrice among women she
Lives blessèd, who, from wife to him, became,
Widowed, partaker of his martyrdom !

" Hosanna to the Son of David, Who,
Beheld of Stephen standing in the heavens,
Received His servant's spirit to Himself!

" The Resurrection and the Life is He ;
He will not leave this body in its tomb;
Stephen and we shall meet Him in the air.

" Descending with the sound that wakes the dead,
Ten thousand of His saints attending Him,
He comes ! He comes ! Even so, Lord Jesus, come !

" Salvation, worship, blessing, glory, power,
Forever and forever unto God,
Our God ; He never will forsake His own."

Uplifted high in heart, they went away.

BOOK X.
SAUL AT BETHANY.

AT the funeral service for Stephen, Shimei was a skulking attendant. He catches at a mention there overheard by him of the name of Saul in connection with that of Stephen, to plot an instigated persecuting visit on Saul's part to Bethany ; Shimei hoping that Saul will thus encounter his own sister identified as a Christian. Saul takes a band of men and makes the visit. He finds his intended victims all together at the house of Ruth condoling with her — Rachel indeed among them. After sharp inward conflict, and much effort put forth without success to make his victims abjure their faith, Saul finally takes them to prison. But Rachel, she vainly entreating to share her companions' fate, he leaves behind. She takes upon herself the charge of Ruth's children in their own home, where Saul, month after month, secretly sends to her supply of every need.

SAUL AT BETHANY.

AMONG the sons of God, when these one day
Came to present themselves before the Lord,
Satan came also ; and so Shimei,
Amid the throng that mourned at Stephen's death,
Intruded.   With smooth face of sanctimony,
Skulking to be unseen or heeded not,
He hovered furtive on the outer edge
Of audience, when those words of praise were said
To hearten — eye and ear alert to mark
All that befell.   His thought was, ' Here perhaps
I shall learn something to the true behoof
And profit of our cause — right aim secure
For the next blow of vengeance to be struck.'
The name of Saul mysteriously conjoined
With Rachel's, in abhorrent prophecy
As seemed — this, Shimei caught at eagerly
And said, ' Aha !'

              Then, as the throng dispersed

All to their several homes, straight Shimei
Went to seek Saul.   Him found that spy malign
With the chief priests in council, plotting deep
To hunt the sect of Jesus to the death.
These had armed Saul with writ and warrant sealed
Empowering him to enter where he would,
House after house, and whomsoever found,
Man be it or woman, guilty of belief
In Jesus as Messiah, such to seize
And drag to prison.

                Instantly conceived
Shimei a subtle snare to enmesh the feet
Of Saul.   The proud young zealot Pharisee
Should be set on to visit first in search
Those homes of Bethany ; where, unadvised
Perhaps, so Shimei guessed, the brother might,
To his dismay, find his own sister one
With the disciples of the Nazarene.
Then to make prisoner his own flesh and blood,
Or openly spare Rachel for kin's sake —
This, scandal against scandal doubtful weighed,
Would be the hard alternative to Saul.

   " Belovéd brother Saul," so Shimei spoke,

"*I* mourned at Stephen's funeral to-day.

Not loud, you know, but deep, my mourning was ;

Not loud, for I am modest, and my wish

Was less to be seen than to see ; but deep,

For there was cause, to one that loved you, Saul,

To be sincerely sad on your behalf.

Incredible it seems, they spoke your name,

Not, as might honor it, with hate and dread,

But very ambiguously, to say the least.

In fact, I fear you may be compromised,

Unless you take prompt measures in the matter.

Hark you, a certain orator stood up

Who, after praising Stephen to his worth,

Distinctly hinted Saul was looked upon

As hopeful future pervert to their cause

Predestined to fill Stephen's vacant room.

The fellow founded on some prophecy

Which, as I gathered, Stephen had put forth.

Now this preposterous notion, with such folk,

Is far more like to prosper, and thus be

Noised undesirably, than you might guess,

As a report injurious to your name.

You will be tainted with disloyalty,

In general esteem — to our great loss.

" What I propose is that you strike a stroke
So sudden and so ringing and so aimed
As shall decisively and neatly nip
This precious piece of prophecy in the bud,
And put you out of reach of calumny.
You have your warrant and commission ; good,
Use them at once, sleep not upon them ; now,
This very night — for domiciliary work
Like what you purpose, night is the best time,
Birds to their nests, you know, at night come home —
This very night, take you a trusty band
And make a bold foray at Bethany.
There Stephen lived, and there a hotbed yet
Thrives of this pestilent heresy.   No place
Fitter than the abode and vicinage
Of your late overmatch in controversy
To make first theatre of the exploits
You aim at in this different field — field where,
With odds so in your favor, you should win.
Easier far, given the right support, to drag
To dungeon and to death a hundred men
Or praying women, all as tame as sheep,
Than one impracticable fellow like
That Stephen manage in fair controversy !

" You have my best kind hopes and all good men's.
Ask for the house that harbored Stephen's corpse
And whence the funeral issued — quarry there
You cannot fail to find.   The widow too
Of Stephen, I watched her, and what I saw
Makes me misdoubt her Hebrew orthodoxy.
Sound her — an ounce of thorough work done now,
Unquestionably thorough, will be worth
A hundred weight of paltering by and by.
Despise the fear that now and then a man
May call you cruel; the worst cruelty,
As you and I well know, is ill-timed softness.
This thing must be stamped out ; it is a plague,
It creeps from house to house, no house is safe.
Your house, Saul, mine — that sister fair of yours,
Yes, treat the thought with scorn, but some fine day,
Why not ? Saul wakes to find his sister lost."

How far unconsciously, Saul could not guess,
But Shimei, in that last home thrust of his,
Either by pure fortuity, or else
With malice the most exquisitely wise,
Had hit the quivering quick of Saul's sore pride.
Saul winced visibly, and Shimei, satisfied,

Left him alone the prey of his own thoughts.

Saul's thoughts were visions rather; first, he saw
His sister as in that farewell with her
Bowed beautiful beneath a brother's scorn,
Like a meek flower broken with tempest; then,
Stephen he saw, his face with God in him
Afire, before the council; next, that face
Toward heaven upturned, he, far within the veil
Agaze, beholding there the glory of God;
Once more, the martyr lifting holy hands
On high, with his last breath praying for those
That slew him, praying also then for Saul!
Rachel the while — she rather felt than seen —
With tears that did not gather, but that made
Her deep eyes deeper than the soundless sea,
Looking at him.   Swift then the vision changed,
And he saw Stephen in the temple court
Turn suddenly round on Saul his blinding face
To threaten him with promise that, one day,
He, Saul himself, should grovel in the dust
Before the feet of Jesus crucified!
Those visions were as when the lightning-flash,
By night, fast following lightning-flash, reveals,

One instant and no more, the world, but prints
Its image on the eye intensely bright.

  The final vision wrought a fierce revolt
In Saul from that relenting which, before,
The earlier visions almost made him feel.
As with a mortal gripe, his vise-like will
Clutched at his heart and held it fast and hard.
Scorning to be diverted from his path
Because, forsooth, the meddling Shimei
Pointed it out to him offensively,
Saul moved at once to go to Bethany.
Seven servitors he chose, strong men whom use
Had, hand and heart, seasoned to such employ —
With these a guide — and started on his way.
Again the moon shone, as the yesternight,
And flooded heaven and earth with glory mild.
But her mild glory now was a rebuke
To human passion, not a balm to pain.
With swords and staves armed, as that night came
        they
Who looked for Jesus in Gethsemane —
The needless lamps and torches in their hands
With flare and smoke affronting the moonlight —

They marched, those seven, following the guide with
     Saul.
At first these chattered lightly as they walked,
But soon the stern, stark, wordless mood of Saul,
And his grim purpose in his pace expressed,
Urgent and swift, taxing their utmost strength
To follow and not fall behind, quite quelled
The social spirit in all, and on all went
In sullen silence like their chief. Like him,
Insensibly each moment more and more,
While thought and feeling they shut strictly up
Within them from all vent in speech, they these
Changed to brute instinct of vindictiveness;
Insensibly, like him, with every step
Of vehement ongoing, vehement
Propulsion gathered they in mind and will
To reach and grapple with their task. So on
And up with speed they pressed toward Bethany.

   At Bethany, meanwhile, the flock in fold
Abode the coming of those prowler wolves—
Unweeting, in sad sense of safety lulled.
The sisters, with the brother Lazarus,
Had to Ruth's house at eve repaired; they there

With Rachel sat together, in the court
Under the open sky, and spake with Ruth,
Or spake for Ruth to hear, comforting her.

"' I am the Resurrection and the Life'"—
Thus Martha—"how the very words to me
Were spirit of life, were resurrection power,
So spoken, from such lips, at such a time,
When Lazarus lay sleeping in that swoon
Which we call death!   I did not need to wait
Until my brother should indeed again
Arise, obedient, at His word, to feel
The utterer of that saying was the Christ."
" But when He wept, when Jesus with us wept,"
Said Mary, " I felt solace in His tears
Such that almost I would have always grieved,
To be always so comforted. "   A pause,
Then eyes on Lazarus turned, and he : " From where
I was — but where I was, although I seem
Well to remember, yet could not I tell
In any words, or show by any signs,
However I might try — I heard His voice
Say, ' Lazarus, come forth. '   Those round me heard,
I thought they heard, with me, that potent voice,

And they were not surprised, as was not I,
Seeming to know it and to understand.
That voice goes everywhere and is obeyed,
To all the perfect law of liberty,
And I obeyed as naturally as I breathe;
And I am here, in witness of His power,
Whose power is universal through all worlds."
"His power is great," said Ruth, "and wide His sway,
Yet seems His grace the sovereign of His power."
"Yea," Rachel said, "for doth not power in Him
Bend to the yoke and service of His grace?"
"We easily err," said Lazarus, "seeking here
To comprehend the incomprehensible.
All difference is in us, for all in Him
One and the same is; power is grace and grace
Is power, in Him, nay, power and grace is He.
And He is ours and we are His, and one
Are we with Him and in Him one likewise
Each with the other, all." "How blest!" they said,
"And the whole family in heaven and earth
Are one, and Stephen is with us or we
With him, and heaven is here or here is heaven!"

A little while in silence and deep muse,

And, by the Holy Spirit, fellowship
With the Almighty Father and His Son.
Then, " Lo, let us join hands," they said, "and sing
That psalm which breathes of unity like this."
With braided tones, in unison they sang :
 ' Behold, how good it is for brethren here,
 ' How pleasant, thus in unity to dwell
 ' Together! It is like that costly chrism
 ' Upon the head which overflowing ran
 ' Down Aaron's beard and down his garment's folds,
 ' Abundant as the dew of Hermon drops,
 ' Distilled, upon the heights of Sion where
 ' Jehovah fixed the blessing, life, even life
 ' Forevermore.'

      " A sweet strain and a rich,"
Said Lazarus; " David touched it to his harp,
Taught by the Holy Spirit. Nevertheless,
Something it lacks to fill the measure up
To that deep sense of oneness which we feel
In Jesus, since He came, since Jesus came
And spake, then went, but came again, in us
Forever to abide. Cannot we sing
Some words of His, as tunable, more deep?
Such words He spake in a celestial rhythm

That night before He sought Gethsemane.
They sat as in the Holy of holies with Him,
And John leaned on His bosom where He sat.
I have heard John rehearse the heavenly words
Until at length I too have them by heart."
Then Lazarus gave them sentences, which all
Chanted in simple measure low and sweet:
 ' Let not your heart be troubled, ye believe
 ' In God, also in Me believe.　Within
 ' My Father's house there many mansions are.
 ' I should have told you, had it not been so,
 ' Because I go to fit a place for you.
 ' And if I go and fit for you a place,
 ' I shall return and take you to Myself,
 ' That where I am there ye may also be.'

 Was it a premonition, or did grief
Surge up through peace and joy to claim its own?
Said Lazarus: "Yet He told us, 'In the world
Ye will have tribulation, though in Me
Ye shall have peace.'　With tribulation, peace!"

 His closing words they took from Lazarus' lips,
" With tribulation, peace!" and of them made
A musical refrain half sad, half glad,

Or wholly glad in sadness, which they sang.
When ever were there cadences more sweet,
More sweet or more pathetic?   Thrice sang they
Those words together; but, at the fourth time,
Just in that breath between the rise and fall,
Before from ' tribulation ' they touched ' peace ' —
A shock as of a mace struck on the door,
Which yielded, and abrupt there strode in — Saul!

  Saul was alone; his men he left without.
The band had first the sisters' dwelling sought,
To find the inmates gone — fled, as Saul guessed.
Without delay, they came to Ruth's abode,
Fiercer from disappointment Saul.   But though
Ruthless he came, he now, arrested there,
Ruthful a moment stood at gaze.   He saw
Four women and one man in simple sort
Sitting together in communion still.
They did not look like culprits, nay, a light
Purer than purest moonlight seemed to shine
From out their faces underneath the moon.
It was a feast of comfort that they kept,
Those four, with Ruth the widowed — this Saul saw,
And his heart thawed to pity and sheer shame.

He would have turned and left them, but — his men
Without! The chief priests and the Sanhedrim!
And Shimei! And Saul, with all Saul owed
To Saul's fair fame, his conscience, and his God!

   This all was in an instant, while he yet
Only the group and not the persons saw
Who made the group, and so before he knew
His sister in her sombre different garb
Disguised and in the half light of the moon.
As Rachel now he fully recognized,
Dismay almost unmanned him once again.
Then anger to dismay succeeding made
His brother's heart in him against her burn
The hotter that it was a brother's heart.
Speechless he hung, because he could not speak
For anger; but when she, adventuring, drew
Near him and said, " Brother, I pray thee let
Me speak with thee apart a moment," then
The vials of his speech he broke on her :

"'Brother'! Thou shalt not 'brother' me.   Thou hast
No brother more, no sister I.   Once, yea —
But that is long ago, and she is dead,
My sister, and in *her* name will I hear

No woman speak henceforth. Thou hast missed thy
    mark
In that appeal.   Better hadst thou bode dumb.
Go, woman !   Thither !   Sit thee with thine own !"

    Saul, with his finger pointing to her seat,
Just left, in added scorn, spurned her from him.
Then Lazarus spoke: " With me do what thou wilt ;
But these are women, let me stand for them."
"Stand for thyself," said Saul, "and answer me.
Thou art called Lazarus, I trow ?" " Thou hast said,"
Lazarus replied.   " Well, friend, with thee," said Saul,
" I have to speak.   Disciple art thou, then,
Of Jesus Nazarene, late crucified ?"
"Of Jesus," full confessing, Lazarus said,
" Of Jesus, whom, not knowing what they did,
Men crucified, but whom God glorified,
Raising Him from the dead and seating Him
At the right hand of glory in the heavens —
Of Him I am disciple.   Bless His name !"

    "Thou art young to utter blasphemy," said Saul ;
" Sure unadvisedly thou hast spoken this.
Unsay it instantly, and swear it false,
Or, by the warrant of the Sanhedrim,

Thou goest with me to prison, perhaps to death,
The way of Stephen and all heretics!"

"Thou speakest idly," Lazarus said to Saul;
"Prison and death no terrors have for me.
The Lord I serve is Lord of life and death."

"Yea, I have heard," said Saul to Lazarus,
"Thou boastest to have been from death itself
Called back to life by whom thou namest Christ.
Let him, once more, call thee from out the tomb
To which I shall consign thee — if he can.
Saul then perhaps will his disciple be!
Poor fool, fanatic, what shall I call thee?
Persist not in this folly.   Be a Jew,
A Jew indeed, nor fling thy life away.
 Anathema be Jesus!' say but that,
Thou, Lazarus, and all the rest, with thee,
And I go hence taking the sword away,
The sword of just authority, undrawn,
Asleep within its scabbard, ye all safe,
All Jews indeed, and I given back again
A sister, Rachel mine, won from the dead!
'Anathema be Jesus!' say those words."

Saul ceased, awaiting what those five would do.

They did not look at one another; all,
As with one will to all — their eyes upraised,
And their hands clasped in ecstasy of awe —
Together "Alleluia Jesus!" said.
On Saul a power like lightning fallen from heaven
Fell, at that adoration from their lips.
A moment he stood stupefied, and then,
With a great wrench of scornful will, he freed
Himself and summoned his retainers in.

    These entered rudely, but abashed they hung,
And wondering saw their master half abashed,
Before that little company clothed on
With virtue like a dreadful panoply.
Half with the air of one subdued, or one
Feeling he acts by sufferance not by power,
Saul bids bind all — save Rachel — and forthwith
Lead them to prison.
                         " Also me, bind me,"
So Rachel to the men said eagerly,
And offered her fair wrists.   They looked at Saul,
But Saul vouchsafed to them nor word nor sign.
Still, ' No,' they gathered from that cold aspect
In him which seemed to say, ' That which I bid,

Do, further, naught.'   Rachel to Saul himself
Beseechingly then turned and said:" O Saul,
Full well I know thou doest this, constrained
By conscience.   Then by conscience be constrained
To let thy men bind also me, who am
As guilty as these are and with them should share
One lot. "

          " I did not come here to be taught
My duty, " Saul said, " least of all by thee.
And least of all from thee will I abide
To be adjured as by my conscience.   Once
I had a sister, she was conscience to me,
But, as I told thee, that was long ago,
And she is dead, my sister !"

                    Sadness mixed,
Unmeant, resisted, irresistible,
With Saul's enforced hardheartedness, which broke
His tone to pathos, and, despite himself
With those last words he burst in tears.   He shook
In shudders of strong agony, while all
Wondered, but Rachel did not wonder, she
Knew far too well her brother, far too well
Knew their joint past, the two pasts they had had
Together, long and happy one, and one

So brief, so bitter,—and she pitied Saul.
She pitied him, but strongly did not weep—
Though afterward, alone, remembering,
She wept as if her eyes were fountains of tears—
With him now Rachel would not weep, for she
Knew far too well her brother, that he scorned
Himself for weeping those hot tears, and would
Be vexed to see tears wept in sympathy
As if with will he let his mood relent.
So Rachel held her pity hard shut up
Within her heart, which ached the more denied
Its wished-for vent in tears, and Saul soon curbed
His passion and in other passion veiled.
" Haste, there!" he said, sharp turning on his men,
" The night flies, while ye loiter."

                          Now the men
Already had bound Lazarus.   He, ere yet
The shameful needless bonds upon the wrists
Of those four gentle women were made fast,
Said : " Saul, what evil have these women done
That they deserve roughness like this?   I go
Willingly with thee, albeit innocent,
For I a man am and can well endure
Bonds, stripes, dungeon, or death, having such hope

Within me as makes all afflictions light,
Whatever they may be, compared with that
Eternal weight of glory nigh at hand.
Like hope have also these, and they will bear,
Doubtless, supported, whatsoever ill
Unmerited thou choosest to inflict.
But wilt thou choose to inflict indignity
And pain on such as these?"

       "I do not choose,"
Said Saul; "I without choosing do, not what
I would, but what I must.   I too wear chains,
Am bond of conscience, heavier chains wear I
Than these light manacles that bind the hands
But leave the heart free and one's will one's own.
Chained am I and driven.   Conscience drives me on,
  on,
Both will and heart in me under the lash
Cower, and I here as but a galley-slave
Do what my conscience bids, joyless, and fierce
From lack of joy, more miserable far,
Binding, than ye are bound, with your fool's joy
Of windy hope!   For me, I only know
That, in whatever way, this thing accursed,
This craze to think *that* man the Christ, must be

Curbed, checked, stopped, crushed, brought to an utter
    end,
Forever.   All the future of our race
Hangs on it.   Woman, tempted, fell, she first,
In Eden, whence is all our woe, and now
Women it seems are the peculiar prey
Of this new trick of devilish subtlety;
And, as of old, woman deceived becomes
Deceiver, and through her the mischief spreads
Ungovernably.   So women, too — the cause
In part of the disease — must in part pay
The price of cure.   For remedy this is,
Not punishment.   Ye for the general health
Suffer — for your own health not less, if ye
Yield wisely, and not foolishly resist.
Yield wisely now, and let me hence depart
Cheered to have healed a little here the hurt
With which the daughter of God's people bleeds!"

How little prospered this his new appeal,
Saul learned, when Ruth, as not having heard even,
    said:
"At least let me, if I indeed must leave
My children double orphans so, let me

Now go and see them in their helpless sleep,
And take a farewell of them with my eyes.
But who will care for them when I am gone?
I cannot, will not, go away from them.
Nay, ye may bind me, ye may slay me, drag
Me hence may ye, alive or dead, but make
Me go with my own feet away from them,
My children, in their innocent infancy,
And leave them to pine motherless, forlorn,
And perish in their innocent infancy —
That is beyond your strength — I will not go —
A mother may defy the Sanhedrim !"

    Ruth spoke dry-eyed, with holy mother's wrath,
Sublime in her indignant eloquence.
Saul, not unmoved, although inexorable,
Said : " Woman, as thy wish is, thou shalt go
Freely to see thy children.   May the sight
Dispose thee to a better mind !   Come back
Ready to say, ' For their sake, I renounce
My folly, I will be true Jewish mother
To them, so let me stay,' — and thou shalt stay.'

    Ruth going, Rachel thought, ' Shall I too go
With her, that I may help her bear to part

From her dear babes ?'   Quickly resolved behind
To tarry, she, Ruth gone, went up to Saul,
And said : " I pray thee, Saul, let Rachel go
Instead of Ruth to prison.   Let Ruth bide
To nurse her children.   I will take her place
Gladly in her captivity, and be
A surety for her.   Young and strong am I,
And I will be a firm good surety, Saul,
Not fleeing and not complaining, always there,—
And if, hereafter ever, it should seem
Needful to have Ruth come herself to prison,
Why, she will still be here, under thy hand,
As now, so then, to be hence thither led.
Be kind, and have me bound straightway, before
Ruth comes again, that she be left no choice
But to let Rachel have her wilful way,
Perceiving that I have my bonds on me
To go to prison with her, if not without,
While much I wish to go without her — wish,
And, by thy kind permission, have the power.
Dost thou not think, Saul "— wherewith Rachel smiled
On Saul a starlight smile, which made him feel
How high she was above him in her sphere
Unconsciously — " Dost thou not think that I

Will make as good a prisoner as Ruth?"

Had she not smiled that smile, Saul might have
    thought,
'Infatuated child!' and thought aloud.
But that bright smile of almost humor sad
Showed him how sanely her true self she was,
And he was baffled, sudden-smitten dumb.
He could not answer her; much less could he
Bid bind those slender wrists with manacles
And send his sister to imprisonment!
So there Saul stood before her, marble-mute.
Not long — for Ruth soon now came back, more calm,
She having prayed beside her sleeping babes,
And trusted them again to the Most High
As Father, and from the Most High received
Grace to bear graciously her testimony,
Even by imprisonment, and children reft,
For Stephen's Lord and hers.   The others marked
Ruth's placid changed demeanor, and gave thanks
Silent to God who thus their prayer had heard.
" I go," she said to Saul, " for Jesus' sake
Wherever thou mayst lead.   My babes I trust,
As Stephen trusted them before he suffered,

Unto the Father of the fatherless.
Lo, I am ready — bind me — for His sake!"

Never so ruefully had those hard men
Bound any hands for prison as they bound hers;
And scarcely Saul found steady voice to say:
"Thy children shall be cared for tenderly,
Till thou return to them in sounder mind;
The fathers of our tribes will see to this."

Then Rachel said, and saying it wept at last:
"They would not bind me, Ruth, to take thy place,
Though I entreated them while thou wert gone.
I shall be left, unworthy to be left,
If ye, beloved, are worthy to be taken!
But, Ruth, if thou wilt let me, I shall stay
And myself be a mother to thy babes,
Nurturing them most lovingly, alike
For thine, their father's, and their own sweet sakes.
And I will daily bring thee word of them,
Treasuring for thee each little syllable
They lisp from day to day of loving speech
Concerning father or mother gone away.
They shall not lack whatever I can give
Of mother's tendance, so as yet to feel

That I am not their mother, only one
Less wise, less good, less loving, and less fair
Than she, who for their mother's sake loves them !
All this, I trust, will not last very long,
This motherlessness for them, this childlessness
For thee — thou wilt come back — but, O Ruth, pray" —
Thus Rachel softly for Ruth sole to hear —
" For surely now thou understandest well,
Too well ! what then I meant when once I told thee,
'I too am widow as thou art, yet not
As thou, since me stroke heavier has bereaved !' —
O Ruth, pray thou and never cease to pray
For Saul, my brother ! "

                So they went away,
And, lodged in prison, those four captives sang,
A silent melody making in their hearts,
" With tribulation, peace ! " until they slept.
But Rachel, having followed at remove
Behind them, saw where they were put in hold,
Then, hedged about meanwhile with purity,
With convoy doubtless too of angels hedged,
Gladly on such an errand earthward come,
Invisible bright legion hovering round ! —

Safely returned to sleep in Stephen's house.

    There she abode, and thence, an angel she!
Went daily to and fro between Ruth's house
And Ruth in prison, bearing messages,
Refections often bearing, food or drink,
Her own housewifely skill and instinct nice,
With other comforts portable, sometimes,
Pillow or cushion, rug or robe or shawl,
Such as might serve to cheer the homesick heart
In any there imprisoned, with sweet sense
At least of loving thought from one for those
In bonds, as herself with them bound ; the while
That for the orphaned children she made home.
Nor ever failed to Rachel full supply
Of all whatever need there was to her.
Month after month, her cruse was brim with oil,
With meal her measure, large replenishment.
God put it in the heart of Saul to send,
Diverted like an irrigating rill
Full all its season from the affluent Nile,
A secret stream of various providence
For Rachel and for Rachel's fosterlings
Fed from the fountain of his patrimony.

BOOK XI.

SAUL AND HIRANI.

Saul, ill-content with his own prosperity in persecution, retires gloomily, late at night, to his desolated home. He vainly tries to sleep, and, rising very early, goes to consult Gamaliel. Returning, he encounters Shimei, who, with gibes, instigates a further act of persecution on Saul's part, cunningly contriving it to make refusal impossible. Saul attempting the arrest proposed by Shimei meets with opposition, which the latter has secretly inspired. The persecutor in consequence narrowly escapes violent death, being rescued at the critical moment by Shimei ; who himself, with a band of servitors, makes the arrest unsuccessfully attempted by Saul alone. The man arrested confesses Jesus before the Sanhedrim, constant against every inducement to deny his Lord. He is scourged, at the instance of Shimei, and finally, at the instance of Mattathias, stoned ; Saul in both cases giving his vote against the man.

SAUL AND HIRANI.

With large prosperity and little joy,
Thus the first stage of that 'straight path' foreseen
By him to Rachel, 'traced in blood and tears,'
Saul had accomplished, and the night was late ;
He parted from his men and was alone.
Alone and moody, by the westering moon,
His face downcast turned absently toward what
Late was his home, home longer not to him,
With footstep slow suspended by sad thought —
Which had no goal, but ever round and round
On one fixed centre hopelessly revolved —
Saul paced the still streets of Jerusalem,
Like a soul seeking rest and finding none.
Before the door at length he finds himself
Of his own house forsaken yesterday.

For an uncertain absence, but for long
As he supposed, Saul thence that morn had fled

In haste and bitterness.   He could not bear
To think of meeting Rachel day by day,
And that great gulf impassable between
Her and himself yawning ! he hands imbrued
Perhaps in blood of those she counted dear
But he most hateful counted bringing home,
Her innocent white hands to touch, and feel
The difference !   Therefore he fled because
' Rachel,' thought he, ' must bide, and bide we twain
Cannot.'   But now Rachel was gone, and Saul,
Alone and lonely, sojourner might be
Where brother and sister late had shared a home.
He enters noiselessly, and unperceived
Steals to his chamber ; there upon his couch
To restless thought, he, not to rest, lies down.
Restless and fruitless, save that, morning yet
Pearl-white, untinted with that ruddy flush
Of color in the east before the sun,
Saul rose, and, after joyless orisons,
Went to Gamaliel's house, sure him to find
Already on his roof to greet the dawn.

  " In anguish sore and sore perplexity
Of spirit, master," Saul said, " lo, I come

To thee, not knowing whither else to go,
For solace, and the solving of my doubt."

"Welcome thou comest ever, even or morn,"
Gamaliel said; "but what disquiets thee?
When in the council last I heard thee speak,
Thou wert all firmness, as one wholly clear
In purpose, and thou hadst that glad aspect,
Though serious, which befits the mind resolved.
Whence, Saul, the change in thee?"

      "Thou knowest," said Saul
"How prospered my attempt, ventured upon
Without thy counsel, in that issue joined
With Stephen."

     "Yea, my son," Gamaliel said;
"But I, meantime, after my counsel given
Dissuading thee, had learned myself to feel
How failed the hand of brute authority
Against this strange faith of the Nazarene.
Thine undertaking I less disapproved
After our hearing of the Galilæans.
Something perceived in them, or through them felt,
Disturbed me with a strange solicitude,

Which the ill fortune of thine own assay
Did not relieve.   But thou, thou still wert clear,
Wert thou not, Saul?   Thine action did not halt ;
Promptly in Stephen's stoning thou took'st part."

    " I acted promptly, that I might be clear
In thought,"   said Saul ; "this, rather than because
I was so clear.   My halting urged me on.
Yet now, O master mine, I might perhaps
Be clear, but that my coadjutorship
Offends me so, torments me with such doubt.
In the right way how can I be, and be
In the same way with Shimei?   My soul
Sickens at him, at all his words and ways
Sickens, and still he dogs me every step,
Clings to me like my shadow, whispers me
Over my shoulder, pointing me out my way,
Until I hardly can do that which else
Freely I should, because he bids me do it !"

    " Yea, Saul, my son, trust thou thine instinct there,"
Gravely Gamaliel said, with slow reserve
That warned how more than he would say was meant ;
"Our brother Shimei is a dark man,
Whose public zeal is edged with private spite ;

Him well, son Saul, it thee behooves beware.
Since when thou scornedst him in those high words
Before the council, Shimei hates thee, Saul,
And hate like his is sleepless till revenge.
Ill for a cause that must be served by him !
But some are tools, and others ministers,
Of God, Who works His holy will with all !"

Unwarned by warning, but in conscience pricked,
And following his own tyrannous thought, Saul spoke :
" Those infamous false witnesses of his —
Say, master, did I on my conscience take
The guilt of their suborning, when consent
I gave to Stephen's death thereby procured?
My conscience like a scorpion stings me on,
But whether a good conscience before God
It be, or rather a conscience violated,
Which I must quiet by not heeding it,
And by confusing it with din of deeds
Forever doing — this I cannot well
Resolve me, and — but, nay, for that were false,
I do *not* wish thou shouldst resolve me it.
Forgive me, and farewell !   But pray for Saul !"

Therewith, and pausing not, like one distraught,

Or one goaded, and wildly seeking fast
Enough before the goad to fly, which flies
Only the faster, following, for his speed,
And pricks the harder — so Saul broke away
And left Gamaliel on his roof alone
Astonished.

           Swiftly now, yet with a haste
As of one wishing to leave far behind
Some spot abhorred, much more than as of one
Eager a goal before him to attain,
Say rather as of one insanely fierce
Somewhither, anywhither, from himself
Pursuing hard himself, to fly, Saul flew
Back toward his dwelling.   At the door arrived,
He well-nigh stumbled — for his hasting feet
Against some shapeless heap struck that alive
Seemed, for it moved, and from the threshold, where
He in a kind of ambush crouching lay,
Slowly into the semblance of a man,
Under Saul's eyes down bent, upgrew — Shimei !

   ' Sin coucheth at the door !' thought Saul; he
      thought
Half of himself, as half of Shimei,

For, ' If thou doest not well, thou Saul !' thought he,
Then, " Reptile !   How beneath my heel should I
His serpent head have bruised !" hissed hotly out
Between his set teeth, and perused the man.
Half under breath this, then to him aloud :
" What art thou ?   Imp of hell spawned hither new
Up from the pit ?   Avaunt !   I loathe thee hence ! "

   " Nay, brother Saul," grinned Shimei, therefore
       pleased
Thus spurned to be, because the spurning was
With anguish of disgust to him who spurned,
Malevolently yet storing reserve
Of hatred and revenge therefor, to be
Afterward feasted when the time should come,
" Nay, brother Saul, you look with eyesight dazed
From undersleeping, and from rash surprise
At this encounter.   I am Shimei,
Your special coadjutor tried and true.
I am a little early, I confess —
Or late, which shall I call it ? early and late —
Like moral good and evil, Saul — ofttimes
Change places with your point of view — become
The one the other, as you look at them.

" You see I hardly slept myself this night,
Thinking of you, and pleasuring my mind
With fancies of the odd coincidences
That might be happening you at Bethany.
I got prompt information how it all
Fell out, and hastened hither to advise
With you.   Upon your sleep, already much
Cut short, I would not thoughtlessly break in,
And so I dropped me at your threshold here,
To wait a proper hour for seeing you,
And yet not let you pass out hence unseen.
I must have fallen asleep, and, brother Saul,
Be sure I was no less surprised than you,
When you just now came on me unaware.
Ha! ha!   How naturally you mistook your friend
For something not so pleasant from the pit
Vomited suddenly up under your feet !
Another might have taken it amiss
To be so little courteously greeted,
But I — why, give and take, say I, in joke,
You have bravely evened up the score between us ! "

" I do not bandy jokes with such as you,
Suborner of false witnesses !" gnashed Saul.

Saul's look, his tone, had withered any man
Save Shimei, who grew blithe in sultry heats
Of human scorn as in his element.
So Shimei flourished lustier hearing Saul
Despise him with the question further asked :
" What is there common between you and me ? "

  " Oh ! Ah !" sneered Shimei ; " I had thought you
        dazed
In eyesight only, but distempered mind
You show now, taking this high strain with me.
' What common 'twixt us ? '   Yea, yea, very good !
' Suborner of false witnesses ' — hence base,
Shimei, but very, very virtuous, Saul,
Who, with much flourish of disdain, his hands,
His lily hands, washes, for all to see,
Quite white and fair of all complicity
With ' lies,' ' devilish lies,' ' lies damnable,'
You know, and so forth, and in due course then,
His moral indignation unabated,
Takes profit of said lies to make away
With Stephen, through more weighty argument
In stones found than conveniently to hand
Came when he crossed words with that heretic !"

The mordant sneer corrosive of such speech
Ate through the thin mail of Saul's scornful pride,
And bit him in his wincing sense of truth.
Against these thrusts in no wise could he fence,
Having the foothold lost whereon he stood
Firm in the conscience of integrity.
Unbidden would those words of Stephen, " Pricks
To kick against!" returning come to him
In memory, while ever, with each return,
Fiercer waxed Saul's resistance, fiercer wound
Infixing in his secret-suffering mind —
As should the bullock battle with the goads
Behind him, shrinking flesh on sharpened steel.
So now his wild heart Saul pressed sternly up
Against the cruel points of Shimei's jeer,
And suffered them in silence.

      Shimei
Felt his own triumph, and at feline ease
Leisurely played with his proud captive.   " Saul, "
He added, " you and I are men too wise
To waste strength here in mutual blame.   Forgive
Me that I was so far led on to speak
As if retorting word for word unkind.
I should have made allowance for your state,

Devoid of that just self-complacency
So needful to a happy health of mind.
Now you and I at bottom are such twins,
We ought to understand each other well ;
It is a shame that this has not been so.
Here we are one in aim, and unity
In aim — what deeper unity than that
Joins ever man and man ?   Let us strike hands
Together, since our hearts beat unison."

Not less revolted at these words was Saul,
More, rather, that he knew how insincere
They were, how hollow, as how void of truth,
Spoken in pure malicious irony.
The sense of difference his from Shimei,
Browbeaten in him, badgered, stunned, ashamed,
Could not rejoice in thought, in speech far less,
Against that flourished claim of unity.
He stood silent, ignobly helpless, while
Maliciously his pastime further took
With him his captor, who then, sated, said :
" Well, Saul, I shall excuse it to a mind
In you disordered through late loss of sleep,
That you do not invite me in to sit

A little at my ease while I disclose
The thought I had in coming to you now.
Nay, nay "— for Saul, broken in self-command
False shame to feel, and false self-blame, as found
Defaulting dues of hospitality,
Instinctive moved toward making Shimei guest —
" Permit me to decline the courtesy.
You are tired, you are very tired, and you should
      rest.
Once within, seated, I might stay too long,
Bound by the charms of your society.

" I pray you be not overmuch disturbed,
But really you should know it, Saul, the chance
You fell in with this night at Bethany —
I mean your meeting of your sister there
Confessed a bold disciple of the Way —
Is likely to engender consequence.
It was a noble chance, Saul, from the Lord,
Pushed to your hand — would you had used it nobly !
Alas, at the extreme pinch, your virtue failed !
I can excuse it, while regretting it,
I myself, Saul.   Not every one, I fear,
Is naturally so lenient as I am.

My sympathy is facile, but the most
Will say, ' Why did not Saul send *her* to prison ?'
Now what you need is, to forestall such talk
By giving people something else to say.
Fill their mouth full with daily fresh report
Of other, and still other, great exploits
Achieved by you in the same line, and then
They either will forget that one lapse yours,
Or cease, from the perversion of a sister,
Connived at or colluded with by you,
To accuse a taint and pravity of blood
Inclining you yourself to heresy.

  " I give myself no end of trouble for you,
And I have made discovery of the man
You must not fail to move for as next prize.
He is a notable fellow, full of quip,
Quaint turn of phrase, and ready repartee,
Each trick of tongue to catch the common ear,
And mischievous accordingly ; for he
Boasts everywhere how, having been born blind
And grown to forty years of age in blindness,
He one day met Jesus of Nazareth,
When that deceiver spat upon the ground

And mixed an unguent of the clay, therewith
Smearing his sightless balls, and bidding him
Go wash them in the pool of Siloam ;
He went and washed, and came a seeing man.

  " Such is his story, and so plausibly
He tells it that a wide belief he wins.
' Hirani ' is the name by which he goes ;
Name self-assumed since his pretended cure,
A kind of label that he boldly thrusts
In people's faces to placard his lie.
' He made me see ' — he, to wit, Jesus, mind —
As were no other ' he ' in all the world !
Well, this Hirani to be weaver feigns,
Mere cover to that other trade he drives —
A famous flourishing one with him, they say —
Proselyte-making for the Nazarene.
Clap him in prison, Saul, let him repeat
His marvel to the unbelieving walls.
At present, many of the Way are fled
Hither and thither through the countryside,
But this man tarries to rehearse his tale.
So there your plan is, ready-wrought for you ;
Now, Saul, go sleep upon it, and farewell."

Man through malicious mind more miserable,
More miserable man from every cause
Of inward sorrow save malicious mind,
Never were met and parted than when there
Shimei found Saul and left him thus that morn.
Once more Saul visited his couch in vain ;
Sleep could he not, could not but round and round
Tread the treadmill of painful barren thought,
On this fixed only, with resentful will,
Not to do that which Shimei pressed him to.
So, having eaten, without appetite,
He flung forth in the street dispirited —
Aimless, nor on the way through hope to aim,
Hopeless, nor on the way through aim to hope - -
Irresolute, deject, energiless,
Therefore the destined prey of whatso snare
Should sudden first waylay his nerveless foot —
Forth in the street flung, at his door to meet
An ambushed messenger of Shimei's,
Who from his master gave him written word:
" The Sanhedrim to sit this afternoon
In council on the case you will present.
All feel the utmost flattering confidence
That Saul will promptly bring his prisoner in.

The bearer of this can guide you to your man."

' Himself false witness now become, the wretch !'
Thought Saul. ' This buyer of false witnesses
Has falsely told my brethren that I put
Myself in pledge to do a special task,
His bidding, and has got the council called
In expectation on their part from me
That I will bring them in this man to judge —
Death doubtless meant, instead of prison, for *him* !
The wretch, the perjured wretch, and damnable !
Yet for me what escape ? Alternative
None offers. Yea, denounce might I the man
Even to his teeth before them all a liar —
But to what profit ? He could truly say
I listened, not demurring, when he broached
This his new plan, as I had done before
Concerning the arrests at Bethany
By him projected, meekly made by me !
I should seem caviller, than he more false,
And trifler with the ancient majesty
Prescriptive of the Sanhedrim.'

                              Saul writhed
With all the frail remainder of his force,

Writhed — and submitted.   With the guide he went,
And the man found whom he, under duress
Resented, sought.   The invisible chains which then
That captive captor wore, far worse galled him   .
Than those whereof he plained at Bethany.
Master more cruel yet the devil can be
Than vehement conscience blinded by self-will.
Pride driving makes an intimate misery,
But a more intimate misery pride driven !

At his loom seated — there his handicraft,
Late learned by him after sight given him late,
Busily plying — Saul's intended prey,
With his hands weaving, as the shuttle flew,
A fabric of coarse cloth, wove with his tongue,
That subtler shuttle in the loom of thought,
Discourse simple yet sage, for those to hear,
A goodly audience, who had gathered round
Him in his place of labor out-of-doors
Under an awning stretched that fenced the sun —
Drawn thither by the fame of what he told,
A strange experience never man's before.

" Thou art disciple of the Nazarene ? "
Abruptly so, intruding, Saul inquired.

The accent of authority that spoke
In him, the masterful demeanor his,
All felt, and of the listeners some, afraid,
Withdrew in silence ; but the sifted more
Who stayed clouded their aspect, and, with grim
Mutter in undertone exchanged between
Them, each with other, asked or answered who
This was that rudely thus and threateningly
Broke in upon them.   Saul! the Sanhedrim!
Were dreaded names, but red runs Jewish blood,
And hot, and quick, and those affronted men
Scarce waited for their neighbor seen thus scorned
To answer yea to his stern challenger,
Ere they together moved in mass about
Saul unattended, naked of all arms
Save his authority, and, hustling him,
Seemed on the verge of using violent hands
To thrust him forth — nay, to Saul's ears there came
That pregnant word, ready on Jewish tongues,
Yet readier hardly than to Jewish hands
The deed, word full of instant menace, " Stones !"

   Saul knew his danger and his helplessness;
But, far from terror, though not void of fear,

Blanching not blenching, he a tonic breath
Drew, in an air that to another man
Had softened all his fibre or dissolved.
Vanished that mood of feebleness he brought,
And in its place a resolute, alert,
Defiant sense of self-sufficing strength
Supported him, nay, buoyed him almost gay,
As thus, with bitter words, he taunted them:
" Yea, now ye show what lessons ye have learned
Of unresisting meekness at the feet
Of this your teacher — *then* not to resist
When ye are certain to be overpowered !
But twenty of you to one man are brave !
Nay, but one man may twenty of you scorn.
Back, there ! Stand back !   This man my prisoner is.
I, Saul, commissioned by the Sanhedrim,
Summon and seize him to appear this day
Before their just tribunal to be judged
As self-confessed disciple of the Way.
Follow me thou !   Make way before me there !"

   The peremptory tone, the audacity,
The prompt aggressive movement, with the proud,
High, lordly speech disdainful, the assured

Serene assumption of authority
Enforced by personal will as strong as power —
These for a moment's space surrounded Saul
With that inviolable immunity,
The nameless spell which perfect courage casts ;
Nay, so far gave him full ascendant there
That he quite to his man his way had made
And on a shoulder laid the arresting hand.
But stay ! not quelled, suspended only, seems
The indignant angry humor of the crowd.
Scarce has Saul uttered his last scornful words
And turned to front the men about him massed —
Not doubting but, with only the drawn sword
Of his fixed forward countenance, he shall
This side and that before him cleave a way
Wide from amid them forth to pass — upon
Such hinging-point scarce poises Saul, when they,
With many-handed violence, seize him
And, irresistibly uplifting, bear
Helpless, headforemost, ignominiously,
Whither they will.

   In vain Hirani cries,
By turns rebuking and beseeching them ;

In vain he follows, warning them beware
To involve themselves in risk fruitless for him ;
In vain implores them even for Jesus' sake,
Whose name will be dishonored by their deed ;
Presents himself in vain a prisoner
Willing to go with Saul unmanacled ;
In vain avouches he, in any case,
Shall yield his person to the Sanhedrim,
Doubtless to suffer but the heavier doom
For what is doing, unless they refrain.
Hirani had adjured them by the name
Of Jesus, but those heady men, that name,
That mastership, owned not, Jews only still,
Still in the changed new spirit all unschooled.
So by their own mad motion ever mad
Growing, they hurtle Saul along the way —
He the while musing, with mind strangely clear,
How like to Stephen's lot his own is now ! —
Till chance unlooked-for their wild turbulence stays.

All had been teemed from Shimei's fruitful brain.
First, he had mixed the listening crowd around
The weaver at that moment with base men,
His creatures, who, for hirelings' pay, should stir

Their neighbors up to wreak indignity
Upon Saul's person, wounding to his pride,
And in the public view disparaging.
Then, at the point of need, to succor Saul,
Bringing his haughty colleague under debt
To himself, Shimei, for his very life —
This was that crafty plotter's next concern.
A band accordingly of men-at-arms,
Sworn in the service of the Sanhedrim,
He had made ready ; and these now appeared
Confronting that tumultuary crowd.
Saul rescued — not without some disarray
And soil of rent apparel, hair and beard
Dishevelled, and disfigured countenance,
His person thus disparaged to the eye,
Hirani, as ringleader of the rout,
Chained and brought forward, while go free, but
    blamed
For being misled, the others — Shimei then
To view emerges.   He addresses Saul :
" Well met !   That fellow, with his crew of like,
Treated you badly, Saul.   You might have prayed
To be delivered into Stephen's hands
From tender mercies such as theirs !   I trust

You have not suffered worse than what I see,
Some slight derangement of apparel shown,
Your hair and beard less sleek than might beseem,
With here and there a scratch scored on your face —
Nothing more serious, let me trust? Our men
Were at the nick of time in coming up.
It was not pure coincidence.   You see,
Both knowing your mettle and the vicious ways
These sanctimonious ruffians have at times,
I had misgivings that you might be rash,
And suffer disadvantage at their hands.
So, as in like case you would do by me,
I, with these faithful servitors of ours,
Run to your rescue here, and not too soon !
A little later would have been too late.
You were well started down the steep incline,
Which, very happily, as I learn, you styled
'The way of Stephen and all heretics.'
Droll, very, with of course its serious side,
Queer irony, you know, of will Divine,
Supposing they had really stoned you, Saul !
Well, well, it turns out better than your fears.
You will not, true, and I lament it, make
Quite a triumphal entry with your man

Before the Sanhedrim, leading him in,
With air of captain fresh from glorious war,
Who brings proud trophy of his single spear
Redoubtable ; but the main point is ours,
The man we want is safe in custody."

Thus Shimei with his devilish sneering glee
Nettled the heart of Saul and cheered his own.

Before the council Shimei stood forth,
Instead of Saul, to accuse the prisoner.
With plausible glib mendacity, he said :
" Not only is this fellow heretic
After the manner of those Galilæans,
But myself saw with mine own eyes just now
How he the idlers in the street stirred up
To most unseemly act of violence
Against our brother Saul, worthy of death,
As being aimed at death, unless that I
Had ready been at hand with force enough
To rescue one of our own number thus
To the most imminent brink of stoning brought.
Saul, if he would, might show himself to you
In lively witness of the things I say."

Hereon to Saul he signed with hand and eye;
But Saul arose and calmly, with disdain,
Thus spoke : " The man here present prisoner
Is, out of his own mouth, disciple proved
Of Jesus Nazarene.   As such I sought
To bring him hither before you to be judged.
This my attempt, most unexpectedly,
A crowd of idlers round about him drawn
Vacantly listening to discourse from him,
Resented ; they, resisting, thrust me back —
I had ventured single-handed and alone —
And, borne to madness, might perhaps have wrought
Some harm to me — I know not ; but one thing
I know, and that I freely testify,
This man, our prisoner, did nought of all,
Contrariwise, with all his eloquence
Endeavored to dissuade those violent,
Constantly saying and averring he,
In any case, should, of his own free will,
Give himself up to you — thereby to clear
The Name he sought to honor of reproach
For wild deeds done as in defence of him."

A moment, having heard Saul testify,

The Sanhedrim sat silent in fixed thought.
Then Shimei, ever easily equal found
To his occasion, when need seemed to him
Of whatsoever fraud in word or act,
Said that of course from brother Saul was heard
Never aught other than he deemed was true ;
But the fact was, as he by witnesses
Would amply prove, that all this culprit's show
Of zeal to stay those rioters back was show
Merely, dust in the eyes of Saul to cast,
Or rather sport to make of him, the prey
Secure supposed of his, the prisoner's,
Malicious machination through the hands
Of his confederates, or tools, who knew
Better their master's purposes, his real
Purposes, than his feigned dissuasive words
To heed, and let his victim go.   Saul's state
Was at the moment such, so ill at ease
His mind — why, even his body in that vile
Duress was hardly to be called his own —
Saul — and without offence would Shimei say it —
Might be regarded as not competent
On this particular point to testify.
At all events, here were good witnesses

Who, from a safer, steadier point of view
Than Saul's, and longer occupied, could tell
Both what the prisoner's wont had been to teach,
And what he instigated in this case.

   With such preamble to prepare their minds,
Minds used to guess the drift of Shimei's wish,
This arch-artificer of fraud produced
As witnesses the men whom he had late
Mixed with Hirani's audience to foment
That lawlessness.   Such serviceable tongues
Failed not to swear, in all, as Shimei wished.

   Saul, in his secret mind with anguish torn,
Gazed at the man forsworn against, maligned,
And almost envied him.   A look of peace
Was on him like a light of fixéd stars,
So constant, and so inaccessible
Of change through jar, through stain, so clear, so fair!
He listened to the voices round him loud,
As if some softer voice from farther sent
Made ever an inner music to his mind
Charming him with a melody unheard.
He saw the things, the faces, and the forms,
About him nigh, as if he looked beyond

Or through them, and beheld far, far away
Or whom or what to others was unseen.

So when the high-priest, from his middle seat
Among the councillors, accosted him,
Asking, " To all these things what sayest thou ? "
The prisoner, like one absent-minded brought
To sudden sense of present things, replied :
" I hardly understand what ' these things ' are,
For otherwhither I was drawn in thought.
But if it be inquired concerning Him
Whom lately they not knowing crucified,
Why, this I answer for my testimony :
' Let there be light,' said God, and light there was.
Almost thus did that Man of Nazareth,
Creative, speak for me, and changed my world
Of native darkness to this cheerful scene
Above, beneath, about me, sudden spread,
And sun and moon and stars for me ordained.
I praise Him as the Lord of life and light,
And Giver of light and life to dead and blind.
All glory to His ever-blessèd Name ! "

The simple ecstasy from which he spoke,
Illuminated, and the holy power

Of truth, in witness such, meekly so borne,
Wrought even upon the jealous Sanhedrim
An influence which they could not resist,
And a pang shot to the inmost heart of Saul.
A faltering of compunction close on shame
Made the high-priest half-tenderly, with tone
As of a father toward a child in fault,
Say : " Nay, my son, deceived art thou ; of will
Surely thou dost not utter blasphemy.
If so be demon power had leave from God
To give thee back one day what demon power
Had erst one day from God had leave to take
Away, thy sight — be glad indeed, but fear
To yield wrongly thy praise to demon power
Permitted ; all to God permissive yield.
Glory belongs to God alone.   My son,
Bethink thee now betimes and save thy soul.
' Jesus of Nazareth anathema ! '
Those words repeat for all to hear, and go
Acquitted hence of that thy blasphemy."

    So the high-priest to him, but he replied :
" Blinded again I should expect to be,
My eyeballs blasted to the roots of sight,

Nay, worse, my inner seeing quenched in dark,
Forever and forevermore past cure,
Were I to speak that Name except to praise.
Glory to God and glory to His Son,
Forever and forever in the heavens,
The heaven of heavens, seated at His right hand!"

"A bold blasphemer!" so, discordant, shrieked
Suddenly Shimei, the spell to break
He feared those simple, solemn, holy words
Again might cast upon the Sanhedrim.

The chance for heaven precarious is on earth
Ever, and now the heavenly chance was lost,
Such counter breath unable to withstand.
Those half-rapt souls reverted to themselves,
And brooked to listen — nay, assent gave they,
Even Saul too gave assent wrung out ! — when, next,
" Stripes for his back!" sharply shrilled Shimei ;
"Good forty stripes less one may save his soul !
He loves his blasphemy, give him his fill,
Whet him his appetite, make him blaspheme
His own Lord God, the man of Nazareth.
For that thrice damnéd name require from him,
At every lash, an imprecation loud,

On pain of instant death should one curse fail!"

So there with cruel blows was scourged the man,
At every blow he crying out aloud
Joy that he might thus suffer for that Name,
And, baffled, they gnashing their teeth on him.
" His madness has infected all his flesh,"
Screamed Mattathias ; " cure there is but one.
Destroy his flesh with stones, let his flesh rot!"

This also they, beside themselves with rage,
Rage rabid from the sight of bloodshed vain,
Resolved — resolving with them likewise Saul !
Without the gate they thrust their victim forth,
And there stoned him calling upon the name
Of Jesus to his last expiring breath.

That night, the violated body, left
There where it fell by those his murderers
To be of ravening beast or bird the prey,
Was thence, with reverent rite, by unseen hands
Borne to a sepulchre, with spices wrapt
In linen pure and fine, and laid away
In secret, not unwept or unbewailed
Of such as loved him for the love he bore,
Quenchless by death, to the Belovèd Name.

BOOK XII.

SAUL AND THE APOSTLES.

AGAIN deeply distressed in heart, Saul at set of sun withdraws to the top of Olivet for solitary thought. There falling asleep, after pensive soliloquy, he dreams that Shimei has followed him thither, and that he now pours a characteristic strain of sneer and instigation into his ear. This rouses him, and he goes moodily home. After a long, deep slumber there, he resolves on undertaking what he dreamed that Shimei proposed, namely, the arrest of the apostles. His men fail him at the pinch, and Saul bitterly upbraids them, declaring strongly that their renegade behavior only determines him the more sternly to root utterly out the pestilent Galilæan heresy, at whatever cost of exertion and blood and tears.

SAUL AND THE APOSTLES.

So one day more of bitterness had spent
Saul, and the night, the solemn night, came on,
Grateful to him, for he would be alone.
Whether the thought of home, no home, repelled,
Or longing toward his sister unconfessed
There in that banishment at Bethany
Bright with her presence in it — whether this
Drew him, or wish of lonely room and height
Where more he might from human kind be far —
However listing, Saul to Olivet
Turned him, and slowly to the summit climbed.

The moon not risen yet, the hemisphere
Of heaven above him was with clustered stars
Glittering, and awful with the glory of God.
Upward into those lucid azure deeps,
Withdrawn, deep beyond deep, immeasurably,
Gazing, Saul said: " Deep calleth unto deep!

Those deeps above me unto deeps within
Me cry, as infinite to infinite.
The spaces of my spirit answer back ;
I feel them, empty but capacious, vast
And void abysses of unfed desire,
Hunger eternal and eternal thirst!
Upward I gaze, and see the steadfast stars
Unshaken in their station calmly shine,
I listen to the silence of the skies
And yearn, with what desire! for peace like that,
Vainly, with what desire ! for peace like that!
Beneath the pure calm of the holy heaven,
So nigh! here am I seething like the sea,
That cannot rest, casting up mire and dirt
Continually!   O state forlorn!   Where, where,
My God, for me is rest?   For me, for me!
'Great peace have they,' so sang that psalmist taught
By Thee, 'Great peace have they that love Thy law
And nothing shall offend them.'   Answer me,
Lord God, do _I_ not love Thy law ?   Then why
This opposite of peace within my breast?
Am I deceived ?   Do _not_ I love Thy law ?
Answer me Thou !"

               But answer came there none,

Or Saul was deaf, and the great sky looked down, .
With all its multitude of starry eyes,
Impassible, upon a human soul
Wretched, unrespited from long unrest.

    The weary man upon a spot of ground
Bare to the heaven had thrown himself supine ;
Lying diffuse, his wistful face upturned,
And poring on the starry-scriptured scroll
Above him, he such thoughts breathed out in words.
He had deemed himself alone, aloof from men ;
But seemed had scarce his murmurous monotone
Died on his lips, he skyward gazing still,
When he was conscious of approaching feet,
Feet all at once so nigh, they in the dark
Touched him ere he could rouse himself to stand.

    ‘ Why, brother Saul !   I stumble on you here,
Much as this morn you stumbled over me !’
Such, to the sleeping man, a voice seemed borne.

    ‘ Those odious false-cheery tones once more !
Shimei has watched, and, hither following me,
Lurked overhearing my soliloquy ;
Then, stealthily retiring a few steps,

Comes back, as with the brisk and frank advance
Of one somewhither walking at full speed,
And stumbles against me of purpose rude !'

So Saul divined dissembling Shimei,
Who said, or to Saul, dreaming, seemed to say —
Vision as life-like as reality :
" How naturally appear our paths to cross !
I thought that I would take a casual stroll
Alone, and you the same thought had, it seems,
At the same time, directed both, odd too,
The self-same way — another proof, you see,
What kindred spirits we are !

                                 " You must have marked
How fine the night is !   What a wealth of stars !
Do you not sometimes wish, Saul, you could be
As comfortably calm at heart as stars ?
How wonderfully quiet all is there,
Up in the region of the firmament !
Probably stars have nothing else to do
Than to be calm like that, and smile at us
Fretting ourselves down here with worry and work.
Worry is worse than work to wear us out.
But worst of all is having huge desires

That nothing in the world can satisfy.
Some men moon sighing for they know not what,
Mainly great hollow hungry mouths and maws,
Like void sea-beds; abysses of desire,
You know, that not the world itself could fill.
Better close up your heart than stretch it wide
And never get enough to make it full.
Adjust yourself, say I, to circumstance,
Hard work adjusting circumstance to you!
There's nothing better than to go right on
Doing the obvious duty next to hand,
And let the stars pursue their peaceful way,
As hindered not, so envied not, by you.
The sky is calm, no doubt — the upper sky —
But happens we do not live in the sky,
But on the earth, a very different place,
And man's work we, not star's work, have to do;
So let us be about it while we may.

" For instance now, to bring the matter home
(I trust I shall not seem officious, Saul,
I really must make one suggestion more),
Your pristine prestige has been much impaired
Through slips and ill-successes on your part.

No mean advantage to a man, repute
For what the godless Romans call 'good luck,'
Piously we, ' the favor of the Lord';
This is forsaking you, I grieve to find,
On all sides round, wherever I inquire.
Up, and recover it with one bold push,
Push that dares hazard all upon a cast.
You know twelve men there are in special sort
Dubbed the 'apostles' of the Nazarene,
Who play a part assigned as witnesses
To testify that Jesus rose again,
After his crucifixion, from the dead.
These fellows boldly in Jerusalem
Stay, while the rest run scattering far and wide.
Some kind of superstitious charm or awe
Surrounds them — that is, in their own conceit
And fond illusion of impunity.
Boldly arrest them, Saul, and spoil the spell."

   Thus far, as oft in dreams will chance, Saul lay
And helpless heard what irked him sore to hear;
But now, the loathing irrepressible
Excited· by such hateful speech, roused him
To spurning that asunder broke the bonds,

The nightmare bonds, of sleep.   He, full awake,
Groped with his hands about, dreading to feel
Shimei indeed couched nigh, as he had dreamed,
Breathing into his ear.   No Shimei there !
He sprang upon his feet, and in the light
Of the waned moon, now risen, still large and fair,
Looked round and round — to find himself alone.

" A dream, then," Saul said, " only a hideous dream !
Thank God ! How horribly real it seemed ! How like
Must I have grown to *him*, to have had his thoughts !
What demon's doom only to have such thoughts !
Perhaps a demon whispered these now to me !
I could even pity Shimei, to be haunt
And harbor of his ceaseless evil thoughts —
Could pity, save that I detest too much.
I cannot be like him and loathe him so ;
Or does he haply also loathe himself ?
Then were I like, for sure I loathe myself !
What travesty it was of those my thoughts !
And not ignoble thoughts, though vain, they were.
The mad pranks that our dreaming brains will play !"

So musing, there Saul, on the mountain's brow,
Statue-like stood some moments in suspense ;

Then slow descending to his house repaired.
A deep, deep draught of pure oblivion
In sleep drowned him until the morrow noon.

Prayer then, and then fast broken, and calmly Saul
The ill dream of his yesternight revolved.
What better project for fresh act than that
Which, gladly now he pondered, Shimei
Did not propose, but only Shimei's
False lively mimic counterfeit in sleep?
Yea, he would next, with prompt but circumspect
Audacity, the audacious head and front
Smite of this growing mischief, in those men
Styled the apostles of the Nazarene.

Saul knew within his heart that secretly
He dreaded this adventure ; therefore he,
With will sardonically set, moved on
To undertake it. Twenty men of tried
True mettle, men with muscle iron-firm,
And mind seasoned, through many hazards run,
And long wont of impunity, to scorn
All danger — such a score of men chose Saul,
And, from them veiling yet his purpose, took,
With indirection intricate, his way

Toward where, as he, by diligent quest, had learned,
The twelve apostles used each day to meet
In secret from their prowling enemies;
But to the common people, loving them
For manifold miracles of beneficence,
Their secret meeting-place was not unknown.

As, gradually, Saul with his retinue
Drew near the spot, so large a following
Of arméd men, led by a chief whose fame
Was rife now through Jerusalem for deeds
And purposes of uttermost revenge
Against the Galilæan heresy,
Gathered about their course a growing crowd,
Who, urged by various thought and feeling, watched
What might that minatory march intend.
Reached thus at length the place, Saul stays his steps,
And, turning to his men in halt to hear,
Speaks, with that dense clear voice which tense will
        breeds:
" Here hide the twelve arch-heretics of all.
Ye come to take them hence bond prisoners,
For lodgment in a hold whence no escape,
That they may cease sedition to foment.

Duly the fathers of the Sanhedrim,
Wise warders of our Hebrew commonwealth,
Will thence adjudge them to their doom of death.
No waste of words in parley now, leave asked,
Terms offered, naught of that, no paltering pause,
Instantly, stroke on stroke, down with the door!"

But pause they did, those picked, use-hardened men;
They stood as struck with palsy or with fear.
"Traitors be ye, or cravens, which?" cried Saul—
Amazement, indignation, ire, disdain,
Effacing exhortation in his tone.
Then, mastering himself, less fiercely he
Chode them : "Whence and whereto is this? Mean
      ye,
Ye surely mean not, mutiny?   Rouse, then,
With will; obey, your loyalty retrieve!"

But still they hung there moveless, until one,
Seeming the spokesman of his fellows, said :
"No mutineers, no traitors, cravens none,
Are we.   But look around, and judge what means
This concourse of beholders"—"'Look around'?
Around look?" thundered Saul. "Nay, straight-on
      looks,

These sole, become stout hearts, staunch wills. 'Around'
Cease looking ye, and all right forward stare
To where yon door fronts you and you affronts.
Batter it down, and, staring forward, on !"

   The vehement, vindictive, dense onslaught
Of that impatient, proud, imperious will
Smote like the missile of a catapult
Against the clamped immovable dead wall
.Of fixed inert resistance to Saul's wish,
Which strangely, as one man, those men opposed.
That impact did not shake that stubborn strength,
Nor shiver back in staggering recoil —
Absorbed, annulled, annihilated, waste !

   One infinitesimal instant, Saul a blind
Mad impulse felt — which, that same instant, he
Quenched in a simultaneous saner thought —
To rush single upon the door, with blank
Ridiculous demonstration of balked will
Indignant.   " Me, then, seize, your chief contemned,"
Said Saul, " contemned, since not obeyed, and me
Deliver captive to the Sanhedrim,
Denounced unworthy of your trust, and theirs !"

As, saying this, around he glanced, he saw,
With unintending eyes, a spectacle
Which well had awed him, but that he was Saul.
The frequence of spectators serried nigh
Had armed themselves with stones, and imminent
    stood,
A thunder-cloud of menace on each brow,
Ready those bolts of vengeance to let fly,
In hail-storm that no mortal might withstand,
At whoso dared defy their angry mood ;
Portent so dire Saul could not but peruse.

" It was but question which should overawe,
Ye, or this rabble of sedition here,
And ye have solved it like the cowards ye are !"
So, with his passion humored to its height,
And javelin looks shot at his men in shower,
Cried Saul ; " I had deemed otherwise of you.
And yet, even yet, once wake the dormant man
Within you, and, from hands through fear relaxed,
Harmless will drop those miscreant stones which now,
With your poltroonery, ye invoke to fall
In well-deservéd doom upon your heads !"

Upbraided thus, they, by that spokesman, said :

" Stoning may lightly be despised by men
Like us, whose trade it is at need to die ;
And bloody death were meet for men of blood.
But we are of the people, as are these
Whom here thou seest around us, stone in hand ;
And we, the people, love for cause those men,
Our benefactors, whom thou seekest to slay —
Wherefore, we know not, save perhaps it be
Some ill persuasion thine that slanders them
As enemies of our race, seditious men,
Conspiring to do evil and not good.
But, if we should as lief, as we should loth,
Offer them violence, and if we could,
As we could not, hope then to escape the stones
Here seen uneasy in so many hands
At only brandished threat of harm to them,
Know, there is more than mail enduing these
Inviolate against what human touch
Might mean them wrong.   Something intangible,
Invisible, inaudible, unknown,
A might as irresistible as strange,
Not only arms them proof against assault,
But issues from them in dread strokes of doom,
Silent like lightning, and like lightning swift,

And instantaneous deadly more than that.
What prison-walls can prisoners hold these men?
Hast thou not heard how Ananias fell,
Sapphira too, his wife, dead at their feet,
Fell at their feet stone-dead, when they but charged
A lie unto the Spirit of the Lord
On those twain twinned in judgment as in crime?
A dreadful visitation, as from God;
But, whencesoever issuing, dreadful yet!
No panoply have we against such stroke,
Against the authors of such stroke, no power.
Slay us, or get us slain, we can but die;
But die like Ananias will we not!"

　　Saul listened with illimitable scorn;
And scorn incensed his rage thus crossed to be,
Hopelessly crossed, by crass perversity.
In rage and scorn, he scourged those men with words:
"There is no reasoning with minds like you!—
Too ignorant to guess how ignorant
Ye are, and self-conceited in degree
To match.　Such ignorance, with self-conceit
Such, renders blind indeed.　What boots it I
Should tell you superstition clouds your brain?

Your superstition would not let you hear.
Your very senses, given by God to be
The avenues of knowledge to your mind,
Satan has clogged to truth, and made of them
But open thoroughfares for lies from him
To enter by and capture you his own.
Mere Satan's lies those tales are that ye tell,
Of prison-doors thrown wide mysteriously
To let these men go free, and of deaths dealt
By magic sentence weaponless from them —
Mere Satan's lies those tales, or, were they true,
Yet tokens only of Satanic power
And craft permitted to disport them here
For their destruction who to be destroyed
Prove themselves greedy by such act as yours.
Dupes of the devil, go, I pity you!
This is your weakness, not your villainy.
I thought to make you helpers in my strife
To save the souls of others, but your souls
Themselves need saving first and most of all —
If souls like yours of saving worthy be,
Or capable!   Some different make of men
From you, seems I must seek, to serve my need.
Yet you I thank at least for this, that ye

By your behavior show me what a sore,
How seated, and how wide, into the heart
Eats of my nation!   Lo, I take the cup,
The full, the overflowing cup of shame
Which ye this day wring out for me, that cup
Take I with thanks from you, and to the dregs
Drain it, in pledge, in pledge and sacrament,
That I hereafter give myself more whole,
More absolute, more consecrate, to one,
One only, pure endeavor and desire,
The utter rooting out — at cost how dear,
No reckoning, mine or other's, toil, and tears,
And blood — wherever Jewish name be found,
Of this foul creeping rot and leprosy,
This blight, this blast, this mildew, on our fame!'

    Saul, in the light of luminous wrath, foresaw
Nigh, and saluted, that career, which thence,
After Judæan cities·overrun
With havoc at his hand to Jesus' name,
Will bear him ravening on Damascus road!

BOOK XIII.

SAUL AND SERGIUS.

After further persecution accomplished by him in Judæa, Saul, with spirits recovered, sets out for Damascus to carry thither the persecuting sword. Pausing on the brow of hill Scopus to survey Jerusalem just left, he soliloquizes. At the same moment, there rides up a troop of Roman horse escorting a man who turns out to be Sergius Paulus, an old-time acquaintance of Saul's, also bound to Damascus. The two pursue their journey together, highly enjoying their ride in that charming season of spring weather, and delightedly conversing on the way. They talk over Greek literature, and in particular by starlight at the close of the first day's journey, Sergius Paulus having by occasion recited an apposite passage of Homer, Saul matches and contrasts this first with a psalm of David, and then additionally with a strain from the prophet Isaiah. This gives rise to conversation on ensuing days, in which religious questions are discussed. Sergius declares himself an atheist of the Epicurean sort, and he plies Saul with incredulous inquiries about the religion of the Jews — Saul answering with Hebrew conviction and earnestness. The two part company at Neapolis (Shechem) because Sergius Paulus halts there, and Saul, in the spirit of true Jewish strictness, will for his part not rest till he has quite passed the bounds of Samaria.

SAUL AND SERGIUS.

Not yet his fill of slaughter supped, though forth
Afar the timorous flock of Jesus now
Were from before his restless, ravening, fierce,
Rapacious sword out of Judæa fled
To alien lands remote, beyond the heights
Of Hermon with their everlasting snows,
And farther to the islands of the sea —
Not yet, even so, his fill of slaughter supped,
Saul had from the high-priest commission sought
To search among the Hebrew synagogues
Of Syrian Damascus, and thence bring
Bound to Jerusalem whomever found,
Woman or man, confessing Jesus Christ.

The season was fresh flowering spring ; the earth
Was glad with universal green to greet
The sun once more, returned in his blue heaven
After his winter's sojourn in the south.

How blithe the welcome of the morning was,
Forth looking from his east across the Hills
Of Moab on the just awakening world!
Saul met it with a sense as if of spring
And morning linking hand in hand for dance
Together in the courses of his blood,
As, mounted on a palfrey fresh and fleet,
With servitors attendant following him,
He issued jocund from Damascus gate.
The animal spirits of youth and health in him,
The joy of new adventure, **the** fine pulse
Of life felt in the buoyant, bounding step
With which his steed advanced him on the road,
The secret pleasure of release at last,
Release and long secure removal, won,
Through growing leagues of distance interposed,
From the abhorred access of Shimei —
These, with the season and the hour so bright,
Brightened the darkling heart of Saul to cheer.
He was a radiant aspect, fair to see,
Fronting his future with that sanguine smile!

    The acclivity surmounted of a hill,
Whence downward dipped his road, declining north,

And farewell glimpse gave of Jerusalem,
Saul rein drew on his foamy-flankéd steed,
And, about winding him, paused, looking back.
His retinue, far otherwise than he
Mounted, part even on foot, with sumpter beasts ·
Bearing camp equipage, behind were fallen.
These, presently come up, he lets pass on
Before him in the way, while still at gaze,
There on the back of his indignant steed
Resentful to be curbed in mid-career —
Companion hoofs heard leaving him behind —
Saul sits, perusing, with an inner eye,
Yet more than with his outer, what he sees.
Half-shadow and half-light, Jerusalem
He sees, smitten athwart her level roofs
With sunshine from the horizontal sun,
The temple of Jehovah in the midst,
As if itself a sun, so dazzling bright
With its refulgence of reflected beams;
While, round about, the warder mountains stand,
Bathing their sacred brows in sacred light.
Saul's heart distends immense with patriot's joy,
Yet joy pierced through and through with patriot's
    pain.

"O beautiful for situation, thou,
Jerusalem!" he fervently bursts forth.
" Peace be within thy walls, prosperity
Within thy palaces!   Yea, yet again,
Now for my brethren and companions' sakes,
Say I, ' Within thee, peace!'   Lo, my vow hear:
For that the temple of the Lord my God
Is in thee, I henceforth thy good will seek.
And Thou, Jehovah in the heavens! behold,
Saul for himself that ancient promise claims:
' Prosper shall he Jerusalem who loves.'
For love not I Jerusalem, with love
To anguish, for her anguish and her tears?
Take pleasure in her stones, favor her dust,
O God, my God!   Is not the set time come?
Do I not hear Thee say : ' Awake, awake,
Put on thy strength, O Zion, long forlorn,
And beautiful thy garments put thou on,
Jerusalem !   Henceforth no more shall come
The uncircumcised into thee, nor the unclean!'"

" Amen!" Saul added, with a gush of tears,
The light mercurial feeling in his heart
Less to sad sinking, weighted down, than all.

With fluent lapse, to pleasing pathos changed.
Into that strain, so ardent and so true,
Of patriot prayer, deeply had braided been,
Half to himself unknown, a silent strand
Of subtle self-regard, vague personal hope
That would have spurned to be imprisoned in words:
'The new Jerusalem that was to be,
Should she not Saul her chief deliverer hail!'

Musing, and praying, and beholding, so,
Saul suddenly a sound of clanging hoofs
Heard, and, his eyes quick thither turning, saw,
Between hill Scopus, on whose top he stood,
And the Damascus gate through which he came,
Advancing toward him on the Roman road —
Cemented solid with its rutted stones,
Like an original stratum of the sphere —
A turm of horse, large not, but formidable,
Caparison and armor gleaming bright,
And with a nameless air forerunning them
Of wide-renownéd might invincible
Expressed in that momentous rhythmic tread
Four-footed, underneath which from afar
With pulse on pulse now rock to iron rang.

The cavalcade, by slow degrees more slow,
Moved up the acclivity till, reached the brow,
Sank to a walk their pace, when Saul perceived
An arméd escort was convoying one
Thereby betokened an ambassador,
Somewhither posting on affair of state,
Or haply citizen of high degree
Honored with ceremonious retinue.

This man regarded Saul with curious look
Respectful, which almost admiring grew;
And gravely, as their mutual glances met,
The youthful Roman to the youthful Jew
Inclined in distant salutation meant
For natural courtesy due from peer to peer.
Saul, in like wise, his greeting gave him back;
Whereon the Roman, reining to one side
His horse, and halting, said: " Peace, but methinks
I saw thee late, months since it may have been,
Where that fanatic Stephen suffered death
With stoning at your angry elders' hands."
" I, in that act of punishment," said Saul,
" As loyal Jew befitted, took my part."
" Nay, but as now I read thy features nigh,"

Sudden more earnest grown, the Roman said,
" Labors my brain with yet a different thought.
Somewhere we twain must earlier still have met.
In Tarsus I some boyish seasons spent ;
I there, by chance full well-remembered, knew
A Hebrew-Roman boy whose name was Saul."
" Then Sergius Paulus is thy name," said Saul,
" And Saul am I — and Saul to Sergius, peace ! "
Who but as man and man just now had met
Greeted again in sense of comradeship.

" Thy face is toward Jerusalem," to Saul
Said Sergius ; " but thy look is less of one
Arriving, journey finished, than of one
Forth setting on adventure planned abroad."
" I journey to Damascus," Saul replied ·
" And thither also I," said Sergius.
Damascus-ward turned Saul his horse's head,
And slowly, with the Roman, now resumed
His onward way, while further Sergius said :
" Having a brief apprenticeship at arms
Accomplished, to Jerusalem I came,
Centurion still, urged by desire to see
Thy capital city, famed throughout the world.

Since witnessing — by lucky hap it fell
My military duty to be there —
Since witnessing that spectacle so strange
Of Stephen's stoning — strange to Roman eyes,
Yet to eyes Jewish doubtless quite as strange
Our Roman fashion, hanging on the cross —
All various ways of various tribes of men
From clime to clime, delights me to observe —
What comedy to the gods must we present ! —
Since I saw Stephen slain with stones, I say,
Good fortune, and some interest made for me
At Rome, have given me this my welcome chance
To travel and more widely see the world.
Now to Damascus I as legate go."
" And of our Sanhedrim as legate, I,
Said Saul, "if so without offence I may
From Jewish mode to Gentile dare my speech
Conform — legate, or hand executive,
Say rather, in some certain offices
Deemed needful, to consult my nation's weal."

    With mutual question asked and answered, vein
Of old-time boyish reminiscence shared
Between them as together on they rode —

Their horses pricking each the other's speed —
The two soon overtook their retinues,
Who, seeing their chiefs adjoined in comradeship,
Themselves in comradeship dissolved their sense
Of race and race to mix as men and men.

So all day long together, side by side,
Riding, or resting in the noontide shade,
Sergius and Saul, a frank companionship,
Immixed their minds in speech of many things.
Young life, young health, glad sense of fair emprise,
High-hearted hope of boundless futures theirs,
Delicious weather and blithe season bland,
Blue cloudless heaven forever overhead —
By the sole sun usurped his tabernacle
Whence sovran virtue beaming into all —
Sweet voice of singing-bird, sweet smile of flower,
Sweet breath exhaled from tender-fruited vine,
Joy, a full feast, through every flooded sense —
And, heightening all, that billowy onward sway
Of motion without effort on their steeds,
Made, to those lord possessors of the world,
Their talking like the coursing of their blood,
Self-moved, or like the running of a brook

That laughs and sparkles on its downward way,
As ceasing never from its hope to drain
The fountain, brimming ever, whence it flows.

  Of arms, of art, and of philosophy,
They spoke, and letters; spoke, too, of the fame
Of ancient Grecian masters of the mind,
Who ruled, and rule, by charm of prose or verse.
First, Homer, hoar with immemorial eld,
Pouring his epics in that profluent stream
Which, like his ocean, wandered round the world;
Bold Pindar, with his lyric ecstasies,
On throbbing wings of exultation borne
Into the empyrean, whence his song
Broken descends in showers of melody;
Father of history, Herodotus,
" Half poet, epic, or idyllic, he " —
So, Saul thereto assenting, Sergius said —
" With his Ionic strain mellifluous
Of wonder-loving artless narrative ";
Thucydides, the soul of energy;
Æschylus, Titan; happy Sophocles;
With soft Euripides unfortunate;
Then Socrates, " Who wrote no books," said Saul.

" Or wrote most living books in living men ;
Plato, the chiefest book of Socrates,
Yet mind so large and so original
That, in him reading what his teacher taught,
One knows not whether Socrates it be,
Or Socrates's pupil, that one reads " —
" Knows not, and, for delight, cares not to know,
Full-sated with the feast of such discourse,
So wealthy, wise, urbane, harmonious !" —
Stung to enthusiasm, thus Sergius,
Continuing what from Saul ceased incomplete.
" Our Tully," added he, " from Plato's well
Deepest his draughts drank of philosophy,
And, thence inspired, wrote such sweet dialogue,
Latin half seemed delectable as Greek."
" Yea, and a man of fine civility
In manners as in mind, your Tully was,"
Said Saul; " Cilicia keeps his memory green
For virtues long in Roman rulers rare.
His too a sounding, stately eloquence,
And copious; but Greek Demosthenes
Pleases me better, with that stormy stress
Of passion in him, reason on fire with love
Or hatred, that indignant vehemence

Which overwhelms us like a torrent flood,
Or, like a torrent flood, upon its breast
Lifts us, and tosses us, and bears us on !
He is more like our Hebrew prophets rapt
Above themselves in sympathy with God."

In talk like this the livelong day was spent ;
Hardly the talkers heeding when they passed
Meadows of flowers pied rich in colors gay,
Poppy, anemone, convolvulus,
Bright marigold wide yellowing belts of green
Into a vivid gold that dazed the eye ;
And heeding hardly if upsprang the lark
From almost underneath their horses' hoofs,
Startled to leave her humble hiding nest,
And, soaring, better hide her otherwise
Amid the blinding lightnings of the sun ;
Such sights and sounds and glancing motions swift
Scarce heeded — yet, as subtle influence,
Admitted, each, to infuse insensibly
Into their mood an added joyousness —
The afternoon declined into the eve.
Passed now a fountain on the wayside cliff,
Coyly, through ferny leafage, shedding down

Its weeping waters shown in fresher green,
Up a long glen they mounted to a crest
Of hill where opened a soft grassy plain —
Inviting, should one wish his tent to spread —
And here they twain their double camp bid pitch.

  Supper soon ended, Saul and Sergius,
Ere sleep they seek, a hill, not far, ascend,
The highest neighboring seen, less thence to view
The landscape round them in the deepening dark
Glooming, or even the heavens above their heads
Brightening each moment in the deepening dark,
Than youth's unused excess of strength to ease
With exercise, and to achieve the highest.
But there the splendors of the firmament,
Enlarged so lustrous through that Syrian sky,
Hailed such a storm of vertical starlight
Downward upon their sense as through their sense
Inward into their soul beat, and a while
Mute held them, hushed with wonder and with awe,
Awe to the Hebrew, to the Roman, joy.
Then said the Roman :

                    " This is like that place
Of glorious Homer where he hangs the sky

Innumerably bright with moon and stars
Over the Trojan host and their camp-fires:
    ' Holding high thoughts, they on the bridge of war
    ' Sat all night long, and many blazed their fires.
    ' As when in heaven stars round the glittering moon
    ' Shine forth exceeding beautiful, and when
    ' Breathlessly tranquil is the upper air,
    ' And in their places all the stars are seen,
    ' And glad at heart the watching shepherd is;
    ' So many, 'twixt the ships and Xanthus' streams,
    ' Shone fires by Trojans kindled fronting Troy.' "

    " The spirit of Greece, with Greek simplicity,
A nobleness all of Homer, there I feel,"
Concession checking with reserve, said Saul;
" Our Hebrew, to us Hebrews, rises higher.
Homer, unconscious of sublimity,
Down all its dreadful height above our sphere
Brings the august encampment of the skies —
To count the number of the Trojan fires !
Our poet David otherwise beholds
The brilliance of the nightly firmament,
Seeing it mirror of the majesty
Of Him who spread it arching over earth,

And who yet stoops His awful thought to think
Kindly of us as Father to our race,
Nay, kingdom gives us, glory, honor, power,
And all things subjugates beneath our feet.
Let me some echoes from that harp awake
To which, with solemn touches, this his theme
Our psalmist David chanted long ago :
  ' Jehovah, our dread Sovereign, how Thy Name
  ' Is excellent in glory through the earth !
  ' Upon the heavens Thy glory hast Thou set ;
  ' The heart of babe and suckling reads it there,
  ' And, raised to rapture, utters forth Thy praise,
  ' That mute may be the adversary mouth
  ' Which would the ever-living God gainsay.
  ' When I survey Thy heavens, Thy handiwork,
  ' The moon, the stars, Thou didst of old ordain,
  ' Man, what is he ? that Thou for him shouldst
     care,
  ' The son of man, that Thou shouldst visit him.
  ' For Thou hast made him hardly lower than God,
  ' And dost with glory him and honor crown.
  ' Dominion over all Thy works to wield
  ' Thou madest him, and underneath his feet
  ' Put'st all things, sheep and oxen, roaming beast,

' And winging fowl, and swimming fish, and all
' That passes through the pathways of the seas.
' Jehovah, our dread Sovereign, how Thy Name
' Is excellent in glory through the earth ! ' "

Recited in slow solemn monotone,
As with an inward voice muffled by awe,
Those new and strange barbaric-sounding notes
Of Hebrew music shut in measured words
Smote on some deeper chord in Sergius' ear
That, trembling, tranced him silent for a while.
Then he said, rousing : " What a sombre strain !
From the light-hearted Greek how different ! "

" Sombre thou callest it, and solemn I,
Who find in such solemnity a joy ;
But different, yea, from the light-thoughted Greek. "
Less as in converse than soliloquy
Deep-musing so to Sergius Saul replied.
" Our bard Isaiah modulates the strain
Into another mood less pastoral.
He pours divine contempt on idol gods,
On idol gods and on their worshippers ;
And then majestically hymns His praise
Who made yon host of heaven and leads them out.

' To whom then will ye liken God ? ' he cries,

' Or what similitude to Him compare ?

' The skilled artificer an image forms,

' And this the goldsmith overlays with gold,

' And tricks it smartly out with silver chains :

' Or haply one too poor for cost like this

' Chooseth him out a tree judged sound and good,

' And seeks a cunning workman who shall thence

' Grave him an image that may shift to stand !

' But nay, ye foolish, have ye then not known ?

' Not heard have ye ? You hath it not been
     told

' From the remote beginning of the world ?

' From the foundations of the ancient earth

' Have ye indeed so missed to understand ?

' He sits upon the circle of the earth

' And they that dwell therein are grasshoppers ;

' He as a curtain doth the heavens outspread,

' And makes a blue pavilion of the sky.

' To whom then will ye liken Me ? saith God ;

' Whom shall I equal ? saith the Holy One.

' Lift up your eyes on high, the heavens behold —

' Who hath these things created ? who their host

' By number bringeth out, and all by names

'Calls?   By the greatness of His might, for that
' So strong in power is He, not one star fails.'"

The deep tones ceased, and once more silence fell
Between those two amid the silent night.
But Sergius, lightly rallying soon to speech,
Said, with a ready, easy sympathy :
"There seems indeed to breathe in such a strain
Some solemn joy, but the solemnity
Is greater, and my spirit is oppressed.
Not less your poets differ from the Greek
In matter than in manner, when they sing.
How high you make your deity to be,
Beyond the stature of the gods of Greece !
Homer has Zeus compel the clouds, forth flash
The lightnings, and the thunderbolts down hurl ;
The mightiest meddler with the world, his Zeus,
Yet of the world the mighty maker not.
But your Jehovah reaches even to that,
As with his fingers fashioning yonder heaven,
And fixing in their station moon and stars.
And he in human things concerns himself !
The Epicurean gods are cold and calm ;
On high Olympus far withdrawn they sit,

And smile, and either not at all regard
Our case, or, if so be regarding, smile
Still, unconcerned, our case however hard.
Your Hebrew God is much more amiable,
But much more probable that Olympian crew;
Nay, probable not at all is either; dream,
Fond dream, the fable of divinities
Who either care, or care not, for our case.
We are the creatures and the sport of chance,
Puppets tossed hither and thither in idle play,
A while, a little while, fooled to suppose
We do the dancing we are jerked to do —
And then, resolved from our compacture brief
Into the atoms which once on a time
Together chanced and so were we, we drop
Plumb down again into the great inane
Abyss, and recommence the eternal whirl!
There is that Epicurean cosmogony,
An endless cycle of evolution turned
Upon itself, in worlds forevermore
Becoming, out of worlds forevermore
Merging in their original elements:
No god, or gods, to tangle worse the skein
Inextricably tangled by blind chance!"

Saul was affronted, but he held his peace,
Brooding the while his jealousy for God.
At length, with intense calm, he spoke and said:
" The Hebrew spirit is severe and says,
' The fool it is who in his secret heart,
Rebelling, wills no God.'   ' The Hebrew spirit,'
Said I ?   Forget those unadvised words;
For to speak so is not the Hebrew spirit.
God is a jealous God; His glory He
Will to another not divide; and God
Himself it is, the Living God, and not
What, Gentile fashion, my rash lips miscalled
' The Hebrew spirit,' that charges atheism
With folly.   God His prophet psalmist bade
Write with a diamond pen on adamant
That stern damnation of the atheous soul:
' The fool hath in his heart said, God is not.'
This tell I thee my conscience so to cleanse
Of sin in saying ' The Hebrew spirit' for God."

With tolerant wonder, Sergius heard and said:
" A strangely serious race you Hebrews are ;
I do not think I understand you yet.
I shall be glad to-morrow, if so please

Thee likewise, to renew this night's discourse."
So they descended from the hill and slept.

The herald Dawn, white-fingered, from the east
Had signalled to the stars, 'He comes!   He comes!'
And these, veiling themselves from view with light,
Had all into the unapparent deep
Retired, and left the hemisphere of heaven,
Late glowing with their fixed or wandering fires,
One crystal hollow of pure space made void
To be a fit pavilion for the sun,
When forth from their encampment rode the twain,
Fresh as the morning from the baths of sleep,
And keen with hunger for the forward road.
"The allotment of my tribe," said Saul — "my tribe
Is Benjamin — in measure such, bare rock
And rugged hill, hardly through age-long toil
Of tilth so clothed as we have seen them clothed,
In terrace above terrace of won soil,
With verdure — that, we leave behind, to cross
This day the fatter fields of Ephraim."
Then Saul to Sergius rehearsed in short
The tale of Hebrew history, how God,
Having his fathers out of Egypt brought,

With sign and wonder thence delivering them
And hither led them through the parted sea,
And past the smoking top of Sinai —
Touched by the finger of God to burn with fire
And thunder and lighten more than man could bear
To see or hear, in sanction of His law —
Had lastly parcelled out this land to them
In portions by their tribes to be their rest.

  While Saul to Sergius so discoursing spoke,
Over their right the sun, long since uprisen,
Climbed the steep slope of morning in the sky.
And now the summit of a ridge those twain
Reach, whence, straightforward looking, they behold,
In light so bright, through air so fair, a scene
Of the most choice the eye can rest upon.
A wide and long champaign of fruitful green,
On either side hemmed in with skirting hill,
Stretches before them to the bounding sky,
Where Hermon, scarce descried through distance dim,
Silvers with frost each morn his crown of snows.
Descended, they therein, through billowing wheat
Wind-swayed, might, to a watcher from the hill,
Seem laboring like two swimmers in the surf,

And hardly, in the fluctuation, way
Making whither they went ; yet swiftly borne
Were they, and easily, onward.   Soon Saul said —
And therewith pointed to two mountain peaks,
Seen towering on the left to lordly height,
Twin warders of a lesser vale between,
In stature twin and twin in symmetry —
" Ebal and Gerizim yon mountains are,
And these between the vale of Shechem lies,
Theatre once of oath and sacrament
Enacted by my nation with dread rite.
'A strangely serious race', thou yesterday
Calledst us Hebrews , strangely frivolous race
Surely were we, if somewhat serious not,
For we are heirs of serious history.
Yon natural amphitheatre thou seest,
Circled and sloped against those mountain sides
With spacious interval of plain enclosed ;
There was the oath of our obedience sworn.
On Ebal half our tribes, and half our tribes
On Gerizim, stood opposite, and midst,
The tribe of Levi, God's peculiar tribe,
Stood in the vale about the ark of God,
Whence Joshua, our great captain, read the law —

He and the Levites, ocean-like the sound —
With blessing or with curse by God adjoined
As disobedient or obedient we.
This was when scarce our fathers had set foot
Hitherside Jordan in the promised land;
They from their stronghold camp came here express
To swear such solemn covenant with God.
Six hundred thousand souls of fighting-men,
With women and with children fourfold more,
Ranged on the one side or the other, joined
To them that mustered in the middle vale,
All heard the threatening or the gracious words,
And all, in multitudinous answer, said
' Amen !' — the tribes on Ebal to the curse,
And to the blessing, those on Gerizim,
Replying — choral imprecation dire
Upon themselves of every human ill,
If disobedient found, of promised good
Acceptance at the price, acknowledged just,
Of whole obedience to God's holy law.
It was as if Jehovah had adjured
All things, above, below, His witnesses,
' Hear, O ye heavens, and thou, O earth, give
          ear,

While thus My people covenant swear with Me.'
The host of Israel, though such numbers, heard —
These mountain-sides redouble so the voice."

" Theatric sacramental rite most weird,"
Said Sergius, "thou hast described to me.
Sure never elsewhere did lawgiver yet,
With ceremony such, a people swear
To obedience of his laws.   The laws, I trow,
Subscribed and sealed with signature so strange,
Strange must have been.   Example couldst thou
    give ? "

" Of all those laws," said Saul, " doubtless the law
To Gentile ears the strangest, is the first ;
That law it is which makes the Jew a Jew :
  ' Other than Me no god shalt thou confess ;
  ' Image, resemblance, none, molten or carved,
  ' Of whatsoever thing in heaven, or earth,
  ' Or hidden region underneath the earth,
  ' Fashion to thee shalt thou, or bow thee down
  ' In service or in worship unto them ;
  ' For I the Lord thy God a jealous God
  ' Am, and I visit the iniquity
  ' Of fathers upon children, chastisement,

‘ In long entail, on generation linked
‘ To generation, following hard the line
‘ Of such as hate Me, endless mercy shown
‘ To such as love Me and observe My law.
‘ Cursèd be he who dares to disobey ’ ;
And Ebal, with its countless multitude,
Thundered to Gerizim a loud ‘ Amen ! ’
While heaven above and the wide world around
Hearkened in witness of the dreadful oath. ”

Saul ceased as mute with awe of memory ;
And something of a sympathetic sense,
Communicated, also Sergius made
Silent in presence of such history.
Not long, for, rousing from his reverie,
And looking up before him nigh, he sees
A city with its walls and roofs and towers.
“ Neapolis ! ” exclaims the Roman voice,
The Jewish, in tone different, “ Sychar ! ” said.
“ Neapolis !   And here I halt, ” said Sergius ;
“ Sychar !   And forward through Samaria, I,
Not pausing till this hateful soil be passed, ”
Said Saul ; “ perchance to-morrow met again,
Beyond, we may together forward fare. ”

So there they parted with such slight farewell;
Nor after met, until, two morrows more
Now spent in separate travel, they had reached
The bursting fountain of the Jordan, where,
Forth from between the feet of Hermon born
Forever — in the joy and anguish born,
The certain anguish and the doubtful joy
Tumultuous of an everlasting birth —
Leaps to the light of life that famous stream,
Like many another child — from Adam sprung —
To run his heedless, headlong, downward course
And lose himself at last in the Dead Sea!
Here was what life, all-welcoming, lusty life,
Doom of what deadly worse than death was there!

A city here the tetrarch Philip built,
Or raised to more magnificent, which then,
In honor of dishonorable name
Imperial, Tiberius Cæsar, he
Called Cæsarea, and Philippi too
Eponymous therewith for surname joined;
But Paneas, earlier name, clung to the place,
As to this day it clings in Banias.

BOOK XIV.
SAUL AND JESUS.

Coming together again at Cæsarea Philippi (Paneas, Banias) after an interval of days, Saul and Sergius cross the southern spur of Hermon. A violent thunderstorm comes slowly up during the afternoon, which gives Sergius occasion, by way of mask to his own secret disquietude, to quote his Epicurean poet Lucretius on the subject of Jupiter's control of thunderbolts. As the storm increases in violence, the fears of Sergius overpower him, and he breaks down at last into a deprecatory prayer and vow to Jupiter. Saul then, the storm still raging, rehearses from Scripture appropriate fragments of psalm, timing them to the various successive bursts of tempest. The sound of a tranquil human voice has a quieting effect on Sergius, and even on the frightened steeds of the two travellers. The storm ceases, and they pass the night under a serene sky. The next morning they set out for the last stage of their journey to Damascus.

But now the scene of the poem changes, being transferred to Paradise ; where a group composed of those who had come to their death by the hands of Saul assemble, privileged by special grace to witness from their celestial station the happy overthrow and conversion of their late persecutor. Sergius applies his interpretation of the occurrence, and Saul finishes his journey on foot, blind, led by the hand into Damascus.

SAUL AND JESUS.

THE splendor of the morning yet once more
Was a theophany in Syria,
When Saul and Sergius, met, from Paneas
Started, with mind to overpass that day
The spur of Hermon interposed between
Them and Damascus.

      " Strange the human bent,"
Said Saul, "the universal human bent,
Toward worship of unreal divinities !
'Paneas!' The very sound insults the name
And solitary majesty of God,
Jehovah, Ever-living, Only True.
Think of it ! 'Pan', forsooth ! And God, who made
These things which we behold, these waters, woods,
And mountains, glens, and rocky cliffs, and caves,
Who these things made, and made the mind of man
Capacious of Himself, or capable
At least of knowing Him Creator, such

A God thrust from His own creation forth,
By His own noblest creature thus thrust forth,
That a rough, rustic, gross, grotesque, burlesque,
Goat-footed, and goat-bearded, horned and tailed
Divinity like Pan, foul caricature
At best of man himself who fashions him,
And out of wanton fancy furnishes him
His meet appendages of brute wild beast —
That this deform abortion of the brain
Might take the room, made void, of God outcast,
And, with his ramping, reeling, riotous rout
Of fauns and satyrs, claim to be adored!
I feel the Hebrew blood within me boil
At outrage such from man on God and man!
Phœbus Apollo seems an upward reach
Of human fancy in theogony;
Some height, some aspiration, there at least,
Toward what in man, if not the noblest, yet
Is nobler than the beasts that browse, or graze.
Apollo, too, I hate, but I loathe Pan!"

"We Romans are more catholic than you
Hebrews," said Sergius, "more hospitable
To different peoples' different gods.   Our own

Synod of native deities we have,
But we make room for others than our own.
From Greece we have adopted all her gods,
And all the gods of Egypt and the East
Are domiciled at Rome — all save your god,
Jehovah, his pretensions overleap
The bounds of even our hospitality,
Who not on any terms of fellowship
Will sit a fellow with his fellow-gods.
Him sole except, it is our policy
To entertain with wise indifference
In brotherly equality all gods
Of whatsoever nations of the earth.
A temple at Rome have we, Pantheon called,
So called as to this end expressly built
That there no human god might lack a home.
Such is our Roman way; your Hebrew way
Is different ; different races, different ways."
Sergius so spoke as if concluding all
With the last word of wisdom to be said ;
He paused, and Saul mused whether wise it were
To answer, when thus Sergius further spoke :
" I marked late, when ' Neapolis!' I said,
' Sychar !' saidst thou, in tone as if of scorn :

' Hateful,' thou also calledst Samarian soil —
Wherefore ? if I may know."   " ' Sychar,' said Saul,
" Imports deceit, and there deceit abounds.
From the Samaritans we Jews refrain ;
Corrupters they of the right ways of God.
Across their soil we either shun to go,
Or, going, hasten with unpausing feet."

" Those also have their ways !" said Sergius ;
" Such humors of the blood thou wilt not cure.
Worship Jehovah ye, it is your way,
And let us Gentiles serve our several gods,
Or serve them not, be atheists if we choose —
I, as thou knowest, an atheist choose to be —
Of comity and peace the sole safe rule.
This therefore is the sum — I say it again —
Ways diverse worship men, or worship not,
All as our natural bents may us incline.
Keep your Jehovah, you, He is your God,
Chosen, or feigned and fashioned to your mind —
Keep Him, but not impose your ethnic dream,
Or guess, of deity on all mankind."

" No dream of ours," said Saul, " Jehovah is.

Nay, nay, alas, far otherwise than so,
Our Hebrew dreams of God have, like the dreams
Dreamed by all races of mankind besides,
Grovelled to low and lower, have bestial been,
Or reptile, nay, to insensate wood and stone
Descended ; we have loved idolatry,
We, with the rest, and hardly healed have been,
Though purged with hyssop of dire history,
Constrained — against the subtly treacherous soft
Relentings of our heart, oft yielded to,
Then punished oft full sore, which bade us spare
Whom God to spare forbade — constrained to slay
With our own swords, abolish utterly,
The idolatrous possessors of this land,
In judgment just on their idolatry,
And lest we too be tainted with their sin ;
Yet foul relapse despite, and after, stripes,
Stripes upon stripes again and yet again,
Suffered from the right hand of God incensed,
Defeat, captivity, long servitude,
With the probe searched, with the knife carved until
Scarce left was life to bear the cautery
Wherewith a holy and a jealous God
Out of our quivering soul throughly would burn

That clinging, deep, inveterate human plague
Inherited from Adam in his fall,
That devil-taught depravity which prompts
Apostasy to other gods no gods —
Hardly so healed, with dreadful chastisement,
Has been my nation of her dreadful crime.
Loth, slow, ingrate, rebellious pupils, we
Taught have been thus to worship only God —
Jehovah, only God of the whole earth ! "

Those last words as he spoke, Saul his right hand
Swept round in waving gesture — for they now
A height of goodly prospect had attained,
Wherefrom, pausing to breathe their laboring steeds,
They backward looked beneath them far abroad —
Swept round his hand, as if the circuit wide
Of the whole earth might there his words attest;
Their fill they gazed, then upward strained once more.
At length a stage of smoother going reached,
Sergius, abreast of Saul, took up the word:
" Yea, might one deem thy Hebrew race indeed
Had been the subjects of such history,
So purposed, then sound were thine argument
And thy Jehovah would be very God,

And God alone, and God of the whole earth.
But other races too besides thine own
Have had their chances, their vicissitudes;
Fortune to all has served her whirling wheel,
And every several race has had its turn
Of rising now, now sinking in the dust.
Wherefore should we you Hebrews sole of all
Reckon divinely taught by history,
Taught to be theists in an atheist world,
Or in a world idolatrous, of God
The True, the Only, only worshippers?"

" The other nations all," so Saul rejoined,
" Followed the bent of nature, had their will,
What they chose did, and were idolatrous,
God gave them up to their apostasy;
Us God withstood, His Hebrews He forbade;
With the same bent as others, as headstrong,
We Hebrews strangely went a different way,
And upward moved against a downward bent.
A fiery flaming sword turned every way
Forever met us on the errant track,
And forced us right though still found facing wrong.
God's prophets did not fail, age after age —

Until for that we needed them no more —
To warn us, chide us, threaten, plead, conjure,
Against our passion for idolatry.
Yet, as defying all that God could do,
Such was the force of that infatuate love
Fast-rooted in the sottish Hebrew heart
For idol-worship, that King Solomon,
The greatest, wisest, wealthiest of our kings,
Mightiest, most famous, most magnificent,
The glory and the crown of Israel,
The wonder and the proverb of the East —
This king, at point of culmination highest
To the far-shining splendor of our race,
The son of David, Solomon, turned back
From God who gave him his pre-eminence,
From God, the Living God, turned back, and sold
His heart, his spacious, all-experienced heart,
To gods that were no gods.

　　　　　　　　　　"Against a will,
A set of nature, a prime pravity
Stubborn like this, and tenfold impulse given
Through such example in our first of kings,
That, conflagration of infection round,
We should escape and not idolatrous be,

We only of all nations on the earth,
'This, without miracle, were miracle,
A miracle of chance, confounding chance,
Monstrous, incredible, impossible!
Nay, miracles on-miracles were for us wrought,
The manifest finger of God unquestionable,
Yet to ourselves ourselves, to all men we,
Wisely looked on, are chiefest miracle,
Witness from age to age that God is God."

 With Hebrew heat, thus Saul to Sergius;
The frequent steep ascents meanwhile, the halts
For rest, for prospect, or for dalliance
Under some cooling shade of rock or tree —
Shield from the waxing fervors of the sun —
Slack pace, due to the humors of their steeds
Unchidden while their masters held discourse,
Left the twain still below the topmost crest
Of Hermon when the noontide hour was on.
Large leisure to refection and repose
Allowed, with converse, and mid-afternoon
It was, before to horse again were got
The horsemen, and their forward way resumed.
As, lightly, they into the saddle sprang,

Out of a purple-dark dense cloud that slept
Wakefully now along the horizon's rim
Under the flaming sun in the deep west,
There came a roll of thunder to their ears,
Remote, and mellow with remoteness, rich
Bass music in long rumbling monotone;
They listened with delight to hear the sound.

Then Sergius, as the vibration died
In low delicious tremble from their sense,
Said, coupling this with that in Saul's discourse,
Fresh, or remembered from the days before:
"That thunder and this mountain bring to me,
Imagined, the wild scene on Sinai
When your lawgiver gave his laws to you.
He schemed it well to have a thunder-storm
Chime in and be a brave accompaniment
To enforce his ordinances upon the awe
Of the unthinking timorous multitude.
Popular leaders and lawgivers have
Always and everywhere their tricks of trade,
To impress, hoodwink, and wheedle vulgar minds.
Our Sabine Numa, he Pompilius named,
Had his mysterious nymph Egeria

To bring him statutes for all men to heed;
And that Lycurgus got an oracle
From famous Delphi to approve his laws,
Which having sworn his Spartans to observe
At least till he returned from whither he went
Abroad, he, after, masked in such disguise
That never thence to have returned he seemed.
The herd of men still love to be cajoled,
Trolled hither and thither about with baited lies;
Frighten them now with brandished empty threat,
And now with laud as empty tickle them.
Augustus taught the art to tyrannize
Through forms of ancient freedom false and vain,
The stale trick since of all our emperors.
Your Hebrew Moses in his rude grand way
Well plied his shifts of lead and government."

  Thunder, a rising mutter, broke again,
And Sergius in his saddle turned to look;
But Saul, with forward face intent, replied:
" Nay, but our Moses thou dost misconceive.
All was to lose and naught to gain for him
Then when he left the ease, the pomp, the power,
Of Pharaoh's court — of Pharaoh's daughter son

Esteemed, and to imperial futures heir —
This left, and loth his brethren led, slaves they,
Out of the realm of Egypt to the sea —
For such a multitude impassable,
Yet passed, through mighty miracle, by all —
Beyond the sea, into that wilderness
Led them, where neither food nor water was,
Yet food found they, and water. in the waste,
Full forty years of error till they came
Next to a land set thick with bristling spears
Against them — though land promised them for theirs —
And land that Moses never was to see,
Save as afar in prospect from the mount,
Because unworthy judged to enter there,
Who unadviséd words in haste let slip,
Unworthy judged, and meekly by himself
Recorded judged unworthy — such a man,
To such a people, so long led by him,
Through such straits of extremity, not once
Spake words to humor or to flatter them ;
Thwarted them rather, balked them of their wish,
Upbraided, blamed, rebuked, and punished them,
Each art of selfish demagogue eschewed.
To rule and leadership like his, nowhere

Wilt thou find precedent or parallel;
One key alone unlocks the mystery — God!"

At that last word from Saul, like answer, came
A deep-mouthed boom of thunder from the west,
After a sword of lightning sudden drawn
Then sheathed within the scabbard of the cloud,
Which now, spread wide, had blotted out the sun.
A vagrant breath of tempest shook the trees,
And the scared birds flew homeward to their nests.
Sergius remarked the stir of elements
Uneasily the more that he alone
Remarked it, Saul, involved in his own thought,
Seeming unconscious of the outward world.
The Roman, groping in his secret mind
Vainly to find support of sympathy,
Faltered to feel himself thus fronted sole
With danger he could neither ward nor shun,
In presence yet forbidding sign of fear.

In this distress he buoyed himself with words,
Cheer seeking in the sound of his own voice:
" A merry place that in Lucretius
Where this bold poet rallies Jupiter —

The whole Olympian crew, Jupiter most —
In such a rattling vein of pleasantry,
On his plenipotence with thunderbolts!
Lucretius, thou shouldst know, interpreter
Of Epicurus is to Roman minds;
From whom we moderns learn the truth of things
And generation of the universe.
 ' If Jupiter,' Lucretius sings and says,
 ' If Jupiter it be, and other gods,
 ' That with terrific sound the temple shake,
 ' Shake the resplendent temple of the skies,
 ' And launch the lightning whither each one wills,
 ' Why is it that the strokes transfix not those
 ' Guilty of some abominable crime,
 ' As these within their breast the flames inhale,
 ' Instruction sharp to mortals — why not this,
 ' Rather than that the man of no base thing
 ' To himself conscious should be wrapt about
 ' Innocent in the flames, and suddenly
 ' With whirlwind and with fire from heaven con-
    sumed ?
 ' Also, why seek they out, the gods, for work
 ' Like this, deserted spots, and waste their pains ?
 ' Or haply do they then just exercise

' Their muscles, that thereby their arms be strong?'"

Sergius so far, from his Lucretius,
When the cloud, cloven, let out an arrowy flash,
And, following soon, a muffled muttering threat
Prolonged, that ended in a ragged roar —
As if, with angry rupture, violent hands
Atwain had torn the fabric of the sky.
A shuddering pause, but again Sergius,
Flying his poet's gibes at Jupiter :
    "' Why never from a sky clear everywhere
    ' Does Jupiter upon the lands hurl down
    ' His thunderbolts, and thunder-booms outpour ?
    ' Or, when the clouds have come, does he descend
    ' Then into them that nigh at hand he thence
    ' The striking of his weapon may direct ?'"

One sheet of flame the bending welkin wrapt,
And a broadside of thunder roared amain.
With mortal strife against a mortal fear,
Hidden, the Roman struggled, not in vain —
As, faltering yet from his feigned gayety,
He, in a forced voice almost grim, went on
With that Lucretian blasphemy of Jove :
    "' Why lofty places seeks out Jupiter,

' And why most numerous vestiges find we
' Traced of his fires on lonely mountain-tops ? ' "

No farther — flash on flash and crash on crash,
Chaos of light and universe of sound ! —
For the wind roared a tumult like the sea
Which the gulfs filled between the thunder-peals.

One mighty blast, frantic as battle-charge
When, mad with last despair, ten thousand horse
Headlong into the hell at cannon-mouth
Plunge — such a blast rushed down the rent ravine
Whereby, along a shaggy side, the twain,
Now nigh the utmost mountain summit, climbed.
The glacial air, as in a torrent rolled
Precipitous or vertical sheer down
Some dizzy height in cataract, so swift !
Unhorsed them both ; but, crouching, man and steed
With one wise instinct instantly to all,
Which equalled all — supreme desire of life —
They huddling crept transverse to where a rock
On their right hand lifted its moveless brow
And, safely founded in the mountain's base,
Made, leaning, an impendent roof which now
Proffered a dreadful shelter from the storm.

Hardly this refuge gained, the tempest, loosed,
Hailstones and coals of fire commingled, fell.
The wind, with such a weight oppressed, went down,
And, with the sinking wind, a water-spout,
Whirled roaring in its spiral from on high,
Those watchers saw peel off, with one steep swoop
Descending, a whole mountain-top and roll
Its shattered forest into the ravine
Suddenly thus with foaming torrent filled.
Therewith, as weary were the storm, a lull ;
Lull only, for the welkin seemed to sink
Collapsed about them, and what was the sky
Became the nether atmosphere on fire,
Enrobing them with lightning fold on fold
And thunder detonating at their ears.

Sergius, ere shut had seared his eyes the glare,
Saw a gigantic cedar nigh at hand,
Under a flaming wedge of thunderbolt,
Riven in parted halves from head to foot,
Fall burning down the frightful precipice.
Spite of himself, his terror turned to prayer :
" O Jupiter," he said, " it was not meant,
What I spoke late against thy majesty !

Spare me yet this once more, and I a vow,
A pledged rich vow, will in thy temple hang,
Then when I first shall safe reach Rome, inscribed
' From Sergius Paulus to King Jupiter,
Lord of the lightning and the thunderbolt.'"

"'Give ye unto Jehovah,'" so at last,
Fragments of psalm responsive to the storm —
As in antiphony of worship joined,
He and the elements! — chanting, Saul burst forth,
At intervals, between the swells of sound,
And varying to the tempest's varying phase,
    "'Give ye unto Jehovah, lo, all ye
    ' Sons of the mighty, to Jehovah give
    'Glory and strength; unto Jehovah give
    'The equal glory due unto His name;
    'Worship Jehovah in fair robes of praise!"

    "' Deep calleth unto deep' at the dread noise
    'Made by Thy waterspouts.   The earth, it shook
    'And trembled; the foundations of the hills
    'Moved and were shaken for that He was wroth.
    'The heavens moreover bowed He, and came down,
    'He His pavilion round about Him made
    'Dark waters and the thick clouds of the skies.

" 'Jehovah also thundered in the heavens,
'And therein the Most High gave forth His voice,
'Hailstones and coals of fire!

       " 'Jehovah's voice
'In power!

    "'Jehovah's voice in majesty!

   "'Jehovah's voice is on the waters! God,
'The God of glory thunders!

       " 'Lo, His voice,
'Jehovah's voice, the mighty cedar breaks,
'Jehovah's voice divides the flames of fire!

  " ' Praise ye Jehovah, heavens of heavens, and ye
'Waters that be above the heavens, Him praise!
'Praise ye Jehovah, from the earth beneath,
'Thou fire, thou hail, thou snow, and vapors ye,
'Thou, stormy wind that dost fulfil His word!'"

So Saul, in dialogue with the elements,
That heard him, and responded voice for voice.
Sublimity into sublimity
Other, immeasurable heights more high,
Was lifted and transformed, the terror gone,
Gone or exalted to ennobling awe —

In converse such, God, with His image man!
The thunder, and the lightning, and the hail
Falling in power, the pomp of moving clouds,
The sound of torrent and of cataract,
The multitudinous orchestra of winds —
Trumpet and pipe, resounding cymbal loud,
Timbrel and harp, sackbut and psaltery —
The majesty of cedars prostrate strewn
In utmost adoration, the veiled sun,
The kneeling heavens, face downward on the earth,
In act of penitence as found unclean
By the white-burning holiness of God —
All this wild gesture of the elements
And deep convulsion of the frame of things,
Appalling only erst, interpreted
By interjections such from Saul of phrase
Inspired, seemed from confusion and turmoil
Transposed and harmonized to an august
Service and symphony of prayer and praise
And solemn liturgy of the universe.

Sergius was charmed insensibly to peace,
And a calm human voice had subtle power
To soothe to breathing rest the trembling steeds.

And now began the cadence of the storm ;
Lifted the sky was from the burdened earth,
The lightnings flashed less imminent, less thick,
The thunder dulled his stroke, retired to far
And farther in the muffling firmament,
The hail ceased falling in a fall of rain,
Through which at last the low descending sun
Smiled in a rainbow on the opposite cloud.
"God's sign," said Saul, " His seal of promise set
Oft on the clouds of heaven when storm is past,
In radiant curve of blended colors fair,
That He with flood no more will drown the 'world."

  Therewith they got them to their path again,
And, forward hastening, on the farther slope
Of Hermon overpassed, were met by some
Returning of their escort companies
Who sought their laggard masters left behind.
These had crossed earlier, and, before the storm,
Housed them in covert, where all now with joy
Welcomed their chiefs from threatened scath escaped
They slept that night beneath a starry sky
Fair as if wrinkled never by a frown ;
To-morrow they would see that paradise,

Renowned Damascus, pearl of all the East.
This their sleep filled with dream of things to be,
Until the morning breaking radiant made
The desert seem to blossom as the rose
Wherein Damascus sat an oasis.

   Meanwhile a morning in true Paradise,
Far hence and hidden in a world unseen,
The Paradise of promise from the Cross,
Dawned to the saints forever summering there
In bliss and glory with their glorious Lord.

   Morning in the celestial Paradise
Is not as morning here, new-springing day
Crescent the same out of eclipsing night:
No night is there, and therefore no vicissitude
Of dark and bright to separate the days.
Yet condescends our Father to their frame,
Still finite though immortal, still in need
Of changes to diversify their state,
And punctuate into periods the smooth lapse,
Else cloying with prolonged beatitude,
Of that eternal dateless life serene
Lived by the happy souls in Paradise;
Our Father condescends and gives them days

And days, with difference of each from each,
That they may reckon up and date their bliss;
No night is there, but without night a morn.
Morning in Paradise is perfect light
Ineffably more fair become to-day
Than yesterday, forever, through more fair
Disclosure, dawn on dawn, eternally
Made of the glory of the face of Him
In whom to His belovéd God still shines.

Morn such had risen once more in Paradise,
When there a group elect together drawn,
Wearing a brow of expectation each,
Stood on a flowery hill enringed around
To be almost an island with a loop
Of river, the river of life, that lucent flowed
Mirroring ranks of trees along its banks
Ruddy or gold in gleams of fruitage seen
Glimpsing against the rich green of their leaves —
Here stood a chosen group who waited now
Tidings a messenger to come should bring.
These were those all who lately on the earth
Had suffered death for Jesus' sake through Saul —
All saving Stephen; he, at point of dawn

That morning, had been summoned by his Lord
To bear from Him some embassy of grace.
·The man born blind was there whom Jesus healed
To double seeing, seeing of the soul,
As of the body, and whom not the threat
Of stripes, of stones, and not the blandishment
Of gentle words from lips with power of death
Could bribe to live at cost of least unfaith
Toward his Light-giver and Redeemer Lord —
He, and a little company besides,
Women with men, who like him lightly recked
Of loss but for a moment then and there
Compared with that far more exceeding weight
Of glory now, in over-recompense,
Forever and forever sealed their own.

This little group, beyond their happy wont
Beatified with hope that heavenly morn,
Soon greet one coming whose irradiate brow
Bespeaks him fresh from audience with the King;
Stephen it was, whose earthly-shining face
Was shadow to the brightness now it wore.
The martyr to his fellow-martyrs brought
Glad tidings; they were all that day to see

Break forth in power the glory of the Lord.
"Saul," Stephen said, "still breathes his threatening out
And slaughter aimed against the church of Christ;
He journeys to Damascus in this mind.
But the Lord Christ will meet him in the way
And overthrow him with resistless light.
Ours is to tarry on this pleasant hill
Of prospect, and, hence gazing, all behold,
Tasting a sweet revenge of Paradise,
To see our prayers fulfilled, in Saul become
From persecutor brother well-beloved,
And builder from destroyer of the church."

So these there sat them down upon the mount.
Here, gaze turned ever earthward, they in talk
Of earthly things that still were dear to them
Consumed the happy heavenly hours, until,
To those their native Syrian climes, drew nigh
Noontide; then, in a new theophany,
The transit of a shadow! — seldom seen
There where was neither sun, nor moon, nor star,
But all was equal universal light —
Came sudden notice to their eyes to watch
The Messianic dread procession forth,

Christ in the majesty of solitude,
Swifter than meteor's fall, from Paradise.

Hᴇ, purposed not to slay, only cast down
Saul from the top of his presumptuous pride,
And break him from his disobedient will,
Would not in His essential glory meet
His creature, lest he be abolished quite,
But dimmed Himself with splendor which, more bright
Than the supreme effulgence of the sun
At mid-day in a crystal firmament,
Fixed, but more vivid than the fleeting flash
Of lightning when its beam burns most intense,
Was splendor yet of ray less luminous
Than the accustomed radiance of His face,
And showed as cloud against that shining sky.

For, in that unimaginable world
Of perfect, purged from sin and sin's defect,
The senses of the blest inhabitants,
Their organs and their faculties, are all
Inured to bear with ease, with pleasure bear,
Continuance and intensity of light
That mortal frames like ours would quite consume.
Those there from light need neither change nor rest.

Their proper substance is illuminate,
And their bliss is to bathe themselves in light,
And light, more light, drunk in at every pore
From the bright omnipresence of the Lord,
Revealed each day brighter forevermore,
Makes their eternal life eternal joy.

But on this day select of many days,
The happy people all of Paradise
Saw Jesus as a darkness of less light,
A glancing shadow, pass from out their sphere —
The most unweeting whither or why He went;
But those knew who kept vigil on the mount.
These had their sense for sight and sound that day
Exalted to seraphic keen and clear
Beyond the glorious wont of Paradise;
While a circumfluous ether interfused
For their behoof between where thus they stood
And where they earthward looked, a subtile air,
A discontinuous element rare like space,
Was now such vehicle, so voluble,
For lightest appulse to both eye and ear
Supernal, thrice sevenfold refined, as made
Seem nigh things seen or heard, however far.

Fixed to behold and hearken thus at ease,
They saw afar two pilgrim companies,
Where, near Damascus, these a shady tuft
Of grove or thicket, in the arid waste
Of burning sand, at noontide hour had found,
For rest and coolness ere their goal they gained.
Those pilgrims just in act, as seemed, to start
Anew upon the way for their last stage
Of going, one, well recognized for Saul —
Remounted not from halt, but some few steps
Leading his horse with bridle-rein remiss
Along his destined path — comrade beside,
Was by this comrade asked, as in discourse
After suspense renewed : " How was it, then,
Through what offence, that he deserved his death ?
Since atheist not, and not idolater,
Nor yet of those Samaritan heretics,
Wherein did Stephen fail of loyalty ? "
" Traitor was he," said Saul, " to our chief hope,
He taught that Jesus Nazarene was Christ;
Nay, that impostor, he, blaspheming, made
Coequal partner of the eternal throne
And solitary majesty of God ;
Worst of idolatry such blasphemy !

Jesus of Nazareth anathema ! ''

Almost, at this, a shudder of horror ran
Chill through the spiritual pure corporeal frames
Wherein were housed those blessed essences,
Hearing from earth such words in Paradise !
They then considered at what cost were bought
Perpetual consciousness of things terrene !

Watched they meanwhile that cloud of glory go
Darkened wherein the Lord of light was hid.
Incredibly though swift its far descent,
Yet answerably swift their vision was,
As swift likewise the motion of their mind ;
And so they plainly saw how, by degrees,
What shadow was, in the celestial sphere,
Became a growing brightness as it went,
Until, within the bounds of sunshine come,
That mild beclouded glory, still unchanged,
Paled with its bright the brilliance of the sun.
Hardly those watchers dare keep looking, pierced
With a redeemed fine sympathy for Saul,
And marvelling, " Such light can he bear and live ? "

To Saul himself no interval there seemed ;

Instant, with his anathema, down smote
That awful light on him, and straight to earth
Prostrate as dead he fell, yet heard a Voice,
Awful not less, speak twice his name, " Saul, Saul,'
And, " Wherefore dost thou persecute Me ? " ask.
Then further these deep searching words to him :
" Hard findst it thou to kick against the pricks!"
"Who art Thou, Lord ?" came trembling forth from
      Saul,
Whereby their brother yet alive those knew.
" Jesus I am, Jesus of Nazareth,
The crucified, whom thou dost persecute,''
They heard Messiah say, and thrilled with joy
Of gratitude to feel afresh that He
Suffered when any suffered for His sake,
And bled in wounds that made His brethren bleed,
Joining Himself to them, by fellowship
Of passion, they in Him and He in them,
The living members with the living Head
Mysteriously incorporate in one.
Thus a sweet thrill of grateful love to Him,
Their Saviour, trembled in those heavenly breasts,
While in suspense of balanced hope and fear —
The fear but such as made the hope more bliss —

They waited what their brother next would say.

But in the prostrate man, at such reply,
Felt from amidst that imminent light descend,
" I Jesus am whom thou dost persecute,"
Thought following thought, a fleet succession, flew.
The boundless blank astonishment was brief
Which, as with wing world-wide of hurricane,
Shadowy, his mind bewildering overswept.
'Such power of splendor his, the Nazarene's!
Jesus had launched that thunderbolt of light!
The Lord of Glory then the crucified!'
The momentary hurricane was past,
But passing it had overturned the world.

Saul vividly saw Stephen as that day
'He shone Shekinah in the temple court
Effulgent with a milder light like this;
' And this was that which Stephen prophesied!
How madly had he kicked against the pricks!'
Next, Stephen martyr stood before his eyes
Uplifting holy hands to heaven in prayer,
On poise for that translation to his Lord
Wherein his, Saul's, the murderer's part had been!
And Rachel flashed in vision on his mind,

Pathetically beautiful, once more,
As on that moonlit eve at Bethany!
The sisters there, and Lazarus — with Ruth
Exalted in her mother-majesty!
Hirani, then, in his simplicity
Perplexed before the Sanhedrim, but borne
In ecstasy above them far away,
Thence looking down upon them all, a light
Fair on his forehead like the light of stars ;
All these things in his past, with many more —
Instant, at sudden summons of his mind,
To swear against him his own blasphemy —
Shot through Saul's spirit, as the lightning leaps,
Rapid, one leap, from end to end of heaven.
'This dreadful splendor was not vengeance all,
It had not slain him, he was thinking still!
A grace was in the glory, oh, how fair !'
The features of a Face began to dawn
Upon him in the darkness of that light ;
As the sun shineth in his strength, it shone,
An awful Meekness mild with Majesty!

The outward light light to his soul became —
A light of knowledge of the glory of God

To Saul, seen in the face of Jesus Christ!
'It would be freedom to serve such a Lord!'
The passion of rebellion all was gone,
A passion of obedience in its place;
The will that hated had dissolved away,
And will no more was left, but only love
This love which was obedience spoke and asked,
" Lord Jesus, what wilt thou have me to do?"

The Brightness of the Father's Glory said:
" Rise thou, and stand upon thy feet, for I
Have to this end appeared to thee, to make
Thee minister and witness both of what
This day thou hast beheld and of those things
Wherein I after will appear to thee,
Delivering thee from Jewish enemies
And from the Gentiles unto whom I now
Send thee, their eyes to unseal and them to turn
From darkness unto light, and from the power
Of Satan unto God, that they of sins
Forgiveness may receive, and heirs become
Among those sanctified through faith in Me."

Saul heard, and in his heart of hearts obeyed;
And his whole life thenceforth obedience was —

Whereof the greater song remains to sing,
If so be God vouchsafe such grace to me.

But Jesus to His servant further said,
" Hence now into Damascus city go ;
There fully shall be shown thee all thy way."

A way indeed stain-traced in blood and tears,
As Saul foresaw to Rachel ; but in tears
And blood his own thereafter to the end,
Even to the end of that apostleship.

Yet glorious end !   Already then afar
Will kindle the dark earth with many a ray,
Never to be extinguished, of heaven's light
Caught from the torch that this world-wandering
    man,
This flying angel fledged with wingéd feet
Tireless, this heart of love unquenchable,
Has borne abroad, when, now the good fight fought,
Finished his course, the faith full kept, he, last,
With aged eagle eyes strained forward, sees
The crown of righteousness laid up for him
Which Christ, the Righteous Judge, will give him
    then,

Give him in that forever-imminent Day —
Nor him alone, as his vicarious soul
Swells to remember, but all them likewise
Who shall have loved the appearing of the Lord.

The transit of a thought athwart the brain —
What computation for such speed in flight !
What reckoning of the number of the thoughts
That in an individual instant will
Chase one another through a human mind
In never-sundered continuity
Of change ! The measureless diameters
Of being that a mortal man may cross
From one pulse to another of the blood !
How, in the twinkling of an eye, become
The spirit its own polar opposite !
Between his Lord's reply, " I Jesus am,"
And his own further question instant asked,
" Lord Jesus, what wilt Thou have me to do ? "
That prostrate proud young Hebrew penitent
The utmost stretch of longitude traversed
That can divide two different selves in man —
He from rebellious to obedient passed,
Blasphemer was adoring worshipper,

The Pharisee was Christian, Saul was Paul.

At witness of the wondrous change, the joy,
The grateful joy, within those friendly minds
Above who saw it, borne to ecstasy
Of gladness, was triumphal, and broke forth
In singing such as heard in Paradise :
" Glory to God, and to our Saviour Lord,
For one more captive to the heavenly thrall ;
For one more human soul to heaven reclaimed
From hell, and star set in Christ's diadem !
For one more witness, an apostle new,
Like angel flying through mid-heaven, to fly
And wing the Gospel wide throughout the world !
Thanks to thee, Christ, for that his name is SAUL ! "

Heard was this quiring song afar, and heaven
Her other joy suspended at the sound :
And every echoing hill of Paradise,
Each grove, each grotto, every fountain-side,
With every bank of river, every glen,
And every bowery, flowery wide champaign
Where angels bask in bliss, took up the strain
And rang it swelling to the highest heaven ;

While harpers harped it to their harps, and palms
Were rhythmic waved in music to the eye,
And the trees clapped their hands, and God was
      pleased.

   So they in Paradise, who saw and heard
Truly; Saul's fellow-pilgrims nigh at hand
Vacantly wondered, who, though they the light
Beheld, and heard the voice speak, missed the sense.
Sergius, recovered from his first surprise
And terror, mused within himself, and found,
Remembering words from Saul against the gods,
Easy solution of the mystery;
'Pan roared at him from out the copse-wood nigh,
With wholesome punishment of fear infused
Avenging his despised divinity;
While Lord Apollo twanged his silver bow
And shot at him a shaft of blinding light;
The gods of right are wroth to be reviled!'

   Saul from the ground arose a sightless man;
The glory that not slew had blinded him.
His steed he would not mount again to ride,
But chose, humbly, and guided by the hand,

Footing to go among his followers.
Who, that blithe morning, as the morning blithe,
Forth for Damascus from Jerusalem
Rode breathing threat and slaughter quenchless sworn
Against the church of Jesus Nazarene,
Entered the city walking, led and blind,
Bondslave thenceforth to the One Worthy Name.

THE END.